THE Corpse WITH THE Amber Neck

CATHY ACE

FOUR TAILS PUBLISHING LTD.

The Corpse with the Amber Neck

PRAISE FOR THE CAIT MORGAN MYSTERIES

"In the finest tradition of Agatha Christie…Ace brings us the closed-room drama, with a dollop of romantic suspense and historical intrigue." – *Library Journal*

"…touches of Christie or Marsh but with a bouquet of Kinsey Millhone." – *The Globe and Mail*

"…a sparkling, well-plotted and quite devious mystery in the cozy tradition…" – *Hamilton Spectator*

"…If all of this suggests the school of Agatha Christie, it's no doubt what Cathy Ace intended. She is, as it fortunately happens, more than adept at the Christie thing." – *Toronto Star*

"Cait unravels the…mystery using her eidetic memory and her powers of deduction, which are worthy of Hercule Poirot."
– *The Jury Box, Ellery Queen Mystery Magazine*

"This author always takes us on an adventure. She always makes us think. She always brings the setting to life. For those reasons this is one of my favorite series."
– *Escape With Dollycas Into A Good Book*

"…a testament to an author who knows how to tell a story and deliver it with great aplomb." – *Dru's Musings*

"…perfect for those that love travel, food, and/or murder (reading it, not committing it)." – *BOLO Books*

"…Ace is, well, an ace when it comes to plot and description." – *The Globe and Mail*

Other works by the same author
(Information for all works here: **www.cathyace.com**)

The Cait Morgan Mysteries
The Corpse with the Silver Tongue
The Corpse with the Golden Nose
The Corpse with the Emerald Thumb
The Corpse with the Platinum Hair
The Corpse with the Sapphire Eyes
The Corpse with the Diamond Hand
The Corpse with the Garnet Face
The Corpse with the Ruby Lips
The Corpse with the Crystal Skull
The Corpse with the Iron Will
The Corpse with the Granite Heart
The Corpse with the Turquoise Toes
The Corpse with the Opal Fingers
The Corpse with the Pearly Smile

The WISE Enquiries Agency Mysteries
The Case of the Dotty Dowager
The Case of the Missing Morris Dancer
The Case of the Curious Cook
The Case of the Unsuitable Suitor
The Case of the Disgraced Duke
~~The Case of the Absent Heirs~~
The Case of the Cursed Cottage
The Case of the Uninvited Undertaker
The Case of the Bereaved Butler
The Case of the Secretive Secretary
The Case of the Unfortunate Fortune Teller

Standalone novels
The Wrong Boy

Short Stories/Novellas
Murder Keeps No Calendar: a collection of 12 short stories/novellas
Murder Knows No Season: a collection of four novellas
Steve's Story in "The Whole She-Bang 3"
The Trouble with the Turkey in "Cooked to Death Vol. 3: Hell for
the Holidays"
Wax in "CrimeFest: Leaving The Scene"

Dedication

In memory of Mum – always my first "Cait" reader, until now
For my sister – thanks for everything, especially this year
For my husband – my rock…we'll always have "our" Paris

Un

The past six weeks had been a blur of preparation, travel, lectures, tutorials, and grading, bearing out my suspicions that my head of department at the University of Vancouver had strategically under-explained the teaching schedule I'd been invited to deliver for a month at the *Sorbonne Université*, in Paris. However, with my responsibilities completed, my husband had finally joined me, and we had the wonderful prospect of a week to ourselves, enjoying the City of Lights – and we'd already thrown ourselves into it.

On Friday afternoon, Bud had helped me clear my bits and bobs out of the disappointingly small office I'd been allocated within the equally disappointing utilitarian building that housed the lauded university's department of Applied Psychology, then we'd headed off to take one of those boat rides along the Seine. Later on, we'd enjoyed a delicious dinner – roasted leg of lamb for me, and steak with *frites* for him – at a brasserie close to my hotel, which had become my sort of regular dinner spot. The people who worked there were delighted to meet my husband, and we'd been treated exceptionally well, with profiteroles on the house with our after-dinner coffees. We'd laughed like drains at the dreadful selfies we'd managed to take during our river trip – with the Eiffel Tower growing out of our heads – and promised ourselves we'd make a better effort when we visited the famous landmark itself…which, of course, we both knew we wanted to do.

Now it was as close to the end of a Saturday morning as you could get. We'd had an early start, with a quick breakfast of *croissants* and strong coffee, reveling in the sight of the sun glinting on the water of the futuristic fountains that splashed in a square in front of one of the *Sorbonne*'s magnificent, gated entrances, while nattering about our beloved black Lab Marty. I'd missed him almost as much as I'd missed my husband; I'd been separated from them both for too long. However, we'd both agreed that Bud hanging about all day in Paris while I was busy teaching would be a waste of his time, so I'd focused on getting my job done, and he'd stayed at home…then he'd arrived on Thursday night.

We'd left our bags at the hotel the folks at the *Sorbonne* had provided for me while I was teaching – knowing we couldn't check into our new hotel, one of our own choosing, until the afternoon. We'd decided to visit the *Opéra Garnier* first thing, then take a trip on one of those buses where you can get on and off wherever you fancy, to wend away whatever hours remained. One of the stops on the route wasn't far from the place where I'd been staying, and we planned to get a ride-share car across town with our luggage later in the day.

Luckily for us, we'd only had to wait a few moments for a bus to show up, and we'd even managed to snag two seats next to each other on the open-air top deck.

"I can't believe how quickly the time disappeared at that place," said my husband as he reached across me, trying to stick the toggle at the end of his pair of earphones into the little socket on the side of the bus, so that he could hear the recorded commentary.

"I warned you there'd be a lot to see," I replied, possibly a little too tartly; in my defense, my feet were killing me.

Bud pulled back his arm and stopped fiddling. "Are you okay? You sound a bit…off. You were the one who wanted to go to the *Opéra Garnier*, after all. Not my thing, as you know."

"It's not as though we had to endure an actual opera," I said, feeling a bit miffed. "And it is a magnificent place, you have to admit. That Chagall ceiling in the auditorium, and the opulence of the main staircase? Stunning. And I do think it's a nice touch that they have a box with a plaque saying that it's to be used by The Phantom."

Bud managed to connect his ear-thingies and stuck one into his right ear – the one farthest from me. "I'll admit it wasn't what I'd expected," he conceded. "Better than I'd hoped, to be honest. Though I'm glad we decided to wander the place on our own, not with one of those guides. They all seemed a bit too bossy for my taste."

"I dare say they have to develop techniques for keeping their groups moving along," I replied. "A bit like I have to with my students."

"Were the ones you were dealing with here in Paris different to the ones you teach back home, in Canada, in any way?"

I gave the question some thought as I sorted out my own set of headphones. "Not really. I mean, there are always types…you know, the normal group dynamics. But I'd say they took their studies a little more seriously than my usual students, if anything. My one big relief was that my French was in good order before I started. Being in Tahiti for so long, and speaking so much French there, really helped – though it took me a while to get my technical vocabulary up to snuff…so that's where I put my effort before I headed here. Getting them for only four weeks meant that they – and, therefore, I – had to cram a lot into a short time, or else the subject wouldn't have received the coverage it needs. And, of course, they'd all signed up for it…which makes a difference, because it means they actually wanted to be there – for the extra credits – unlike when I teach compulsory courses back in Canada. To be honest, I was delighted to see so many young people interested in the concept of victim profiling. Maybe there's hope that the discipline will grow in popularity as time passes, and as the role it can play in solving crimes becomes better understood…oh, we're off. Right – no more shoptalk, let's just enjoy the trip. It'll be nice to sit down for a while after all that walking. Did you pick up a map when we got on?"

Bud unfolded the colorful, cartoonish plan of where our route would take us, and we settled back to take in our surroundings – as best as we could, in the unyielding seats – while accordion music played through our headsets and the bus pulled away, crawled along for a bit…then stopped.

I really didn't care that we were already caught in a knot of Saturday lunchtime Parisian traffic; all I wanted to do was enjoy the sights and sounds of the city in a way I hadn't been able to for the past month. Finally, the bus lurched into motion again, and I turned to focus on some sort of flash that I'd caught out of the corner of my eye. As I swiveled my head, one of my earbuds popped out and smacked me in the face, but that wasn't foremost in my mind: what grabbed my attention was the sight of a pair of hands around the throat of a person sitting side-on to a window we were passing.

I must have made some sort of noise, because Bud asked, "What's the matter now?"

Although the bus was hurtling forward, meaning I couldn't see the unsettling scene any longer, I didn't take my eyes off the building in question. I shoved my elbow into my husband's ribs and yelled, "Someone's being strangled, Bud – stop the bus!"

Deux

Bud pulled out one of his earbuds and said, "What do you mean, someone's being strangled? Who? Where?"

I was still staring at the rapidly receding building, and ignoring the people behind me who were giving me funny looks, so couldn't see the expression on my husband's face.

I replied, "Someone inside a room I could see into. Stop the bus, Bud. Isn't there a button you can push or a string you can pull?"

The bus rounded a corner, meaning I could no longer see the building, and I finally turned my head. Bud was on his feet, grasping the back of his seat, his disconnected headset dangling from one ear. He was bobbing up and down.

I shouted, "There – at the top of the bit that surrounds the stairs, there's a big red button saying 'stop'. Push that, and let's get going."

Bud dutifully pushed the button, and a yellow light illuminated a sign above the windows at the front of the bus, but the vehicle didn't even slow down, let alone stop. Nevertheless, I shoved Bud toward the stairs, and we made our way down, jostled by the motion of the vehicle.

When we reached the lower level, the bus driver shouted to us in French, then English, "Please sit down when the bus is moving. Take a seat, please."

Bud made his way toward the driver and spoke to him so quietly that I couldn't hear what he said. The driver's response of a loud, "*Non, c'est impossible,*" suggested that whatever Bud had asked of him wasn't something he felt he could do.

Bud moved even closer to the man's little cabin and spoke in an even lower voice. The driver's only reaction was to hit a button and announce into a loudspeaker system, "We are soon arriving at stop number three, the Louvre Museum."

Bud glanced over his shoulder toward me with an expression of helpless frustration. I planted my feet as we rounded a sharp corner, then as the bus aligned with a narrow archway, through which we drove – emerging into the expanse of the *Cour Napoléon* courtyard of the Louvre Museum, with its stunning pilastered façade and Ieoh Ming Pei's iconic glass pyramid.

The moment the driver opened the doors, I jumped off the bus and paused only long enough for Bud to reach my side.

As I strode off, I said, "We've got to get back to the building where I saw…what I saw."

Bud grabbed my hand, but didn't try to hold me back. "How will you manage that? Those buildings all…well, a lot of them look similar to each other."

"Building on the corner, emerald green shutters, second floor, first window along," I said, dropping Bud's hand to better negotiate a gaggle of Japanese girls who all appeared to have shopped at the same backpack store.

"Which corner, Cait?"

I turned to see Bud's worried expression above a bouncing procession of sky-blue neoprene.

I waited until the throng had passed, then kissed Bud's cheek. "Husband, I didn't see the street name, but I saw the building. I saw the side profile of…" I dared to close my eyes within the bustling crowds for a few seconds, then said, "A woman, with long dark hair, wearing a dark dress or shawl. Hands were at her throat…they were dark against something that was glowing in the sunlight…not glittering, but glowing. Something was covering her entire neck, from her chin down onto her chest…maybe a scarf, or a silk blouse? And the hands were large…possibly gloved. I didn't see whose they were…no body, just the hands. The woman being throttled was looking up at her assailant…then the bus moved on. That's all I saw…but I know that's what I saw. You believe me, don't you?"

Bud's face creased into a broad smile. "Always, Wife. Always. And I trust your eidetic memory to have grabbed onto not only what you saw, but also where you saw it. My only doubt is about our ability to find the place, not yours to remember what it looks like."

"Got the bus route map?"

Bud passed it to me.

I pointed. "We got on here – the second stop, just beyond the *Opéra Garnier*, outside that biscuit shop, *La Cure Gourmande*. We pulled out, then stopped quite soon afterwards, so this is the corner – though I'm not sure what the address would be, because that triangular block could belong to either street, I suppose. Come on, let's go. It might have only taken us ten minutes or less to get here, but that driver put his foot down on his one-hundred-percent-electric whotsit…so it'll take us longer to get back there."

I paused…realizing what that meant for the potential victim, and Bud's concerned expression left me in no doubt that he understood what had just dawned on me. He held me for a moment. "We can only do our best, Cait, and – without an address – what else can we do but find the building, then alert the authorities?"

The poor woman's probably dead by now, was what I thought; "I know, you're right," was what I said.

We trudged along the busy street past the *Hôtel du Louvre* – wonderfully located, but beyond our budget – and skirted the courtyard outside the *Comédie-Française*, where it appeared that an impromptu display of juggling by a group of people dressed as clockwork ballerinas had broken out. Finally reaching the *Avenue de l'Opéra* I walked as fast as I could, meaning that the otherwise noteworthy fountains, pavement cafés, and general ambience were all completely lost on me, because the only thing in my mind's eye was that poor woman – who, upon reflection, didn't seem to have been trying to rip the hands from her neck, nor attempting to rid herself of her attacker in any way.

Odd.

As we drew closer to our objective, I said, "We should cross over – the block was on the other side of the road."

We waited, as patiently as possible, for the light showing the little standing man illuminated in red to be replaced by the one where the little walking man was illuminated in green; I'd learned that it really wasn't worth trying to dash across any road when you sensed a break in the traffic in Paris – especially with so many electric cars and bikes in use, which are both dangerously silent.

Bud took his chance to observe, "So you saw into a window that was higher than the level of the top deck of the bus, and across two – or even three – lanes of traffic?"

I felt my multipurpose right eyebrow shoot toward my hairline. "Yes. Exactly. The height wasn't an issue, due to the distance."

Bud's tone was gentle when he suggested, "Maybe we adopt a softly-softly approach, rather than run into the place shouting about a murder, eh? I believe you saw what you did, but it was just an instant, so you might have…misinterpreted something."

"A woman was being strangled, Bud. That's what I saw. How could I misinterpret that?"

Bud checked that his feet were still at the ends of his legs. "It could have been…play-acting, something…innocent?"

Just as I stared at Bud with an expression that I hoped would suggest he'd lost his marbles, the urgent beeping that accompanied the crossing lights jolted us into action, and we hurried across the wide avenue, reaching the opposite side just before the traffic shot along the road again. I marched on, until

I stood in front of the place where I'd seen a woman being killed. The building was, of course, as I'd remembered it: we stood at the point of a typical triangular Haussmann block, with intricate metal balustrades on the balconies and one of the mansard roofs that everyone envisions when they think of the Paris skyline.

I pointed to a window. "It happened there."

Bud looked up. "I thought you said it was on the second floor – that's the third."

I smiled. "I know that growing up in Canada you'd think of the street level of a building as the first floor, but here in Paris they use what I think of – as a Welshwoman – as the 'normal' names for floors. These buildings were planned and designed to house commercial activities on the ground floor, at street level, you know…shops, services, and cafés or restaurants. Look around – there isn't a single place we can see that doesn't still do that, except, weirdly, this building. That layer of short, stumpy windows above the ground floor, the first floor, was either where the business owner lived, or it was used for storage. The floor above that – where I saw that poor woman – has taller windows than any other floor, and a balcony running the whole length of the façade. That's where the richest people had their apartments. Above that there's another floor with rooms and windows that are almost as tall, but there are no balconies – or maybe just a few Juliet balcony things that have been added later – and they were designed for well-off families. Above that are slightly smaller rooms and apartments, some with balconies, some without – the balconies weren't just useful for the people who lived there, but were also designed to give balance to the façade. Then there might be another level or two of those smaller rooms, with the final floor – the rooms in the roof itself, with those dormer windows – being reserved for servants' quarters. Napoleon the Third approved of Haussmann's organization of Parisian society, as well as the streets of the city."

Bud stared at me. "Thank you, Professor Morgan. Really, Cait – architectural lessons when we're here to try to find a possible victim? Or…not a victim at all, of course. I know I said we shouldn't be all gung-ho, but can't that sort of stuff wait?"

I felt my neck flush with heat. "Sorry. Sometimes I can't help myself…and you're right about finding the victim – or not – and about adopting a more cautious approach, but – now that we're here – I can't see a way in. There's no obvious door. Can you see anything?"

"You go down that street, I'll go along here," said Bud, striding off down the left-hand side of the wedge-shaped block.

I scurried along the right-hand street – passing a long row of parked pick-up-and-drop-off electric rental bikes – and noted again that this was the only building in the area that didn't have any type of commercial undertaking using its ground floor. What would have been shop or café windows were all glazed with darkened, mirrored glass, and there wasn't a door to be seen. At the end of the building farthest from the *Avenue de l'Opéra*, Bud's head popped around the corner.

"This way, Cait."

I turned the corner to see a small garden set in the road, like a roundabout: tall horse chestnut trees – just coming into bloom – were planted around the perimeter, offering shade from the sharp late-April sunlight; a massive fountain, topped with statues of three women wearing diaphanous gowns, each holding…something…aloft, bubbled and splashed at its center. A walkway was set inside the tree-lined perimeter, and circumnavigated the entire thing, which was about thirty feet across. Its diameter matched the width of the building, which made up for the total lack of doors anywhere else by having its entire lower-level façade filled with one of the most magnificent entrances I'd ever seen. It looked as though someone had stuck a small bronze version of the *Arc de Triomphe* onto the building, within which gilded, ornately patterned gates were pushed open revealing massive glass double doors, in front of which stood an upright, bearded man elegantly attired in an emerald green greatcoat and top hat. One of the glass doors bore the gold-painted word "*Maison*", the other the word "*Églantine*".

Bud and I exchanged a glance. I whispered, "A hotel?"

Bud shrugged. "Let's ask."

It was only as we approached the doorman that I could see that his overcoat was made of deeply carved velvet, rather than the wool I'd expected, and even his top hat was velvety and intricately embossed. His facial hair was styled in a manner that reminded me of King Edward VII, with a full beard, trimmed to a point, and a long mustache, which completely hid his top lip; it worked well with the style of his outfit – definitely era-appropriate.

Very fancy, was what I thought; "Good morning, I wonder if you could help us, please," was what I said – in French, of course.

When we got close, I realized the man was older than I'd originally imagined; his dentist had missed a trick or two, and the skin on his face was sufficiently wrinkled that I suspected he'd never heard of sunscreen.

He walked down two steps toward us, beaming. "How may I be of service?"

Maybe that poor woman was a guest here, was what I thought; "Is this a hotel?" was what I said.

The man's grin grew even wider, revealing that however woefully misaligned his front teeth might be, at least he had some – whereas the rest of his mouth had none. "No. This is *Maison Églantine*," he replied – thereby giving us no more information than that which was painted on the doors behind him, which frustrated me.

Bud stepped in. "And *Maison Églantine* is…what?"

The man's smile disappeared, and his brow furrowed. "You do not know *Maison Églantine?*"

Bud and I looked at each other blankly and shook our heads.

The man asked, "You are American?"

Bud and I chorused, "Canadian," then grinned. I added, "I'm originally from Wales, but now I'm a Canadian, like my husband."

The man's face brightened. "Ah, Wales. I love rugby."

Pounce now, Cait!

I smiled my best smile. "Me too…of course, it's in my blood, being Welsh. We're here on holiday, and wondered what this building is, but we don't know what *Maison Églantine* means. Could you tell us? Is the building open to the public?"

The man took the final step down to join us on the street. He leaned in. "It is not for sightseers, but I could allow you to come inside to enjoy the reception area, which is wonderful. Which team do you support?"

I gushed, "Wales, internationally, of course…even if they're playing Canada. And I'm from Swansea, so the Ospreys…or maybe the Scarlets – Llanelli – if Swansea's not playing…though I only dare switch allegiance like that because I live in Canada."

The man thrust out his hand. "I am Lucienne, and I'm for *Stade Français Paris*, of course. You know them, I am sure – they are a great team…even though they have off games."

"I'm Cait, and this is Bud, and we'd love to have a little peep inside here," I replied, eager to try to find out more about the building behind Lucienne, rather than his rugby interests.

Lucienne glanced around. "Now is a good time; it is a special day for us – everyone has arrived for the board meeting, and they are all upstairs. Come on in."

As Bud and I followed him up the wide, elegant steps, I asked, as casually as I could, "So this is an office building? People work here during the week?"

Lucienne held open one of the massive glass doors for us to enter as he replied, "It is the heart of Madame Églantine's empire: there are offices and workshops and meeting rooms, as you might imagine. She used to sometimes show her collections here, but that is now always done elsewhere."

The penny dropped even as I took in the magnificent interior, where marble floors and warm cream paintwork showcased a massive arcing staircase defined by an elegant and sinuously delicate black-metal balustrade, all illuminated by spectacular chandeliers. Pieces of almost-welcoming furniture – all exceptionally modern in design, and upholstered exclusively in jewel-toned velvets – were dotted along the walls.

Good grief, it's like a palace, was what I thought; "This is a fashion house?" was what I said.

"Impressive," said Bud, "though fashion's not something I know much about."

Lucienne whispered, "I see many things working here, and my uniform is, of course, created by the house – but I, too, am not normally interested in clothes…except that they do their job."

We all shared an almost conspiratorial smile, but I knew I had to – somehow – try to work out who it was I might have seen being "strangled". However, I was beginning to doubt what I'd seen, because I reckoned that a murder was unlikely to have gone unnoticed in such a place, and there weren't hordes of police running about…nor would the accommodating Lucienne have been likely to invite us into a known crime scene.

I opened with: "Earlier today we passed the building on an open-topped bus. I caught a glimpse into one of the second-floor windows. Did I see a woman in there, by any chance?"

Lucienne shrugged. "A woman?"

I dared, "She was wearing something that gleamed gold, that covered her entire neck." I didn't mention the gloved hands.

Lucienne half-smiled. "Madame Églantine wears a collar made of amber stones that comes from her chin to her chest. She has always worn it. It is one of her…symbols. Amber is important to her — as well as velvet, of course. Her house is known for its velvet."

With the doorman's response telling us both that what I'd seen might, in fact, be something…real, I saw Bud tense up. He asked, "And Madame Églantine is…well?"

Lucienne's exaggerated response spoke volumes. "She is Madame Églantine…I do not see her…often. She chooses not to mix with society at all. But she will attend the meeting of the board on the second floor today. When did you see this person?"

I checked my watch. "It would have been around noon."

Lucienne shook his head. "Lunch began at twelve thirty, or so. Madame will join the others when the meeting begins, at two. She would not have been on the second floor at that time. Possibly you saw Mademoiselle Avril. When she first arrived today, she was wearing a gold velvet scarf. It was very long…though she is a tall woman, as tall as me, so it must be this way. But I do not think she was here at noon…though she arrived…then left…then returned, so…maybe she was."

I jumped in. "Does Mademoiselle Avril have long, dark hair?"

"It is short, white, very…angular," said Lucienne. "Her daughter Joanne is also here, and she has long hair. It is on top of her head today."

I glanced at Bud, who was nibbling his upper lip; I hoped he had an idea of how we might progress our "investigation", because I was running out of options. I threw myself into gushing about the architectural details of the building — as a normal tourist might be expected to do — then made my way to a glass-enclosed, headless mannequin which stood near the rear wall of the deep reception area.

"That's stunning," I said. "The way the velvet has structure at the shoulders yet drapes so softly to the floor is quite amazing, as is the fabric itself." The long evening gown was made from *devoré* velvet that appeared to be both emerald green and purple at the same time – depending on how the subtle lighting caught it. And the pattern that had been created in the fabric by using chemicals to burn away the velvet tufts was an intricate concoction of paisley, swirling *fleur-de-lys*, and something that looked like a ragged peony head. It was astonishingly complex, and it mesmerized me for a moment.

Lucienne joined me and offered, "This was in Madame's first important collection, in the 1970s. It will soon be on display as part of an exhibition showing the development of all the famous fashion houses in Paris through the years. There has been a great deal of activity here at the Maison today because of this exhibition – this will be the final piece to be delivered. They collect it tomorrow morning, in its case, which might be…a challenge."

I admitted, "I'm embarrassed to say I've never heard of *Maison Églantine*, which is a great shame if this is the sort of thing you make here. It's…stunning."

"It is a gown to flatter every woman, they say," observed Lucienne.

If you're six feet tall and as thin as a whip, was what I thought; "I dare say you'd need to be quite well off to be able to afford it," was what I said.

Lucienne grinned. "Ah yes, it is only for every rich woman, not every poor woman – but that is couture. As I said, I know little about clothing, but the business of fashion is known throughout Paris. There are few who can afford such clothes, but Madame has made garments other than gowns. Her clothes have been worn by many rock stars, and many famous people. Mick Jagger and Stevie Nicks know Madame personally, they say. But we have a website – you could read all this there. Here, allow me to give you a card with the address, then you can see it when you are at home, after your vacation."

I took the card – emerald green, and embossed – then decided I had to say something that might help us. "I know this might sound a little strange, Lucienne, but – when we passed this building, on that bus – it really looked to me as though a couple of people were…messing about in front of a window. It was the first window on the left-hand side of the second floor…the first window along from the point of the building, on the *Avenue de l'Opéra*. And it looked as though…well, as though one of the people involved might be in medical distress. Has there been…an emergency here at all today?"

Lucienne shrugged. "Busy? Yes. But no emergency. Not today. Not since last week. Then one of the cutters had an accident and she went to the hospital. But today, everything has been normal. You say you saw the windows on the second floor near the *Avenue de l'Opéra*? Those are the windows for the anteroom, beyond the room where lunch is being served. At noon the people working for the catering company were in there – they arrived around…oh, eleven thirty and carried up many boxes. They could not use the elevator, because that has been used all morning by the people taking garments to the exhibition. Not that this is unusual – we have a great many deliveries and collections here, it is normal for such a business, though not on a Saturday…as a rule. The time was when I knew most of the people who would do this work for the fashion houses – for all of us. Now? Now it seems that anyone who owns a large vehicle can sell their time to deliver bolts of fabric, or take away crates or samples…whatever is needed – but they often do not understand how careful they must be with such precious items. Times change, this is true. Today? The caterers complained a great deal because they had to use the stairs."

I was puzzled: a room being used by a number of caterers would be unlikely to simultaneously host a strangulation.

Maybe Bud was right – I merely witnessed some sort of tomfoolery, was what I thought; what I said was, "I'm going to be honest with you, Lucienne – I thought I saw a woman, with something glowing gold beneath her chin, being attacked, in that room, around noon. Bud and I left the bus as soon as we could and hurried here to try to find out…anything. Please – could you do something to establish that everyone is alright up there? Is there someone you could talk to? Or could you maybe check inside the room to which I'm referring?"

Lucienne stared at me, then at Bud – who nodded – then at me again. I reckoned he was trying to work out if I was some sort of madwoman.

Bud approached us and said quietly, "I used to be a police officer, before I retired, and Cait's been teaching at the *Sorbonne* for a while – she's a criminal psychologist. We're not two people who would make this up, Lucienne. I understand that you don't know us at all, and that what we're saying sounds…odd. But if something did happen, it would be good to know about it, I'm sure you'd agree."

The doorman did the staring thing again, then his beard shoved forward, and he strode to the massive marble-topped desk that held pride of place at the foot of the staircase. He didn't say anything to us, but used an ornate telephone that looked as though it had been on the table since the nineteenth century. He spoke quietly, and hurriedly, leading me and Bud to walk toward him, hoping we'd be able to hear what he was saying…though we couldn't.

He all but glared at us as he spoke, listened, then spoke again. He slammed down the seemingly antique instrument. "The caterers have been in and out of the anteroom as I said. No one has been attacked there. Everyone is enjoying lunch, and the caterers are busy with service. I cannot disturb people more, so I cannot help you. I must ask you to leave now. This is a private company and nothing has happened here that is unusual today. I wish you an enjoyable vacation."

It was clear that we were being dismissed, and I could tell by the look on Bud's face that he agreed with me that there was little we could do but leave…which we did, thanking the doorman for his hospitality and kindness. As we walked across the road into the circular park in front of the building, I managed a backward glance, and saw Lucienne staring at us before he disappeared behind the gleaming glass of the imposing internal doors, which closed slowly, then merely reflected the trees beneath which we were walking.

We plopped down on one of the narrow wooden benches set around the inner pathway of the garden, picking a spot where we could feel the sun on our faces.

Bud grabbed my hand and said softly, "We did our best in there, Cait. Any suggestions about next steps?"

I stared at the fountain, glad that the sound of splashing water was drowning out the traffic that surrounded us. Now that we were close enough for me to see what each of the figures at its center was holding, it was clear that the trio of women were the Three Fates: the carved marble figure of one held up a small spinning wheel made of bronze, from which a thread of bronze ran to the hands of another who measured a length, which was being cut with a bronze knife by the third.

I observed, "That's cheerful. Not."

Bud's gaze followed mine. "How d'you mean?"

I explained the Greek and Roman myths about the three sisters who spun, measured, and then cut the thread of each human life as briefly as I could, concluding with: "They were known collectively as the *Moirai* in Greek mythology, and the *Parcae* in the Roman version. Clotho – the Greek spinner of the thread – is Nona in Roman mythology. Lachesis – who measures the length of a life and its experiences – is also called Decima. And the sister who cuts the thread – signifying the end of life – is Atropos in Greek but Morta in Roman. You can see where our word 'mortality' originated."

Bud chuckled, "Thanks for making that lesson so painless. I dare say you know all that from reading a book when you were fifteen – right?"

I chuckled back. "I was about ten, and – for some reason I never quite fathomed – a book by E.M. Berens, entitled *Myths and Legends of Greece and Rome*, was in the small library at my junior school. I took it home to read, and loved it, despite the fact it had been first published in the 1880s. I read the tenth edition, but don't think it had been updated much from the original. It's what started my love for ancient myths – all those wonderfully labyrinthine relationships, and feuds. And I suppose some of the tales were truly grisly – so they had that going for them, too…though, thinking about it now, there is an awful lot of violence against women in those stories. So maybe they had something to do with me wanting to speak for victims later in life…who knows."

Bud managed a smile. "Not me, for one."

"And not me, for two."

Bud sighed. "I'm at a bit of a loss, Wife, and I'm really not sure what we should do next. If everything's been 'normal' at the Maison all day, as Lucienne said, and if the caterers were really in that anteroom from eleven thirty onwards – making it unlikely that someone was being strangled in there at the same time – then…well, what do you think?"

I kissed Bud on the cheek. "Oh Husband, I do love you…you just don't want to accuse me of having 'seen things that weren't there', do you? And I adore that about you. But…I know what I saw – and where, and when, I saw it. And…well, we know nothing about Lucienne, other than that he's one person who's told us one version of what was happening in that room I saw into at the time. He might not be telling the truth. I didn't see the body attached to the hands around that woman's throat, after all, so…it could have been…him."

Bud raked his hand through his hair – which told me how stressful he was finding the situation. "You think we've just been in the company of a killer?"

I shrugged. "We both know how good some people can be at disguising their true self…though, to be fair, I didn't get 'strangler vibes' from him."

Bud's eyes grew round. "'Strangler vibes'? That's a very un-Cait-like thing for you to say."

I nodded. "I know – but I'm not feeling very Cait-like at the moment. I'm getting a distinct whiff of Christie's *4:50 From Paddington*, which is irritating me, and making me feel a bit…otherworldly, I suppose. But, honestly, I do know what I saw, Bud."

My husband kissed my cheek. "Right then, let's go to the police and tell them that. I don't know if my track record, or yours, will carry any weight – but we should do what we think is right, and report this."

I held up my phone. "Good, because I've just found the nearest *commissariat* – or police station, to you and me – on this map, and it's not too far from here."

Bud hugged me. "I knew you wouldn't let us do nothing about it. Come on then, let's go."

Trois

It didn't take us long to reach what turned out to be a flag-bedecked and imposing building of significant age. It had been retrofitted with some incredibly high-tech security measures, which meant that our entrance was overseen by multiple cameras mounted upon antique marble balustrades which lined a mezzanine floor above our heads, as well as the watchful eyes of the officers on duty inside a cubicle built out of what I assumed was bulletproof glass.

I imagined them sizing us up as we crossed what felt like acres of echoing marble, and believed I could hear the cameras swivel to focus on us as we proceeded toward them. Having explained who we were, and why we were there – a bald statement that I wanted to report what I believed was a murder, or at least a violent attack – one of the officers impassively typed something on the keyboard in front of him, then we were told to take a seat. We did, which wasn't a comfy experience; it would appear that plastic bucket chairs suitable for being permanently attached to the floor are designed to accommodate a narrower *derrière* than mine.

From above us, a voice called out, in English, "Professor Morgan? Is that really you?"

I looked up. "Good grief – Pierre Bertrand?" I couldn't believe it; I hadn't seen Pierre since that terrible business in Nice when my old boss had collapsed, dead, into a bowl of escargots, almost five years earlier.

"Stay there – I'll be with you immediately," called the young police officer, who'd been a uniformed lieutenant back then, but was now wearing a smart suit and tie, and had much longer hair than he'd worn beneath his uniform's cap.

The two officers in the glass booth stared upward, then at us, as we hovered in the middle of the yawning atrium awaiting the arrival of Pierre.

I bet you're really curious about us now, was what I thought; "This could be…good for us, Bud," was what I said.

"He's the guy you told me about in Nice, right? The one you kept in touch with after you got back from that nightmare. Did you know he was in Paris?"

"No. I have to admit that I haven't been too good at emailing him. In my defense, life's been quite busy…especially the past couple of years…though I know I sent him some photos from our honeymoon trip. There he is…" I immediately used my best French to address the young man, just so that I could show him how I'd improved, since we'd first met. "Pierre, what a wonderful surprise. How are you?"

A great deal of cheek-kissing ensued, as well as formal introductions, and then an explanation that Pierre had been urged by none other than Captain Moreau – his superior back in Nice – to sit exams to allow him to become a detective, and seek a post in a place that stretched him: Paris. He'd been in the city for a little more than a year, and was loving it.

Bud and I exchanged a glance, and I opened with: "I've been teaching a course at the *Sorbonne* for a month, and now Bud's come over to spend a week with me here – just the two of us, on a break."

Pierre smiled widely; his grin had lost none of its impishness, even though – now in his late thirties – his face had matured in other ways. "This explains why your French is good. Did you find out somehow that I was here? But no, you said it was a surprise to see me," noted the detective, with a twinkle in his eye. "So, why are you here…at this place? I saw something pop up on my screen about a Professor Cait Morgan being a witness to…something, and I came to see if it was you. And it is!"

I thanked him for bothering to do so, then continued, "The reason we're here, now, is that…well, I think I saw a murder today – or at least someone being attacked, and we came here to report it."

Pierre's demeanor changed in a heartbeat: his back straightened, his shoulders settled, and his smile disappeared. When he spoke, his tone was grave. "We must speak about this in the proper manner. Follow me."

He marched toward the men in the glass cubicle and spoke to them abruptly; one of them indicated a door to the right which Pierre pushed open. He motioned for us to enter. Inside were two sofas, a coffee table, and a barred window; the room felt bleak, but hardly forbidding.

Waving toward one sofa, Pierre sat on the other. He pulled out his phone. "I shall record this," he said, suggesting we had no option but to agree. "Please tell me everything – but start with…is there any action I should be taking at this moment to save a person's life?"

"I don't believe so," I replied, looking at Bud.

Bud's tone signified resignation. "Cait witnessed the scene at approximately noon."

Pierre looked shocked. "Then why have you waited…no, forgive me, please, Professor Morgan, state your name, and make your statement. This is a formal report, yes?"

I nodded, and explained exactly what had happened from the moment I'd spotted the woman in the window, until our arrival at the police station.

When I'd finished, Pierre asked, "You agree with this account, Monsieur Anderson?"

"I do. I believe that your initial contact with Cait means you know about her abilities to recollect things in an unusually accurate way. I didn't see what she saw, but I believe she saw it, and the rest of her explanation of our actions after that moment is, as you might expect, not only highly detailed, but also accurate."

Having now had a chance to study him a little, I could see that Pierre's face had taken on a leaner appearance, with his bone structure being better defined than it had been five years earlier; also, what had once been an open and happy expression was now more guarded. He'd certainly slimmed down a great deal, and the tan he'd had when I'd met him in the south of France had paled to an almost jaundiced pallor, though he looked, for the most part, to be in excellent health. As his eyes flicked between me and Bud, I wondered what was going through his mind, and whether his abilities as an officer of the law had matured alongside his physical appearance.

You can't decide how to handle what I've just told you, was what I thought; "I understand we might have put you in a delicate situation," was what I said.

Pierre nibbled at his lower lip, then said, "You have, but that isn't just because of what you've told me. It's also because of my position here. I am still a lieutenant, but I have a more senior role than when you first met me, and am now with the judicial police. So, yes, I am a criminal investigation detective, though I have developed some specialism in criminology – inspired by my meeting with you, Professor Morgan. Captain Moreau in Nice encouraged me to pursue both academic and police advancements, so I am here to…suggest ways that the study of criminal psychology can help officers in their detection of criminals. Maybe you can understand that this means that I am not always…popular?"

Bud and I both laughed aloud, then realized that our reactions might be misinterpreted, and shut up.

I said, "I'm delighted to know that I inspired you, but – you're right – both Bud and I understand what that means when it comes to working with experienced detectives who've always handled their cases in certain ways, and don't often agree that new ideas have a role to play in their day-to-day work."

Pierre's expression cleared. "Good. You see, I'm inside the department, but am often treated like an outsider. Of course, there's also always the normal reaction to someone from the south of the country being placed in a role here in the capital, but I can cope with that. It's just that I will have to present what you have told me…carefully. Not only is it the weekend, but my immediate superior is on vacation at the moment, and his superior is a person who is…not often on my side. However, there is an officer of equal rank to my boss's boss who is on duty today, and she is more sympathetic to what I am trying to do."

Bud noted, "There aren't a huge number of female senior officers in the French national police, are there?"

Pierre shook his head. "Not yet, though this is changing, slowly. But this woman? I think you will like her. She is strong, intelligent, and has a quality that some of her equals here lack – empathy. I believe this is critical when investigating crime. If you cannot understand other people, how can you truly understand why a criminal might have acted in a certain way?"

I jumped in. "Thank you, Pierre – a point I make over and over again in the classes I teach…when it comes to profiling a victim, as well as hunting for a perpetrator."

Pierre smiled warmly. "We all agree then. But, if I'm to find this person, I must leave you now. I shall return as soon as possible. There's a small refrigerator there – help yourselves to water."

Alone in the barren room, sipping on chilled water, Bud and I remained silent for a few moments. Eventually I said, "He's grown up a lot. When I first met him, he was almost too afraid to speak in the presence of his superior officers, though he was always most helpful to me…and I took a shine to him, as I know I've told you."

Bud grinned, "Says Mother Hen, eh?"

I play-thumped him. "Now, now. He was always thoughtful – he even kept me up to date with how the folks I'd met in Nice got on with their lives…and it was thanks to him that I got all those insights into the court case that followed. Pierre Bertrand is one of the good ones, and it's nice to know I've inspired someone to find a path that suits them, which can also benefit others…even if that's in the long run, by the sounds of it. I know that all police services are like oil tankers in that if you want them to change direction you have to do it carefully – by degrees – and allow time for it to happen. However, without people like Pierre making suggestions about how that shift might be undertaken, it'll never happen at all."

Bud nodded. "Yeah, I get it that cybercrime units, and even the sort of thing I ended up doing – working with international agencies across many borders to try to control gang activities – can be 'added on to' the existing structures, but the way work is done at the core needs to be addressed too. And I don't just mean by sending every officer to do a few courses about how to interview victims more sensitively…though goodness knows that's needed. No, I mean that the entire mindset has to be addressed – and that happens when you recruit differently, train differently, then manage differently. And all that takes time. It's almost generational, in fact. Young officers with good ideas are needed, and it looks to me as though Pierre Bertrand is everything you told me he was – bright, and dedicated."

As if on cue, Pierre entered the room again, followed by a short, slim woman, with dark circles beneath her eyes that suggested sleepless nights. She wore four-inch heels, a luminous caramel-colored silk shirt, and an immaculately tailored three-piece navy pantsuit that I suspected would have cost me a month's salary. I pegged her at being around forty, a few years Pierre's senior, in any case.

She stuck out a hand. "I'm Captain de Gaulle – no relation – Francine, please. And you are Professor Morgan and Monsieur Anderson?"

"Cait, and Bud, please," said Bud, smiling.

"Sit. I shall stand. Pierre has let me listen to your statement, Cait, and I find it unsettling. I have put out some calls and am awaiting news, though I wanted to…ah, wait, please." Francine answered her phone, listened, sent a text, then returned her attention to the three of us. "This is…concerning. A call has been received stating that Madame Églantine George, the owner of *Maison Églantine*, is missing…with the initial report suggesting a kidnapping. Our department has responded appropriately, and officers are on their way to the Maison at the moment. Given your statement, Cait, I have inserted myself into the case. I must communicate with the officers on site before they begin work."

So…I was right to be concerned – but…a kidnapping? was what I thought; "I'm pleased we came to report what I saw – which might have been an attack to subdue a victim of kidnapping…do you think?" was what I said.

Francine's demeanor plainly signaled she wasn't going to give us any more information. She squared her shoulders and said, "Thank you for your time. Please ensure that Officer Bertrand has all your details so that we are able to reach you. Is the hotel where you will be tonight close by?"

Bud replied, "We'll be in the second *arrondissement*, on *Rue du Sentier*. The Luxsey."

Francine's eyebrows shot up. "The Luxsey? Near the Rex Cinema? The crowd that socializes there is…young and…interesting. Give Pierre your details, settle in, enjoy your vacation, and thank you."

I couldn't help but wonder what Francine had meant by her use of the words "young and interesting", but pushed such thoughts out of my mind as quickly as I could.

"We'd really appreciate any updates you might be able to give us," I said, hoping that a winning smile might grease the wheels.

Francine's eyes narrowed. "You might be a witness to a crime. We might need to question you, so please always have your phones with you. Thank you."

She'd shot out of the room before anyone had a chance to add another word.

Pierre's expression suggested that he might be more than a little in awe of Captain Francine de Gaulle. "The captain will act swiftly and most appropriately," he said, with a flush of…*pride?*

"If you give me your number, I'll text you all our details, Pierre," said Bud.

Pierre smiled. "Ah…but we have a form for that. Wait, and I'll bring it. Though I will give you my number – and I promise to tell you what I can, when I can. In memory of our time in Nice, Professor Morgan. I owe you that."

"Please Pierre, it's Cait and Bud for you too, not just for your boss."

"My boss's sort-of boss, you mean," corrected Pierre as he left us again.

Bud and I exchanged a resigned glance. I said, "We're not going to get a chance to do anything regarding this, are we? Francine made that much clear."

Bud smiled. "Let's try to get on with our vacation as best we can…knowing we've done what we could, and that the cops are all over it. It sounds to me like Francine knows what she's doing – and I reckon Pierre'll pass on as much as he's able. Unless Francine tells him not to. I don't think he'd cross her, do you?"

I grinned. "Oh no…we're seeing a case of a completely adoring puppy there, I think. He'll pant after her, and gaze in admiration at her…but never cross her, you're right. But he did say I'd inspired him to change career path, so – yes – I think Pierre will tell us what he can…if she lets him."

"Then there's hope," said Bud, "because I know what you'll be like about this…until we find out something more about what's going on at *Maison Églantine*."

"I don't know what you mean," I said, as convincingly as possible.

Quatre

When Pierre had taken all our contact details, he announced that his shift was over and offered to drive us back to our original hotel, then deliver us to our new one, but we explained about our luggage, and he admitted that his small car might not be adequate for the job, so Bud and I walked back to the bus stop outside the shop on the *Avenue de l'Opéra* where we'd begun our trip several hours earlier.

As we, once again, passed *Maison Églantine*, I craned my neck to see if there was any obvious investigative presence, but my suspicions that any activity would be at the end of the building farthest from the *Avenue de l'Opéra* were borne out insofar as I couldn't see any police at all.

Bud and I surrendered ourselves to the enthusiastic commentary being delivered by the recorded system on the bus as we took in the sights of Paris from our top-deck seats. The late-April air was a good deal chillier than it had been when we'd begun our original trip, so I sat on my hands, and pulled the collar of my jacket around my chin as the air rushed past us, cooled even more by the fact that the sky was most definitely clouding over; the sun wasn't due to go down until about nine o'clock-ish, but the promise of the sunny morning had descended into gloom – a bit like my spirits.

I gave myself a good talking to as the bus swept away from the Louvre and along the bank of the Seine, heading toward Notre Dame, which looked magnificent, following all the work that had been done to restore its façade. Shortly afterwards we alighted, then walked back to the hotel that had been my temporary home for the past four weeks. Even though I'd been in and out of the place a good many times, I still didn't feel as though there was any real connection between me and the slightly sullen staff at reception, so Bud and I simply collected our bags, then waited outside as he followed the progress of our ride-share car on his phone.

When it had been stuck "five minutes away" for ten minutes, he shoved his phone into his pocket with disgust and said, "I can tell you're stewing on what you saw…but we need to try to put it to one side, at least until tomorrow. Pierre's off duty – he won't know anything to tell us until then, at the earliest, so let's get checked in to our new hotel and sorted out, then find ourselves somewhere to have a nice dinner, eh? When I was looking for a place for us to stay, I picked one where there are lots of bars and restaurants close by, so we can try somewhere different for each meal, if you like."

"I wonder what Francine meant when she said that the people who use the hotel where we're staying are young and interesting? She chose the words…carefully."

Bud shrugged. "Who knows? She was an amalgamation of opposites, wasn't she?"

"You mean it looked as though she hadn't slept for a week, yet was wearing clothes that cost a bomb? Yes, a real enigma."

"It might just be a French thing – you know, investment dressing."

I chuckled as I replied, "And what would you know about 'investment dressing', Bud? You hate shopping for clothes, and always say they're just something you have to wear. Have you been reading up on fashion while I've been here, slogging my guts out?"

"Actually, I've been planning the next five years of forest husbandry for our mountain, and breaking my back in the garden trying to sort out the rhododendrons that needed attention before being left to their own devices at a critical time of year. I've also been Marty-wrangling…which takes a bit of doing, because he seems to be going through a particularly energetic phase at the moment, and you know I've been back and forth to Mom and Dad's a lot. She recovered well from that hip replacement, but I don't think Dad is…thriving, and she seems to be a bit short-tempered with him at the moment, which isn't like them, at all."

"Did he get around to sorting out any hearing aids, like he said he would?" I suspected I knew the answer; Bud's father had maintained he had perfect hearing long after we all knew he didn't.

"As a matter of fact, he has…though Mom says he turns them off when he wants a bit of peace and quiet."

We shared a wan grin – then our car arrived, which was good, because I was starting to get thoroughly fed up with just waiting about.

I'd noticed, when we were on the bus, that the traffic in Paris appeared to have a rhythm, and "at a dead stop" was definitely part of that rhythm, which meant that – twenty minutes later – I was cursing the fact that I hadn't availed myself of the facilities at our last hotel, because we were sitting in yet another snarl-up, this time caused by some significant roadworks, which seemed to be happening on all the major boulevards, and many side streets. Just as I was thinking I might have to ask the driver to stop for me to nip into a café, we pulled up behind a car parked in a side street so narrow that we couldn't get around it, stopping outside a small wooden doorway in a long, blank wall.

"The Luxsey," announced the driver.

One look at Bud's horrified expression confirmed this wasn't what he'd expected. He said, "It didn't look like this online."

"That car ahead of us is in front of the entrance," added the driver, then switched off his engine and got out.

"It's only a few yards to wheel the bags," said Bud with a suspicious amount of enthusiasm, and he, too, got out of the car. He stuck his head back inside and added, "You go on ahead, I'll bring your suitcase."

Clever Bud — you spotted all the signs that I need the loo.

I didn't hesitate; knowing there was a washroom in my near future, I cantered toward the steps that led to a massive, arched portico, then entered a bar area with a cobbled floor. Ahead of me a glass wall partitioned the bar from an open-air courtyard, filled with tables, chairs, trees wreathed in lights, and jolly umbrellas. I gratefully caught sight of a sign for toilets, and shot off in that direction, following a circuitous route downstairs to a bank of beautifully appointed all-gender stalls, each with their own washbasin and hand dryer. I couldn't have been happier.

Refreshed, I made my way back up the wide, curving stone staircase, following signs directing me to the reception area, where I found Bud, who looked like the cat who'd just lapped up all the cream.

"Dave here was just telling me about the menu for tonight at the restaurant here," said my husband, looking smug.

A slim Black man was beaming from his spot behind the reception desk.

I said, "Dave?"

Dave nodded. "From London. Ontario, not England. Welcome, fellow Canadians."

I was surprised, and a little deflated — I'd been hoping for a hotel with a real sense of…Frenchness, then I looked beyond the desk, and realized there was no shortage of that. Without the urgent need to relieve myself, I was better able to take in my surroundings, and was impressed.

"The elevators are just through there, and we're on the third floor," announced Bud. "Let's dump these bags — then I'll buy you a G and T, just to help you settle in, okay?"

"Lead on," was all I could muster, because my mouth had started to water at the thought of a gin and tonic.

Once I'd checked that the bed in our spacious room was comfy – it was – that the loo flushed and the water pressure from the shower was good – it did, and it was – and that the view from our window was suitably Parisian – it was, because we looked out over the mansard rooftops beyond our building – I was happy to dump everything…and agree that unpacking later on would do.

Ten minutes later I was sitting at a table in the courtyard with a gin and tonic in my hand, Edith Piaf warbling in my head, and a broad smile on my face.

"These people aren't so young," I hissed at Bud as I sucked at my drink and took in the ornate architectural details surrounding us. "They're in their thirties at least, though their fashion sense is…eclectic. My students were younger, of course, and fell into two camps. There were the ones who looked as though they'd put on something that happened to be clean, but managed to look chic, somehow. The others had obviously worked at it, and often it just didn't…well, work. These people? Effortlessly stylish, I'd say. In fact, I'm quite jealous."

"Yeah…an average age of about thirty or so, I'd guess," he replied. "No, not so young…but, yes, a bit arty, I'd say. Look at that guy with the earrings…they really suit him. And that group of three young women? You're right – they don't look as though they've stepped out of a magazine or anything, but even I can tell they have…a certain *panache* in the way they present themselves. Do you like it here? This sort of crowd isn't making you feel…uncomfortable, is it?"

"It's quite the place, and I don't feel at all uncomfortable. Look – not one person's on their phone…everyone's talking to each other. It's quite wonderful." I acknowledged, "Good choice, Bud."

"It was a grand home back when it was built in the 1700s," said Bud enthusiastically. "Madame de Pompadour used to live along the street, and this place was owned by an advisor to King Louis the fifteenth. Fancy, eh?"

"Fancy, indeed. That's a beautiful staircase, winding its way up to that balcony, above the bar in there," I noted.

"They enclosed that entryway to make the bar area – hence the cobbles – and installed an original eighteenth-century staircase to access the mezzanine they built. I don't think they spared any expense when they converted the place. And there's a second courtyard through that arched passage there."

I turned to see the archway toward which Bud was waving, behind me. "We'll take a look later, but I just want to enjoy this drink, for now. You seem to be incredibly well acquainted with the building's history, Bud."

"It's all on their website – about the building. Fascinating stuff. Funnily enough – given where we found ourselves earlier today – this area, Sentier, used to be the heart of the textile district in Paris, and this place was once a clothing factory."

As I took in the elegantly carved façade of the interior courtyard, and the carefully laid paving which surrounded us, I said, "It's always quite something to imagine the previous lives a building has led, isn't it? Oh…is that a menu?"

Bud handed me a small booklet. "It's for the restaurant, in there–" he pointed toward a door in the wall adjacent to the glass separating us from the bar –"and they serve here, if you want to eat outside. Though it might get a bit chilly, later on."

"We've got our jackets, and they've got heaters – it would be nice to watch the light change in the sky, don't you think?" I read the offerings on the menu, mentally eating my way through every dish as I did so. "Fancy some braised ox cheeks, with vegetables and garlic mash?"

Bud wrinkled his nose. "I was thinking more along the lines of a steak and *frites*, to be honest."

"That's what you had last night."

"But I like it."

We chuckled, and both decided that, even though it would be quite early for dinner, we'd eat right away, because we'd both made ourselves hungry by merely thinking about food. We managed to order quickly, due to the attentiveness of our server – a young woman named Marianne, with a dark ponytail that bounced above her smart black and cream suit, and gifted with an efficient, friendly manner. Moments later she arrived with a basket of bread, a pitcher of water, and a mound of glistening butter. I took a big slurp of gin, slathered butter onto bread, then bit into the moist, crusty deliciousness. I reveled in the textures and flavors…simple, but exquisite.

Yes, there really is something special about fresh French butter, was what I thought; "I knew I was hungry, but didn't realize how famished I really was until just now," was what I said.

"Me too," said Bud, who was chomping on bread with a smile on his face – and he's not usually one for the breadbasket.

It was as though someone in the kitchen had read our minds and had been standing by ready to prepare our meals, because, within moments, Bud and I were comparing dishes, I was pinching one of his *frites*, and he was asking me about the flavor of the ox cheeks – which I did my best to communicate. "The meat's soft and yielding – as it would be, because it's been braised – and it's definitely been cooked in red wine, likely with a mixture of onions, carrots, and celery, because the *mirepoix* is a starting point for many French recipes. The vegetables have been steamed, then buttered to within an inch of their lives, and the garlic mash is fluffy, creamy, and…extremely garlicky. Maybe you should have a couple of mouthfuls of that, just so we both smell the same as each other later on."

Bud chuckled. "Fair enough…but that doesn't mean you can have any more of my *frites*. My steak's perfect, and I'm glad you suggested the *Béarnaise* sauce on the side, which is delicious."

For the next few moments we each indulged silently, enjoying the ambience, the freshness of the evening air, and the aromas of our own food…and that being served around us. The background music was modern, yet pleasant, and most definitely French, though the sound of sirens that reached us from the streets outside spoiled the overall effect a little. Eventually they stopped, and I realized I'd finished my drink. I looked around, managed to catch our server's eye…then spotted a face I recognized peering through the glass wall.

Pierre Bertrand burst into the courtyard, followed by two uniformed, and obviously armed, police officers. "Cait, Bud – you must come with me. Now. It's most urgent."

All eyes turned toward the officers…then us. Our server – who'd been walking toward us – stepped backward, knocking into an adjoining table.

I asked, "Pierre – what's happened?"

The two officers stood beside Pierre, and the taller of the two barked, "You are to accompany us, now. No questions."

Bud and I stood, because we felt we had no choice, and moved toward Pierre. Bud called over his shoulder, "We'll charge all that to our room – I hope that's okay."

I glanced backward to see our server nodding dumbly, as we were hustled through the cobblestoned bar, beneath the eighteenth-century staircase, and out onto the street, where we were bundled into a waiting police car, which set off with its lights flashing, and siren screaming.

And I'd been looking forward to another gin and tonic.

Cinq

I know that back at home, in British Columbia, all drivers do their best to pull over to the side of the road and stop to allow the passage of emergency vehicles. It seemed that the same was true in Paris, but I quickly realized there wasn't the space available for vehicles to get out of the way easily, so the lights and sirens meant that our progress was more rapid than it had been on the bus or in the ride-share car, but it wasn't without its pauses, and some nifty maneuvering on the part of the officer who was driving.

With Pierre in the other car, and Bud and myself in the back seat of the one with the grumpy officer, I didn't think we stood much chance of being told what was going on, but it soon became clear that we were headed toward *Maison Églantine* rather than the police station which – oddly – led me to perk up a bit. I even squeezed Bud's hand and nodded at the circular garden in a knowing way once I spotted it.

He rolled his eyes, then gave me a little smile before hissing, "Try not to look so pleased, Cait. This might not be…good."

I hissed back, "I'll take any chance I can to find out more about the woman I believe was killed here, or at least attacked. You understand why I have to do that, don't you? My work, and my life, is all about acting on behalf of victims…I need to be true to myself."

Bud squeezed my hand and smiled. I thought I caught a quiet tutting noise coming from him…but the siren was so loud that I couldn't be certain. Either way, we had no choice but to sit until our doors were opened by the heavily armed officer a couple of moments after we'd stopped right outside the imposing entrance to the Maison.

Through the glass doors I could see people inside scurrying about, but there was no sign of Lucienne. "Our doorman seems to have disappeared," I whispered as we stood on the steps, awaiting our fate.

Before Bud could reply, Pierre was at my shoulder. "Thanks for coming. Captain de Gaulle requested your presence. She's here herself…which is not usual."

I dared, "To be honest, Pierre, we didn't have any choice about coming, did we? But, that aside, I thought you were off duty…and why do you think such a senior officer has come to the scene of…well, what, exactly?"

Pierre looked panicked. "I don't know. I received a call, and I responded. I have no idea what's going on. I didn't even eat dinner…I live quite some distance from the station – it's too expensive to live close to it."

For a moment, I caught a glimpse of the younger man I'd first met; Pierre looked a little lost. I said, "I'm sure Captain de Gaulle will explain the situation, now that we're all here."

We were ushered into the reception area where we'd stood several hours earlier, then were directed to sit on a vivid purple velvet banquette that was surprisingly yielding, and threatened to swallow me whole. We waited there for the next twenty minutes – completely ignored by all those swirling about the place – none of us speaking…though we all shot occasional glances toward each other; I suspected mine displayed my increasing irritation.

Eventually, Francine de Gaulle walked down the sweeping staircase. She still looked haggard, but she managed to swoosh toward us with an easy elegance.

"Thank you for coming, Cait, Bud. Has Pierre explained why I asked for you to be here?"

Pierre had shot to his feet, but nonetheless dared, "I couldn't do that, because I wasn't briefed, Captain."

Francine's brow furrowed. "You should have been told. All of you." She paced around the yawning space, the sound of her high heels echoing on the marble floor, then eventually stood in front of us and said, "You know we were alerted to the fact that Madame Églantine George had disappeared earlier today. We have now established that she is not only missing from here – her place of business and home – but she is not in any hospital, nor has a person matching her description been reported as 'found'. No ransom demands have been made – which might yet happen, if she's been kidnapped – but I wanted you here so you could show me, and explain to me exactly, *in situ*, what you saw at noon today, Cait. I've arranged for a bus of the type you were on to be brought to the *Avenue de l'Opéra*, where I want you to sit in the same seat, and give the word when you reach the same point at which you saw…what you saw. I have people standing by to enact what you say you witnessed. This will help us all. You agree?"

I wasn't sure what she was asking me. "Do I agree to do it, or do I agree it will help?"

"Both."

"I agree…but I'd like Bud to be with me. Would you and I communicate by telephone when I'm doing it?"

"Yes."

I quite liked the way that Francine didn't waste words, or time.

She turned her attention to Bud. "You and your wife are interesting people. I have researched you both, since we met – at least, my team has done so – and I was surprised to discover that not even my level of security clearances allowed me to find out more about you. I will speak to a colleague in another department this evening – he specializes in organized crime, which includes gangs. I believe he might be more forthcoming. Do you think that might be the case, Monsieur Anderson?"

Bud smiled. "I've already told you, it's Bud…and I'm retired now, so I'm not sure what anyone could tell you about me."

She replied, "We shall see. In any case, now that I am clear about the…reliability of your past roles – both of you – I shall tell you that every member of the board of the *Maison Églantine* organization was here for a meeting today, and they went looking for their boss when she didn't arrive for her appointment with them. Madame Églantine occupies the top floor of this building. It's been her personal apartment for decades. There are no signs of a struggle having taking place there, and no obvious signs of personal trauma there either. I have a team going door-to-door in the local vicinity to discover whether the missing woman has been seen by anyone. So far, they have no useful news. Pierre, and other officers, will accompany you both to the bus, and will remain with you throughout this process. Thank you. Though I had no doubt you would agree to my…request."

Francine tossed her hair – which I noticed had a wonderful cut, and an impressive balayage in honey and caramel hues, with not a split end in sight – and headed toward the door. "I suggest you accept the blankets you're offered. We're not sure how long this will take. We have the bus until midnight."

Midnight? Are you kidding? was what I thought; "I dare say it'll take as long as it takes," was what I said.

When I'd stepped happily onto the bus earlier that day, I hadn't imagined I'd be getting onto the same sort of vehicle hours later – for the third time – accompanied by two armed policemen, another officer I hadn't seen in years, and with a police car as a guide for the vehicle to be able to nose out into the Saturday evening traffic.

The whole area looked completely different than when we'd first seen it: shopfronts were now in darkness, except for their glowing signs; cafés and restaurants were busy and bustling, even on pavement terraces, where customers chatted as they enjoyed their evening, protected from the chilling air by jackets, coats, and lots and lots of scarves; apartment windows were alight, with hints of motion coming from behind partially closed or open shutters.

I hope I can still connect what I originally saw with how things look now.

When the police car drove forward so that the bus could move, unimpeded, out into the heavy traffic I waited until we were close to the angle that had been my original viewpoint, and Pierre ordered the driver to slow, then stop, when I told him to. I spoke into my phone explaining the location of the window where I'd seen the attack take place. As I did, a flashlight was waved at the window, and I agreed it was the correct one. A moment later the entire room was lit, and I saw – once again – the side view of a woman with a pair of hands at her throat.

Speaking to Francine, I had to shout over the cacophony of horns being honked by drivers angry that there was a police vehicle with its lights flashing and a double-decker bus, both of which had stopped, for no apparent reason, in the middle of the road.

I said, "Right – this is different because I can really only see a silhouette, due to the fact that the figures are being backlit, but the woman was a fair bit lower down than that. At the moment I can see her from her waist up, whereas I could only see to the middle of her chest."

"The woman is standing," replied Francine, "we'll have her sit."

Figures moved about, until the scene was reset.

I said, "I can still see too much of her torso. Lower…lower…that's it – so she must have been that short-bodied, or else sitting that far down in the seat…but now I can see arms leading to the hands around her neck, and I could only see wrists…so the woman was closer to the left-hand side of the window, from my point of view, and the wrists weren't angled down – the hands were straight around her neck."

There was a great deal more movement, and I could hear muffled sounds as the scene was reset. Eventually Francine said, "How about that?"

I was satisfied, and said so. I saw flashes, and assumed photography was taking place.

Francine then asked, "Now I want you to focus on the woman herself…is the hair correct?"

I stared at the window, then closed my eyes and hummed; I don't know why it helps me to dredge things up from my photographic memory, but it does. "No – she had bangs…a fringe…long and a little bouffant. Her hair was also a little bouffant on top of her head, and fell down her back beyond my sight."

I could clearly see the woman donning a wig, then there was someone fiddling about with it. I shouted, "That's it," when it looked right.

"Now tell me about the hands at the woman's neck," said Francine.

"I'm sorry, because of the effect of the backlighting, I can't do that, now. Though my impression was that the fingers were thick – so I assumed gloves, as I know I mentioned in my initial statement. Thinking about it, leather might have been the material, though all I could tell you is that they were dark. I didn't see a color, other than they appeared black against the glowing…whatever it was…around her neck."

"Is there anything else – now that you're there, Cait?" It sounded as though Francine were pleading with me to give her…something more.

I replied, "Sorry, no. What I just saw replicates what I saw around noon as closely as is humanly possible, I'd say."

Francine snapped, "Now you're saying 'around noon'. Was it noon, or wasn't it?"

Bud's brow creased when he saw my reaction to what I'd heard. He whispered, "What's the matter?"

I spoke into the phone, "Just a moment, Francine." I said to Bud, "Can we be more specific about the time when I saw what I saw? Francine's picked me up on that…and I can't be certain. I didn't hear anything chime noon, and I wasn't looking at my watch."

Bud shook his head. "Might the bus company know what time we pulled away from the bus stop at least?"

I asked Francine the question, and got an explosive, "The bus left stop number one at eleven forty as scheduled, but the driver only has to 'generally' stick to the timetable, except for certain stops, and was not prepared to be specific about when he arrived at or left stop two, which is where you got on. Come back now, please. Thank you."

The bus moved a little farther along the street, pulled into a gap between the parked cars, and we all trooped down the stairs. As the bus drove off into traffic the accompanying police car screamed away with its siren blaring. We wandered back to the main entrance of the Maison feeling a little despondent. I didn't feel I'd achieved much, and was still – irritatingly – in the dark about what exactly was happening. I reasoned that if Francine had gone to the considerable trouble of recreating what I'd seen, she had to think it meant something…but what?

If Églantine George was "missing", was it really her that I'd seen?

And…more importantly, was she still alive?

Six

A uniformed officer led us toward the staircase inside the Maison, and we trailed after him. Pierre went first, with Bud following me up the wide, shallow, marble steps which wound gracefully across one intricately mosaiced landing, then up to another broad, marble-inlaid one. Double doors stood open, revealing an impressive, massive room with an impressive, massive chandelier hung above an impressive, massive oval table, where it looked as though an actual board meeting was about to break out: the table was half-surrounded by people. Francine, who sat at its head, was wearing a grim expression.

"Sit," she instructed as we entered. Bud, Pierre, and I moved toward three of the empty seats. I felt my mouth fall open as I took in the design details of my surroundings: on the walls, panels of emerald green flock wallpaper…no…actual velvet – employing the same paisley, *fleur-de-lys*, and tattered peony bloom pattern I'd seen in the gown in the reception area earlier in the day – were surrounded by frames of varnished wood, swooping in the sort of curves and delicate twists I'd already seen in the metalwork at some Metro stations; the chair I was pulling out to sit on had been upholstered in the same fabric that was mounted on the walls, and the wooden back had been carved to incorporate sinuous lines. The whole place was an homage to the delight that was *art nouveau* design – and it, most definitely, lived up to the *Maison Églantine* promise.

Once we were settled, Francine announced, "I want you all to state your name, explain who you are, and why you're here. I shall begin. I am Captain Francine de Gaulle – no relation – authorized to investigate the disappearance of Églantine George, of *Maison Églantine*. We'll work clockwise."

All eyes turned toward the man sitting to Francine's left, whose neck immediately flushed with a blotchy patchwork of pink and red. I put him in his mid-forties; he had longer than average thick, lush, dark hair, wore an open-necked pink shirt with a purple velvet cravat, and his jacket was a black-and-white, large-houndstooth-patterned velvet.

He smiled slowly, showing perfect teeth, then said, "I'm Jacques Novello, the head of design and creative integrity at *Maison Églantine*, a position I've held for the past eighteen months. I work as Madame's right hand, and do my best to both embody and creatively continue the spirit of the brand." He nodded graciously toward Bud and me, then at everyone else seated around the table, and waved a hand toward the woman sitting next to him, almost as though he were passing a baton.

That's a smug expression, Monsieur Novello…and the woman beside you thinks so too.

Turning her head on her long neck to face us, the woman beside Jacques Novello dropped her chin, opened her eyes wide – showing off thick kohl eyeliner – and flashed a hint of teeth as she smiled coyly. Her expression reminded me of Princess Diana, though an aged version, because this woman was at least in her mid-sixties. A severely wedge-shaped, short cut of her glossy white hair suggested to me that this was the woman Lucienne had referred to when we'd spoken to him earlier in the day. She was wearing a form-fitting, midnight-blue velvet dress that had oversized, sharply pointed shoulder pads, and was embellished with silver piping around its deeply plunging V-neck; her ornate blue and silver earrings and necklace complemented the dress perfectly. She paused…until I believed she felt she had the undivided attention of everyone in the room.

"I'm Avril. Avril Tambour. Though people always call me Mademoiselle Avril, of course. I was once Églantine's model, and muse. I'm now her confidant, and – I trust – a continuing inspiration for you, Jacques, since I am, as Églantine has always said, the embodiment of the brand."

Oh…just a little rivalry there, I think.

Beside Avril sat a woman who might have been in her thirties or forties; she had dun-colored hair wound into a messy topknot, and was wearing a drab olive-green woolly cardigan over a drab, slightly different shade of olive-green sweater. Her tortoiseshell-rimmed spectacles had thick glass in them, making her eyes look unnaturally small. Her tone was flat. "I'm Joanne. Daughter of Mademoiselle Avril."

Odd way to refer to your mother.

Beside Joanne sat two women who had to be twins: each had short, steel-gray hair; each had an overbite; each wore an emerald green smock of some sort which exposed parts of a gray cotton, long-sleeved dress beneath. Both wore gold-rimmed spectacles, and sat with their hands folded on the table in front of them. Despite the fact that they were sitting down, it was obvious they were both short.

Weirdly, they spoke in unison, "We're Monique and Monica Martin."

The one on the right nodded at the one on the left, who continued, "We run the *atelier* here at *Maison Églantine*. We've been with Madame since she began. We're seamstresses and dressmakers. We're responsible for recruiting the best apprentices, we train them well, and ensure that standards are maintained in all aspects of producing the couture quality for which the Maison is justly renowned. We have approximately seventy people who create the pieces."

Not sure which is which, but the both of you are…interesting.

The man sitting along from the twins said, "I'm Gustav Sutter, the business manager here. I'm the one who actually runs the place, answering only to Églantine." His gravelly tones suggested either heavy smoking, or great tiredness; the bags beneath his eyes supported the latter, though his wrinkles told me he'd spent much more of his life smiling and laughing than frowning. A man who clearly liked his food, and wasn't averse to wearing a blue shirt with a green tie, and a brown jacket, Gustav Sutter was an imposing figure. I pegged him to be in his sixties – or maybe he was younger and just exhausted.

Maybe tiredness explains that slight slur in your speech, eh, Gustav…or maybe not?

All eyes then turned to Pierre, who stammered a little as he introduced himself. I felt sorry for him, because I could imagine how much he wanted to curry favor with Francine, but his performance was a little too lacking in confidence to have made anything but a poor impression.

I was up next, and went with a simple, "Cait Morgan, on vacation in Paris, and a potential witness."

Puzzled looks from the people across the table.

Bud followed my lead. "Bud Anderson, Cait's husband, not a potential witness, but here to be supportive."

We all turned toward Francine, and I asked, "Where's Lucienne?"

Gustav jumped in. "I gave him permission to leave his post before we realized that Églantine…wasn't here. He was feeling…sick. He went home. But…but Lucienne is a trusted employee of the Maison, with many years of service to the house, and Madame herself. He cannot be suspected of…anything."

Bud and I exchanged a glance, but didn't comment.

Francine added, "A car has been dispatched to the home of Lucienne Durand, but he's not there. We're taking steps to locate him. All the lunch caterers have been interviewed and dismissed – none of them had worked here before, and their backgrounds are being thoroughly checked. Unfortunately, they had already bleached all the surfaces in the anteroom, having served lunch, so our forensics people told me there was nothing they could find of any significance in there, except some fingerprints, which we're working on. They were an efficient and diligent group of food handlers, it seems, which – it turns out – is a great pity. Those I have asked to stay are those who knew…*know*…Madame Églantine."

You think she's dead, Francine.

Avril pounced. "I don't know why you let the caterers go. They were on the premises when Églantine disappeared. They should be locked up until she's found. They're the type who might have done…anything. As is that Lucienne. I warned her about him."

Gustav added wistfully, "She was always one for the stray dogs."

Francine responded sharply, "Stray dogs?"

Gustav replied, "Églantine was well known for taking people under her wing who needed a bit of help. As you yourself did when the two of you met, Avril…unless you've forgotten that."

The model-muse – who moments earlier had managed to look simultaneously coy and coquettish – now simply lashed out at the smiling, portly man who'd, seemingly, besmirched her character. "Me? Need help? It was my choice to leave my home, to seek my fortune in Paris with Églantine. It's a famous tale now, of course, but it was all meant to be. It was fate, I tell you…fate."

Turning her full attention to those of us across the table from her, she added, "Églantine happened to see me in Montlyon when I was on my way to school one day. I lived next door, because my father was the caretaker for the buildings…which made life at school difficult. Some of the children were horrible to me because of his job, and because I was so tall, and thin that…well, who's laughing now? Anyway, she spotted me, and she came right over to me and begged me to wear a dress she said she'd sketched. Said she'd make it just for me…that she'd been inspired by how she'd seen me walking through the little park-like area that separated the school from our house. She said I could become a famous model. When she came back two days later with a garment that fitted me like a glove, what was I to do? She was a good bit older than me – at least, it felt that way at the time – so of course I allowed her to photograph me in it, in that same park. She made me promise it would be our secret. I didn't tell my parents, or my classmates…no one. She sent those photographs to every magazine, to every newspaper…and to every agent of every musician in Paris. When she came to me months later and told me how many people had seen me, and how she could make a business based upon how I looked in that one dress, was it any surprise that I did as she wanted, and joined her here? I waited until I turned sixteen, left school, then I secretly escaped to Paris. Of course, I left a letter for my parents. That was how this house started – with me. Because of me. I was no 'stray dog' – I was Églantine's discovery, and her muse."

"It wasn't because of you that she became successful, it was because of herself, and because we made the clothes she sold," said Monique – or it might have been Monica, I still wasn't sure which was which.

The other seamstress added, "Our blood was literally sewn into those garments. Each stitch had to be perfect, and – while she knew how to create a *devoré* fabric like no one else, and how to design and sketch a gown – she didn't understand pattern-cutting as well as we did at that time, and certainly had no idea about how to stitch a garment so that it stood out as a couture piece in a sea of cheap alternatives. Without our skills, she would have disappeared quickly. This Maison would not have existed."

Gustav smiled warmly. "You are all correct, which is why you all have shares in the company. Églantine has always been happy to recognize your roles in her success at the beginning – and in its continuation, Jacques – but you have to admit, she's always been a champion for those who have little."

Joanne said quietly, "But, for all that, she also always had an ability to make those who have a great deal to pay through the nose for her garments."

You're…sad?

Jacques sounded a little hurt when he said, "My new designs continue to attract those with discerning taste. Even in a world of fashion that is changing, we remain who we have always been – the leaders in velvet, with our signature *devoré* at the forefront. Fashion changes. Style is timeless."

"I admit that Églantine's timing was magnificent," said Avril quietly. "With Barbara Hulanicki's *Biba* company getting big enough to move into an old carpet warehouse in London, then getting that entire fancy store on High Street Kensington – and the world going mad for anything *art nouveau* – Églantine's paisley, and nouveau-inspired designs in velvet *devoré* were spotted by those in the know…the early stylists for rock stars in the 1970s. She was the absolute queen of the fabric long before von Etzdorf tried to claim the crown, though it's true that the two of them battled it out through the 1980s and 1990s. But it was the vision of me – wearing garments as I did – that sold them to people who'd never so much as heard of Églantine George. So there."

Francine said, "Enough. You all know Églantine well, and you have all told me you have no idea where she is. You have also told me that she rarely leaves her apartment. Raising the alarm about her disappearance was the right thing to do – but I feel that all of you are not telling me…something…that might help us locate a frail woman in her early eighties, who is not where she should be."

Glances were exchanged around the table suggesting that every member of the group felt…defensive.

Francine added, "Cait – describe what you saw earlier today."

Everyone stared at me, and I did my party piece. I concluded by saying, "The reconstruction organized by Captain de Gaulle a short while ago confirmed for me that I did see what I believed I'd seen – a woman being strangled at a window in that room, there." I pointed toward the doors at the far end of the meeting room, which was where logic dictated the window in question had to be located.

The entire group began to exclaim, and declaim, that nothing of the sort could have possibly happened.

Francine raised her hand. "Enough." Everyone shut up. She asked me, "Have you ever seen a photograph of Églantine George?"

I smiled. "No. I did a bit of Googling about this place when we left, earlier today, but I only happened upon one photograph of Églantine. It was a blurred shot, taken back in the early 1970s, so I have no idea what she looks like today."

Francine stood, pulled a framed photograph from a bag that was on the floor at her feet, and handed it to me. The frame was an *art nouveau* masterpiece in silver; the photograph a portrait of a woman with large, limpid brown eyes set in a wizened face. She was smiling, her face accordioning with wrinkles. Her teeth were small and even, her mouth enlarged with vibrant pink lipstick, her complexion flattened out with what was obviously thick foundation, and her eye make-up was straight out of the 1970s – with dark color surrounding her entire eye, and her lashes caked with mascara. And her neck? From just beneath her chin were row upon row of amber beads forming a collar which fitted all the way around her neck – rather like the chokers that were habitually worn by Queen Mary of Teck – with rows of larger amber stones that extended an inch or two beyond her neck, toward her shoulders, then descended toward an invisible cleavage. Églantine George could have achieved the same effect with any number of scarves, which she could have endlessly switched up to match her outfit – but, no, she'd gone for this necklace, which took on a new and greater significance for me.

She's not wearing a piece of jewelry – she's wearing…armor?

I announced, "The woman I saw in the window wore her hair in exactly this style, though I saw it as merely dark, as opposed to this plum color. And this piece of jewelry she's wearing? That's what I saw glowing beneath the hands at her neck. I'm certain that this was the woman I saw being strangled."

The energy in the room shifted perceptibly.

Francine stood. "If you saw Églantine George being strangled, then where's her body? And if…" The captain glanced at her phone in her hand. "Wait." She answered her call, listened, then put her phone into her pocket.

We were all agog, and Francine didn't disappoint. She said quite calmly, "I want you all to stay here. I have calls to make. Lucienne Durand has been located. His body is on the way to the morgue. Bertrand, you're with me."

Pierre shot to his feet, and the pair left the room. The rest of us just…stared at each other.

You could have heard a pin drop.

Sept

Gustav broke the silence. "Lucienne is…dead? I don't know about anyone else, but I need a drink. A big one." He pushed his seat away from the table and strode – a little unsteadily – toward a magnificent *art nouveau* walnut sideboard that sat snugly against the wall behind me. I turned to see him press a panel that appeared to have no handle, and the entire front popped open, to reveal a collection of bottles on one level, and glasses on another. I was pretty sure this wasn't going to be Gustav's first drink of the day, something that would explain his almost over-the-top level of bonhomie – given the circumstances – up until that moment.

"I'll have one too," chorused Monique and Monica.

Avril added, "And me too – but get some ice, Gustav. I can't drink anything without ice."

Gustav snorted. "And where am I supposed to get ice, Avril?"

Monique – or Monica – said, "There's a refrigerator in the anteroom, so maybe there's ice?"

Gustav straightened up, and we all looked toward the double doors at the end of the room…then I realized that everyone had turned their attention to me.

"You said you saw Églantine being strangled," said Avril contemptuously. "Why should we believe you? You and him," she jabbed a thumb toward Bud, "might have been the ones who kidnapped her."

"She hasn't been kidnapped," chorused the twins.

One of them added, "We said that earlier. You were the one crying 'kidnapping', Avril, when all the rest of us just thought that Églantine had gone out for a walk and lost her way."

The other twin directed her comment to Bud and me, "Églantine's been getting a bit vague recently. We think she's got a touch of dementia. She might have just wandered off. We told the policewoman that when she got here, but she didn't seem impressed. If you think you saw Églantine being strangled – and the policewoman knew that already – that would explain why, I suppose."

The timbre of the two women's voices, the tilt of their heads, and even the smallest gestures of their hands were indistinguishable, though one had slightly longer hair than the other. I was really struggling to tell them apart, which was annoying me.

I took the plunge. "I apologize, but I'm not sure which of you is Monique, and which is Monica."

"I'm Monique."

"I'm Monica."

Right – longer hair is Monica – got it.

I thanked them, then added, "I realize we're strangers to you, but I'm quite certain of what I saw – I assure you all of that. As I told you, we came here earlier today, and met your doorman, Lucienne. It's terrible news about him. Did you all…know him well?"

I had no idea about the relationships in the place, so decided to try to find out.

Joanne rose from her seat. I could see she was crying. Silently. She said quietly, "Lucienne was a lovely man. I've known him since I was a small child. He used to let me tickle his beard when I was little. Not many men had beards back then – not like today – and it fascinated me. I have no idea why Églantine made him keep it as a condition of his employment, which was something I found out about much later, but I'm glad she did. Oh dear…maybe now all bearded men will remind me of Lucienne and the way he'd giggle when I tickled him."

She closed her eyes tightly, squeezing out more tears, then added, "No…I can't let that happen. I must…" She shook herself. "Right, I'll find ice, you find glasses, Papa."

I was surprised. "Papa? Gustav is your father?"

"We divorced many years ago," snapped Avril.

Oh heck.

Bud said, "Family dynamics are always so interesting, especially if you're all involved in the same business."

Nicely defused, Bud.

Avril sniped, "Gustav only managed to get his foot in the door as Églantine's business manager because of me, though he'd like us all to believe he's the one responsible for the value of our shares being what they are."

"And we're off," observed Joanne, sounding as though she'd said, and felt, the same thing many times before. "Please don't start with that old refrain, Avril – I'm getting ice…and I'll have a large scotch when I come back, Papa."

It's interesting that she calls her mother Avril, but her father Papa, was what I thought; "I'll give you a hand, and I can see if there's any tonic water out there," was what I said, also rising.

I managed to whisper, "Dig," to Bud before I followed Joanne through the double doors, which swung open easily and silently revealing a rather disappointing room. There was a low sink set against the left-hand wall between the windows; a large round table that had seen a great deal of wear fitted well within the room which narrowed to a point that housed one single window; the right-hand wall had shelf units between the windows – stowaway places for a variety of trays, collapsible stands, folding chairs, and linens. There was a single door in the wall alongside the double doors through which we'd entered, which I assumed was a cupboard.

A chair was placed close to the first window on the right-hand wall; I knew that was where whomever had been the evening's stand-in for Églantine – and Églantine herself – must have been sitting when I saw them from the bus. The chair's position suggested that someone had been sitting at the table and had turned the chair outward. In any case, I was pleased to have achieved my goal of seeing the scene of what I was certain had been a crime for myself.

"There's tonic, and other mixers, in the fridge here," said Joanne, snapping me back to reality.

"Excellent, now all I have to hope for is gin in that cupboard in the boardroom." I grinned, and Joanne gave me an upside-down smile. I dared, "I can see you're upset. I'm so sorry about Lucienne. You said you've known him since you were young?"

Joanne stared at me through her thick spectacles, then closed the fridge door. She plopped a pile of ice-cube trays into the sink, grabbed an ice bucket, then set about pouring tap water over the ice to release it, before dumping it into the bucket.

She spoke as she worked. "You don't have to be pretty to be a runway model, you know? You just have to develop the right attitude, and learn the right walk. But what you need to possess before they allow you to do any of that is the element that Avril goes on and on about, which people in the business recognize when they see it in someone…but can't name. Avril hoped I would have it. She frequently brought me here when I was a child, believing I'd get fashion into my blood somehow – that the quality without a name would materialize in me one day. It didn't. She gave up on me when I was about twelve. Said then that she knew I was a lost cause. It was at about the same time that she and Papa got divorced, so going away to school was the best thing that could have happened to me. And it turned out that – while I might not have been a natural for modelling – I was rather gifted when it came to the sciences. Chemistry, in particular. And that's not because of Avril, nor even really because of Papa – but because of Églantine. Yes, she was a talented designer, but she was also a scientist – a natural one – who experimented with acids, and dyes, and fibers, and worked with fabric-making artisans and manufacturers to create…her magic. I saw the passion in her to try to find out how things work the way they do, then take them in new directions…and Papa at least indulged me in that. Avril wouldn't let me 'do my silly experiments' as she called them when I was young, whereas Papa allowed me…well, possibly too much freedom, I suppose, because I had a few accidents. But it was Églantine's interest in the scientific method that got me started, and it's why I work, indirectly, for the Maison, too. Though not here, and we have other clients. I'm involved in textile development, you see – the scientific end of things – at a small facility away from the center of the city. But I do have shares in the Maison, which is why I came here today. Do you really think someone strangled Églantine in…this room?"

Joanne suddenly appeared to realize what that might mean, and glanced around as though a killer might be hiding…somewhere. Under the sink, or in the large cupboard, I presumed, because there wasn't anywhere else.

Her quick change of topic had surprised me, as had her unbidden need to tell me…a great deal about herself.

I managed, "Yes, I'm afraid I do. And in that chair. At least, in a chair that was there – not necessarily that specific one."

Joanne stepped away from the chair.

I asked, "So Églantine was starting to wander…even though she'd been a bit hermit-like for some time?"

Joanne wiped the remnant of a tear from her chin. "Églantine was always a fiercely private person. Avril has told me tales of how she used to host amazing *soirées* – inviting people to her apartment in small groups – but that she always disliked attending shows, or anything where a lot of people were in one place. Hated crowds. And cameras, generally speaking. I know for a fact that she's avoided any large gathering that she hasn't absolutely needed to go to. Her shows – yes, but she'd rush onto the runway at the end, bow, then leave as quickly as possible. Avril, of course, played the hostess to the hilt, and partied her way through my entire youth…still does, whenever she can. Papa grew to hate that routine, and now – as an adult – I understand why. I turn forty next year, and plan to spend my birthday alone somewhere, doing what I want – no matter how much Avril insists that I have a big bash."

Forty going on fourteen, was what I thought; "Avril certainly seems to be a very…definite person…sure of herself," was what I said.

Joanne snorted – in much the way her father had done. "You could say that. She's certainly never wrong. Papa and I were talking about exactly that when we were alone for a while, earlier today. He was in a reflective mood. He doesn't often talk about Avril, but he was going on a bit about how she has to have things done just the way she wants them. It was when I'd finished searching about the place for poor Églantine, and he was having a drink…and rambling on about how Avril's got this ability to steamroller people by using her 'womanly wiles'. That made me laugh – Papa using such a phrase. Then Jacques joined us from the first floor, and I didn't get a chance to ask Papa what he'd meant."

Avril's voice floated into the anteroom, "Where's that ice? I'm gasping for a drink – we all are."

Joanne's shoulders fell, and any hint of a smile disappeared from her face. "Let's get what we came for and join the merry band, shall we?"

I grabbed a few bottles of tonic water, she grabbed the ice bucket, and we returned to the boardroom, where it looked as though a cocktail party was about to break out.

Bud looked almost cheerful. "We found snacks, Cait."

Monique sighed. "Which is just as well – I'm starving."

Monica snapped, "You ate a good lunch, dear."

"We all ate a good lunch," noted Avril, "but it was a long time ago, so snacks will have to do. Nuts are good, though I'll pass on those horrid cracker things, thank you, Gustav."

The end of the table where Francine had been sitting was now covered with a variety of glasses, bottles, and little bowls full of nuts, crackers, olives, and tiny pretzels like the ones they give you during a flight. Although I'd eaten a good dinner, a few salty snacks and a gin and tonic seemed quite appealing, so I joined in with the group as we all organized our drinks and then stood, nibbling, and making comments about how good – or otherwise – what we were eating and drinking was. The atmosphere was strange, and strained, to say the least.

Just as I was thinking that I might scream if I heard another person mutter, "Oh, I needed that," Monica asked Bud and me, "Why is your French so good? You both speak it well, though you have a French-Canadian accent, Bud, and you have a…charming one, Cait. You are both Canadian?"

I grinned. "Yes, we're both Canadian now, though I know I still have my original Welsh accent when I speak English, so I suspect that's what you're hearing when I speak French. And we spent an extended period in Tahiti recently, so we brushed up on our vocabulary at that time – though not on our accents."

Monique said, "Well, I'm glad you do both speak French, because my English isn't good. Not as good as Monica's. She's gifted when it comes to languages, which is just as well because good workers at our *atelier* come from all over Europe, these days…and from beyond. Thank you for speaking French with us all – it's polite and helpful."

Avril chose to follow her own train of thought, which didn't surprise me. "Ah Tahiti…it's a magical place. Idyllic. A paradise," she mused.

Bud and I exchanged a wide-eyed glance over our glasses, but didn't say anything; we just nodded and smiled.

Gustav chuckled wryly. "You said at the time that you hated the humidity, Avril, and that it was too hot, as I recall."

"You wouldn't even take me with you," said Joanne sullenly.

Avril laughed. "You were too young at the time, dear. It's such a long trip."

"But now you can go whenever you want, young lady," said Gustav indulgently to his daughter. "You've achieved great things, my dear, and you deserve to reward yourself with a little break now and again. You might find Tahiti to be just the restorative you need…you work such long hours."

Joanne smiled wanly. "You know I'm not good with too much heat, Papa."

Avril observed, "You could do with some sun on you – get yourself out of the laboratory and into the fresh air." She held out her glass to her ex-husband. "Another, I think."

Gustav looked at her empty glass, and said, "The bottle's right there." He walked away, grabbing a handful of pistachio nuts as he went.

Avril rolled her eyes, and poured herself another drink.

Monica said, "If someone's kidnapped Églantine, they'll probably phone with a ransom demand – or would they send a message some other way? Would they email someone do you think?"

She didn't seem to be asking the questions of anyone in particular, so Monique said, "Might they text, these days?"

Avril looked surprised. "They'd need someone's number to do that. How would they get any of our numbers? I don't give mine to anyone…questionable."

Gustav slammed his glass onto the table. "Oh shut up, woman. Look – the police aren't here, so let's talk openly. Cait – you say you saw a woman who looked like Églantine being strangled, in there, at noon. I have to say I find that hard to believe because there have been people coming and going all around the Maison all morning, and I dare say the caterers were here at that time, no doubt in and out of that room preparing our lunch. Monica and Monique came down from the sewing rooms, together, just as I was coming up the stairs, and we were the first three to come into this room. That was at about twelve twenty. Jacques arrived moments later. Joanne was on time, as always, and Avril arrived late, at about twelve forty. None of us was even here, on the second floor, at noon."

Avril said, "I told you all that policewoman should have focused on the caterers, and yet we're the ones nibbling at this rubbish because we've all missed dinner."

Bud spoke quietly. "Lucienne told Cait and me that you came here, left, then came back again, Avril, is that true?"

Gustav spluttered his drink, and everyone looked at Avril, then at Bud, then at Avril again. The model straightened her shoulders. "It was nothing – I had to collect something I'd forgotten at home." She turned to us. "My phone had somehow slipped out of my handbag."

I'd spotted Avril's handbag, and it flitted through my mind that Avril and Jane Birkin had moved in similar circles in Paris for decades, and had possibly – or even probably – known each other, which made her choice seem…strange. To carry a bag so closely connected with a person you know as a friend? *Odd.*

Joanne was also peering at Avril's bag – which was on the floor, at the woman's feet – when she snapped, "Your ruinously expensive bag is equipped with any number of closing and locking devices, but you always have it wide open, so what can you expect?"

Avril slammed down her glass. "I will not be interrogated by my own family, I've done nothing wrong. All I did was misplace my stupid phone…and now…this. I won't stand for it."

Gustav said, "Well, sit down then, dear."

Avril's fists were clenched as she sniped back, "I will not…and don't be flippant. That's you all over – never serious about…anything."

Gustav said gravely, "Except my family. And running this business." He raised his glass toward his ex-wife.

I don't even want to imagine what your private fights were like, was what I thought; "What about the people who were taking the garments to the exhibition?" was what I said.

Monique looked surprised. "What do you know about that?"

Bud leaned in. "Lucienne told us about it, when Cait was admiring that wonderful gown in the glass display case in the reception area. Was that the work of you two, by any chance?"

Both Monica and Monique smiled with a mixture of pride and unsettling coquettishness. "Yes," they said in unison.

Monique said, "That gown was a triumph…and it marked an important step for the Maison. You see, it was the first time that Madame showed her own version of Paris green, which – as I dare say you know – is our house color."

I said, "You mean this wonderful emerald green you have on the walls here?"

Monique and Monica nodded, as though synchronized. Monique said, "Exactly. Though it's not actually emerald green…well, not the original one."

Bud looked puzzled. "I thought that the term 'emerald green' was…generic."

Monica jumped in. "Oh it is, now…except to those of us in the world of couture. But…well, this was all because Madame was so good with dyes, you see. Originally there was a green called Scheele's green, which was invented back in the late 1700s, but it was arsenic based, so highly dangerous. Though that didn't stop people using it to dye fabrics, which then…well, yes, they killed people – the ones who made it, worked with it, and wore it. Then in the early 1800s a German paint manufacturer invented a color they named emerald green…because it really did look like the depths of an excellent emerald. It was still based on arsenic, and it still killed people…in fact, it was known as an insecticide – first one ever – if you can believe it, and yet still people used it to dye thread, which they then spun, and cut, and sewed, and wore. It was more stable than its predecessor, though only just…and it became known as Paris green."

Joanne said, "They do say that a great deal of Paris was actually painted with the color, because it was believed that the paint was weatherproof. Paris green is certainly beautiful…chemically fascinating, and it delivers a shade that's green, but with a slight blue undertone. There's even a self-portrait by Van Gogh with Paris green as a background color."

Gustav smiled warmly. "You would know that, my dear – you're so well read."

Joanne smiled and flushed pink. "Without science there'd be no art, Papa, as I've said many times."

Gustav raised his glass to his daughter, while her mother rolled her eyes…again.

I said, "So you're saying that Églantine adopted the deadly Paris green as the brand color for her Maison?"

Monique said, "No – she went one better. She'd worked for years to come up with a new version of the Paris green dye, a truly safe, stable, and vivid version, with real depth…not like the muddier, or less complex green dyes offered back then."

Monica continued, "The gown downstairs, which is named 'Life Triumphs in Paris', was the first time she showed the new, safe dye in use, and it was a sensation. It's why the gown is so important to us, and the entire industry, because she didn't keep the formula a secret…though she could have done, of course. No – Madame believed that everyone should be able to use it, so she did the right thing and made the formula available to all.

But we know it's her emerald green…her Paris green…and we're the only house to use it as our color, as is our right."

Monique added, "That first, important collection, it was just the two of us, doing everything – patterns, cutting, and sewing – if you can imagine that. Just the two of us."

"And just me, modelling every garment," piped up Avril. "It was exhausting. Days of fittings. No sleep at all. Almost no food. And the show itself? Insane. If there's only one of you, you have to be constantly on the move, with people fussing over you, trying to get you out of one thing and into another."

Jacques – who I'd noticed was being incredibly quiet as he nursed his almost-untouched drink – blurted out, "That was the show with the dogs, wasn't it? That's a legend in the business."

"Yes…there were the dogs," said Monica. She turned to Bud and me and explained, "Madame Églantine always loved dogs, and she found a shelter run by the Society for the Protection of Animals close to the run-down old building where the show was held. She got volunteers to walk dogs that could be adopted along the catwalk – which we all thought was amusing – between garments. Each dog wore a little scarf she'd designed, and lots of people did, in fact, adopt that day – and got the scarf, to keep – which she, and everyone who got one, thought was just wonderful. By doing that, she also created the time we needed to get Avril out of and into the clothes. And fix her hair, which was long and red, back then. She always did her own make-up, and for a few shows she even made herself up in a droopy moustache with those mutton chops things that were so popular at the time, and wore the men's garments, so that we didn't need male models. Simpler times…much simpler times."

"The gown downstairs is stunning," I said, "Lucienne told us it goes to the exhibit tomorrow – the final piece. Were you involved with getting everything else ready to go today?"

The twins nodded.

Monica looked wistful when she said, "It's been a labor of love, because we've had a wonderful opportunity to become reacquainted with garments that were a big part of our lives for a long time. There have been some necessary repairs, of course, and yet we were both impressed by the work of the conservators – it's paid off. Most of the items were in excellent condition. We're due to go to the exhibit tomorrow to oversee the installation. But if you were thinking that the people transporting those items could have been here when you saw…what you saw…then the answer is no – they'd all left before noon – right, Monique?"

Monique shook her head. "No idea. I was giving Justine a good talking to on the phone, because her work on the bugle beads for the gold cape just isn't up to our standards. Her tension is not sufficiently even, and her knotting is quite lumpen. It won't do…as I told her."

Monica said, "Can't you get Leonora to do it? She's so reliable."

"She's still on the mauve cape."

"Still?"

Monique nodded. "Remember – she went back to Cannes for that family funeral? She's been gone for almost two weeks. I have no idea why it takes so long to bury someone down there. Honestly, people from the south are so…slow."

I didn't want to get sidetracked, so did my best to hit the restart button regarding those who might have been in the building at the critical time. "So how many of you were in the *atelier* around noon?"

The twins giggled. Monica said, "Usually there's about seventy of us – all crammed into two floors, the third and fourth. We're on the fourth, where we also have our client fitting area, which is large, as our clients expect appropriately lavish surroundings when they're paying for a unique garment." She sighed. "It's always been that way. The people who make the actual garments get squashed in, while those who buy and sell the stuff, and manage the money, and do all the primping and so on get all the space. But the *atelier* is not staffed on a Saturday, normally, so we two were alone, catching up, and overseeing the removal of the garments to the exhibition, which opens on Tuesday. It's going to be wonderful…our last hurrah, in a way, because Madame has come up with a generous package that will allow us to both retire, shortly, knowing we've trained some excellent people to come after us. The end of an era."

Gustav nodded his acknowledgement and volunteered, "I have an office on the fifth, where the administrative staff is housed. It's also where Jacques conjures his magic. Our PR person was at the exhibition location, sorting things out before our area is set up tomorrow. I wasn't using my office this morning – I came from home, for the lunch and the meeting. I often work there, and – quite frequently – have meetings away from the Maison. But…what can we achieve by discussing this? I honestly believe that Monica and Monique might be correct – that Églantine decided to go…somewhere, and didn't tell anyone. I hate to say it, but I must agree – she's not the woman she was even six months ago. I should have paid more attention. I feel I am to blame for this – I should have taken responsibility for her…insisted that she consult a doctor, at least. But…well, things have been busy here this past year, as Jacques knows only too well."

Jacques finally became animated. "It has, oh yes. I have the design and the production of the collections to oversee for our shows, and there are always the *haute couture* commissions that come in for historic pieces, too. We're known for that. Valued customers will be fitted with select items from our current, or archival, collections, of course, but sometimes they'll even brief me with their specific needs, and I design – and we all create – a brand-new garment, handmade just for them, with no one else ever being allowed to have another. It all means that I, and our valued creators, are constantly in demand."

"We'd be able to keep up if only you didn't change final details so often," noted Monica.

It seemed to me that this group of people might well all be working toward a common goal – the successful continuation of a fashion house with a history going back over half a century – but it didn't seem that any of them were overly happy with their lot…except for, maybe, Gustav, who looked…*resigned?*…if not exactly joyous. But…work's called "work" for a reason.

Abruptly, Joanne said, "Why aren't we talking about Lucienne? We have no idea what's happened to Églantine, that's true, but Lucienne? He's…he's dead. Why are you all acting as though nothing's happened?"

"He's never been a calm person," said Avril. "Always rushing here and there, never allowing life to come to him. He wasn't feeling well earlier today, as Gustav said. Maybe a heart attack?"

Joanne sniffed. "You don't think his death is connected to Églantine's disappearance, do you? Oh…what if he saw her leave the building and didn't have the chance to mention it to anyone…and now we'll never know. Oh dear. Poor Lucienne. Poor Églantine."

Surprisingly, Avril took her daughter's lead. "I know I was the one who thought that kidnapping was most likely, but we still haven't had a ransom demand, so it might be that you're right…Églantine has simply wandered off."

"And I saw someone who looked exactly like her being strangled – by coincidence, right?" It was out of my mouth before I could stop it.

Bud glared at me, Gustav snorted, and Avril rolled her padded shoulders – which was a spectacular show, dislodging the entire V of her neckline, which she then had to readjust.

Bud's phone pinged. He read something, then announced, "They're on their way back – at least, Pierre is. Should be here in about fifteen minutes. Maybe we'll learn…something useful, then."

Joanne wiped a tear from her cheek. "I hope so. Lucienne was always good to me. He used to make coins appear from my ear when I was little, and always had bonbons in his pockets, like you always did, Papa. It just won't be the same here without him…it already isn't. The place feels…soulless, now."

"It is also because Madame is not here," said Monique. "Her presence above us was always felt – even if we saw her less and less…down here."

I checked, "So Églantine lived on the top floor – in what would have originally been the servants' quarters? Aren't those rooms quite low-ceilinged? Why did she choose to do that?"

The twins chuckled. "She was short, like us," they said.

Monica continued, "She was given the building by…well, she always said 'a grateful client', but we had our suspicions, didn't we, Monique?"

Monique nodded, and the pair shared an impish smile. "Indeed we did, Monica. She always was a bit…well, you know, the Seventies and the Eighties were a bit of a wild time for a lot of people, and Madame was always one to enjoy socializing – in small groups. And we think there was a certain gentleman, with a title, who gave her this building as a gift…as a thank you for…you know. Anyway, when she got it, she lost no time in turning it into more or less what it is today – though it wasn't until the Nineties that she added a few of the more expensive details to the place – like the chandeliers in the reception area."

Monica jumped in. "Yes, she had the whole top floor opened up right away – as much as she could – and moved in. The place is wonderful. It was like she made herself into an apartment, the space was so much…her."

I pounced. "I expect it's magical…what I wouldn't give to be able to see it for myself."

It appeared I'd taken a step too far, because there was a gasp from everyone in the room – except Bud.

Gustav said, "No one goes into Églantine's personal space unless they're specifically invited. I mean, I know I went in there after lunch today, but that was because she hadn't arrived for our meeting, and I felt I had no choice. But she'd have a fit knowing the police have been rummaging about up there all afternoon – but that couldn't be helped, either." He chuckled wryly. "I bet more people have been in that apartment today than have been there, in total, for the past couple of years."

"She has help – to keep it clean, and so forth?" I asked, not wanting to be deterred from finding out more about the woman's habits, even if it was clear I wasn't going to get the chance to see for myself how she'd lived.

Avril replied, "Of course she had a cleaner. Everyone has a cleaner. Though she gave up her cook a long time ago. Gets all her meals delivered from a brasserie the other side of the garden. She's like a child – eating the same food on a rota, week in, and week out. It's…odd. But she's always done as she wants, so I don't see why I should be surprised."

Bud asked, "So someone would have delivered food to her in her apartment today, while you were all lunching here?"

Jacques replied, "The police asked that, but, no, Églantine never ate lunch. She said it was because she'd always been too busy in her working life to stop for it, so didn't intend to start eating it now that she was semi-retired."

I jumped in. "So she was still involved with the business…in an active way?"

Gustav walked over to refresh his drink. "Not on the business side of things at all, though she still gave you a fair bit of input, didn't she, Jacques?"

I judged from the designer's micro-expressions that he was struggling to control his demeanor when he replied, "Églantine was always generous when it came to sharing her experience, and I know I'm still young – in the world of exclusive maisons – and have much to learn."

Boy, that was an effort for you, was what I thought; "But she allowed you full rein with the running of the business, Gustav?" was what I said.

Looking at his glass with satisfaction, Gustav replied, "She did. Hasn't been interested in how the place is run for many years – and I don't think profit was ever the main driving force behind her zeal for fashion. It was always all about the garments, the designs themselves."

"Oh yes," chorused the twins.

Monique added, "She would design fabrics then not worry about how much it might cost to create them, and design garments that used expensive materials without consideration. She did not do this because she felt she was above such things as money, but – when she decided that a thing had to be just so…it had to be just so. She was intent upon seeing what she'd imagined being brought into being in the best possible way, not someone who was trying to show off their brilliance to the world. The search for beauty and perfectionism was what drove her…not her bank balance."

Gustav added, "Which is why it's just as well that I came into her life when I did, because you can't keep going like that and hope to survive, and thrive. If I hadn't made such good investments over the years, this Maison would be dust by now."

"And we'd all have been out of work long ago, owning shares in something worthless," said Monica.

"We can retire, soon, and live our dream of opening a cat sanctuary, in the countryside," said Monique, wistfully, "thanks to our shares."

"Just a few months more," said Jacques.

You sound…relieved?

Pierre entered the room with all the enthusiasm of a man being dragged to face a guillotine.

"What news?" Bud sounded bizarrely jovial.

Pierre looked at all of us, glimpsed the bottles on the table, and said, "If you have something without alcohol, I could do with a drink. And maybe something to nibble? It's going to be a long night."

Joanne pleaded, "Tell us what happened to Lucienne. Was it…was it a heart attack?"

Pierre's expression was grim when he shook his head. "The poor man was poisoned. Something…nasty…took him out before he reached his home. His body was found in an alley. It sounds as though maybe…people walked past him for some time, thinking he was dead drunk – then a kind soul called the paramedics. But it was too late."

A chorus of: "Poison? Poison!" hissed around the room.

Huit

Joanne groaned loudly; her father swore even more loudly, then immediately moved to comfort her; Avril sat tapping her nails on the table with what I judged to be…*contempt?*

Bud asked quietly, "Do they know how the poison was administered, Pierre?"

Pierre shrugged. "I've just left the hospital – the body was already on its way to the morgue, as you know. There's been no post-mortem yet, but the medical examiner said it looked like a fast-acting poison…and suggested maybe Lucienne ate or drank something on his way home, though no food was found upon his person, and – as far as we can gather at this time – nothing was found near him, either. But I dare say that an examination will give us more facts, and we shouldn't speculate until then. Though it's clear that someone meant to do him harm, and – well, I have to tell you that the captain is considering whether there might be a connection between his death and the disappearance of Madame Églantine. She was thinking about calling the forensics people back in here – to take another look at the apartment on the sixth floor, this time hoping to find out more about the missing woman."

Bud leaned in. "You know that's what Cait used to do for my homicide squads, right? She'd build a profile of the victim based upon their lifestyle, their home, and so forth. Maybe it's something that might prove useful in this case?"

Joanne said, "What do you mean by *your* homicide squads, Bud?"

I saw Bud's neck flush. "I used to be a cop. Headed up…a few murder units."

The silence was deafening.

Pierre cleared his throat. "I thought you all knew…Bud Anderson is a retired homicide detective of some note, and Cait Morgan is a world-renowned criminal psychologist."

The looks from everyone in the room suggested we'd morphed into cockroaches.

Avril slammed down her empty glass. "You might have told us that we were all chattering in front of two…people connected with the police."

I smiled as warmly as I could. "But we're not connected with the police, Avril. Not in this instance. We're only here because of what I witnessed today."

Avril countered with: "I believe your story even less, now. I don't think you saw anything – you are here as…as a ruse. To flush out the person who…kidnapped Églantine."

Bud said, "So now you're back to thinking that someone has kidnapped your old friend, Avril?"

The woman pushed her glass with her fingertips, looking sullen. "Perhaps."

I sighed. Loudly. "So, Pierre – as Bud said, one of the things I used to do for him was to evaluate homes to help build a victim's psychological profile…going beyond that which was known about them by others, that is. If there's nothing else we can do but wait for Francine, then why don't I 'do my thing' up on the sixth floor? It can't hurt, can it?"

Pierre's eyes widened. "I'll text the captain."

"Good idea," said Bud. "Cait's fast – and you'd be surprised by what she might be able to discern."

Pierre pushed through the doors into the anteroom, while the rest of the group regarded me and Bud with fresh eyes – and unfriendly ones at that.

"Explain what you do," said Gustav.

"Yes, please do," added Joanne. "It sounds rather interesting…even if it's not terribly scientific."

I took a seat. "I'm a psychologist who chose to specialize in criminal psychology, and then shifted my focus to work on victim profiling. I'm a professor at the University of Vancouver, and – for a few years – I was also a consultant to the homicide teams headed up by Bud, in British Columbia, Canada. I've just been teaching a course for the Applied Psychology department at the *Sorbonne* focusing on how building a profile of the life and lifestyle of a victim can aid in the detection of those who have victimized them. By understanding how a person lived their life, and why they lived it that way, we are better able to understand how they might have come into contact with someone who meant to rob them, or victimize them in another way…and that, in turn, means that a team of detectives might spot different leads that can be pursued. When I worked with Bud, my efforts focused on murder cases – because that's what his teams were investigating – but the discipline has other applications. Indeed, the course I've just delivered at the *Sorbonne* considered many non-lethal crimes such as theft, extortion, and so forth – either of real goods and monies, or of virtual items of value, like cryptocurrencies, for example. These days it's a lot easier – and potentially more lucrative – to run an online scam to get someone to send you gift cards worth thousands than try to rob a bank. What Bud was referring to was one of my techniques whereby I visit a victim's home and learn what I can about how they lived, what their home says about their values, sense of self-worth, and so on. It helps me illuminate their vulnerabilities, and make suggestions about how that person might have encountered someone who intended to do them harm."

Jacques raised a hand. I grinned, and said, "You have a question?"

He nodded. "Aren't you saying that people do things that make them victims? Blaming them, in a way? That doesn't sound…well, that's not fair, is it?"

I sighed. "I understand why you might think that, but I'm not blaming the victims. We all make hundreds – thousands – of decisions each day, many of which are made 'unconsciously'. The choices come from somewhere deep within us – representing the truth of us, if you like. Those are the decisions I try to discern – not the ones like: 'Should I walk along this dark alley, alone, in a dangerous part of town?'."

Avril snorted; it seemed to be a family habit. "Rubbish. If you came to my home all you'd be able to say is that I have good taste and an efficient housekeeper." She smiled…cruelly.

Joanne leaned forward. "In chemistry, elements and even compounds act in certain predictable ways. Are you saying that people are the same, Cait?"

I smiled. "No. If only they did, we psychologists would – literally – be mind readers, and we're not that. But there are patterns we can discern. For example, a person is more likely to do, or not do, something because of the values and attitudes they hold, which are displayed, often, by those unconscious – or subconscious – choices they make…which I can deduce from seeing how they lived other parts of their life."

Jacques asked, "Like being a cat person, or a dog person? I can always tell the difference, because I'm definitely a dog person, and cat people are quite…different."

Gustav said, "That's because a dog wants a master, whereas a cat wants a servant. Just ask Monica and Monique – I've lost count of the times they've had to do something 'because one of our cats needs us to'."

The twins giggled. "It's true," they chorused, happily.

I replied, "You make a decent point, Jacques, as does Gustav, though, sometimes, allergies play a part in a choice of pet, too."

Pierre reappeared. "I explained to the captain that you won't disturb anything, and she says that I am to accompany you, and take photographs, as necessary. You have an hour. She's attending Lucienne's post-mortem now. She made them do it immediately, given the possibility of a kidnapping."

Avril stood. "And what about us? Are we all supposed to just hang about here, twiddling our thumbs? We have lives, you know."

Pierre straightened his back. "The captain says you are to remain. She will return when she has more information."

I didn't hold out much hope for any useful news coming from the post-mortem: unless the nature of the poison was obvious, there'd be the need for toxicological testing, which I didn't think would be quick on a Saturday night, even with a captain of Francine's considerable determination in charge of things.

I said, "Let's get on with it then – though I want Bud to be with me, because we're used to doing this together. Do you need us to wear protective gear?"

Pierre nodded. "I'll get some booties and gloves, and head-coverings, to be on the safe side."

Oh, that'll be nice, was what I thought; "Highly professional, Pierre," was what I said.

Neuf

Pierre, Bud, and I left the group of annoyed people sitting in their boardroom, and walked up the flights of stairs which grew narrower, and less decorative, the higher we went. Pierre was a little way ahead of us, with me bringing up the rear.

I managed to pant at Bud, "I thought there was an elevator…somewhere – couldn't we have used that?"

Bud shrugged as he smiled over his shoulder at me. "There might be oxygen when we get there." He paused and held out a hand. "Need a Sherpa?"

"Wait for me before you go in, will you?"

I dragged myself up what felt like the nineteenth flight of what were now quite narrow wooden steps, and finally reached the top. I puffed out, "Next time, we'll definitely take the elevator…when we've found it."

Pierre stared at me. "There's an elevator? Why didn't you say something? No one wants to brief me properly, it seems."

I'm so pleased you're taking a chance to use your English, because it's nice to have a break from speaking French, was what I thought; "We don't know where it is, but Lucienne mentioned one earlier today," was what I said.

As I caught my breath, Pierre mused, "None of those people seem to be emotionally touched, or upset that Lucienne's dead – or did I miss something important while I was away?"

Bud replied, "Joanne was the only one to shed a tear for him. Says she's known him since she was a child. And did you know that Gustav is Avril's ex-husband, and Joanne's father?"

Pierre nodded. "Yes, the captain told me as we were driving to the hospital. And, before you ask, no, I have no more information than that which I shared with the whole group – we really do have to wait until the captain arrives for that. So…shall we? Bud told me you wanted to go in first, Cait, so let's all get kitted out and we'll begin."

Once we were all gloved, booted, and hair-netted – and looking a right old sight – I pushed open the door to Madame Églantine George's apartment, found a light switch, and was blown away by the sight that met my eyes. To all intents and purposes, the large open space was a late-nineteenth- or early-twentieth-century *art nouveau* cocoon.

"Nobody move – let me take it all in, from here," I said – then realized that I'd whispered.

Hard and soft furnishings with sinuous lines and lustrous fabrics and finishes filled the space; richly carved wood with flamed and matched markings paneled the walls; there were dozens of bookcases, their shelves heavy with a jumble of volumes of all shapes and sizes; jewel-toned stained-glass lamps made by Tiffany – and probably designed by Driscoll, I reckoned – must have all been controlled by the one switch, because they simultaneously pooled light here and there, but allowed some areas to remain dim; intricately woven rugs sat on dark hardwood floors; artworks by Klimt, Lautrec, and Mucha – that I recognized – depicting mainly female forms were hung on, and propped against, walls; the scent of peonies – dotted about the apartment in large, impressive vases – filled the air.

I flicked another switch, and external lighting flooded in through the dormer windows, set into the inwardly raked, mansard roof which gave the room a feeling of being wide, but squat, with its sloping walls suggesting the apartment was offering me a luxurious hug.

I want to move in, and never leave.

I stepped forward carefully, and saw that, outside, a garden extended along at least both sides of this main indoor area, which was itself set with what modern-day interior designers would call "zones": lounging, sitting upright to read, dining, and more lounging just about summed it up.

There were two doors in the wall, facing me. I headed to the right-hand one, which led to a short corridor, along which the windows, and the balcony garden beyond them, continued. The first door on my left opened onto a shallow, though wide, kitchen, where there would have been room to swing a couple of cats – if they'd been handy – and even boil an egg or two, but not much else. It was decorated from floor to ceiling with iridescent peacock-turquoise tiles embossed with a stylized flower, and the meager fixtures seemed to have been salvaged from the turn of the previous century, though the refrigerator was a newer model. The next door on the left surprised me by not opening. I peered through the glass panel set at eye level, then spotted a button on the wall. I turned to see Bud and Pierre hovering and said, "I found the elevator…but it must be pretty compact."

The door at the end of the corridor, facing me, opened into a bedroom that filled the entire wedge-end of the building, and was larger than the anteroom that led off the meeting room on the second floor. It was decorated with the same pattern of velvet wallcovering I'd seen in the boardroom, but this time it had been made in a shade of blueish teal, and all the trim had been painted to match. In this room – because the ceiling sloped inward not just at the sides, but also toward the point – I had the feeling that I was on a ship, sailing toward the Paris skyline…and what a skyline it was.

Églantine's bed was set against the wall facing the point, which would give the occupant a perfect view through the window in the very end of the building, where the floodlit statue of Napoleon on top of the column at the center of *Place Vendôme* was visible, just a block or two away. I'd first seen that column when Maurice Chevalier's private detective character used it as a lookout spot in *Love In The Afternoon*, with Audrey Hepburn as his daughter.

I wonder if Églantine thought of Napoleon himself when she saw that column, or of Coco Chanel who lived at the Ritz there…or of any of the other fashion houses that had their headquarters there over the centuries?

"Big bedroom," said Bud behind me, making me jump. He flicked a switch – wall sconces and bedside lamps glowed. "And that's quite a bed…it's almost like a boat. But…no closets?"

The wooden structure of the bed was, indeed, boat-like, completely encasing the four sides of the mattress in a wooden box, with sinuous carvings leading from the curvaceous headboard to a triumphant prow-like point at its foot.

A boat…on a ship, in the ocean of Paris…amazing.

Above the bedhead were four massive, framed prints by Alphonse Mucha, each representing a flower, in the shape of a diaphanously clad young woman, and the bed itself was mounded with so many cushions – each covered with a differently patterned and hued velvet – that I wondered where the elderly woman would have put them all when she slept. I suspected that the trunk at the foot of the bed, with stylized cast-iron tulips as brackets, solved that one.

And Bud was right: other than the bed, the posters, the trunk, a pair of matching nightstands, and a mustard velvet *chaise longue* placed in front of the window at the point of the room, the large space was empty. I said, "I wonder where she kept all her clothes? I'm guessing a fashion designer would have a lot."

Bud chuckled. "I'm still wondering how on earth she got that bed up here. The elevator must be tiny, and I know the staircase is impressively wide in the reception area, but the way it narrowed as we got up here? I find it hard to believe that this bed even got through the door to the apartment. Do they…disassemble all large pieces of furniture – here in Paris – to move it into a place like this?"

Pierre was distracted by something on his tablet, so I replied, "Moving companies have a special sort of lifting device. It looks like a fireman's ladder, attached at its base to a wheeled trailer or vehicle, and they extend it until it's set against the window, or the rail of a balcony. Then there's a large flat platform on runners that they winch up and down the ladder, with items of furniture secured to the platform."

Bud shook his head. "Good grief…the things you know."

I smiled back. "I only know that one because I saw it happening at an apartment close to the *Sorbonne* a few weeks back. I found it fascinating…especially the way that no one seemed to think much of the fact that the entire narrow street had to be closed to accommodate the operation – and all just because someone on the fifth floor was having a new fridge delivered."

Bud shrugged. "I suppose we should be grateful we never faced that sort of challenge at our house."

"Indeed. Right…on we go."

There was a door on the other side of the bed that matched the one we'd entered by, so we all trooped through that. The first door on the left opened into a large dressing room which answered my question about clothes storage – in spades. The door beyond that allowed access to a tiny bathroom – which would have backed onto the kitchen, but was even smaller than that compact space, with only enough room to house a toilet, washbasin, and miniscule shower; it was also covered from floor to ceiling in the peacock tile. Then we were back in the main room.

Oh yes, I could live here…if the shower were larger – I wouldn't fit in that one.

Once we reassembled in what was about the only area of the room that wasn't hosting a piece of furniture – standing, almost in a row, in front of the bookcases on the back wall – I said,

"Right, I won't disturb anything – unless you specifically allow me to do so, Pierre – but now that I've got the lay of the land, so to speak, I need to get to work with what I can see…and I'm starting in the bedroom, and dressing room."

"Why not here?" asked Pierre.

"This is a public space – even if Églantine didn't really entertain any longer. The bedroom and dressing room were exclusively hers, so I might learn more about the private Églantine there. Come with me and tell me what I can touch, and how."

Bud added, "And take pictures – Francine told you to do that, didn't she?"

Pierre sighed. "She did, and I shall obey her orders, of course. I'll follow you, Cait – and you point out things you might want to mention to her so I can record them for…posterity."

The dressing room had racks of garments hanging around most of three sides – allowing for a make-up table – with a large, dark wood *armoire* each side of the door…the back of which had been fitted with a full-length mirror. A seat-height pouffe upholstered in mustard velvet occupied the center of the room. The illumination wasn't given by period lamps in this space; low-wattage daylight globes hung, bare, in all four corners, flooding the room with "natural" light as though it were noon. I noticed they were operated with a modern dimmer switch.

"I can open drawers, and so forth, as long as I don't fiddle – is that correct, Pierre?"

Pierre nodded. "The captain told me that the entire apartment has been searched – but in the manner of establishing that Madame George was not here, that there were no signs of an attack having taken place here, and that she'd left no note saying she'd planned to leave the Maison, or anything like that – rather than in a full, forensic manner. The team will come back to do that – so, no, please don't move anything, until I have photographed it in place, and use caution when touching surfaces, even though you're gloved. Thank you."

Bud and I nodded, and I began to pull open doors and drawers, as well as peering at the stunning gowns, tops, skirts, and trousers…plus the dozens of scarves, shawls, and – my personal favorites – the magnificent kimono-style over-thingies in various lengths, and finishes.

"Right, bedroom next," I said.

"No photographs?" Pierre sounded disappointed.

I relented and held open one of the *armoires*. "These shoes and handbags, and those canes and umbrellas in the corner, and her make-up table, thanks, as well as some general shots, please."

I left Pierre snapping and moved on to the bedroom. The bedside tables held few surprises, except that the small bookcases beneath the drawers were full of crime novels which Pierre allowed me to examine – paperbacks, mainly in French, but some in English.

"Bathroom next, and you can take some photos of all the book titles here, please, Pierre," I said, and, once again, left Pierre snapping away.

When Pierre arrived outside the bathroom – it was only big enough to accommodate one person at a time with any comfort – I held open the medicine cabinet, which was a mind-boggling construction in walnut, carved to look like an arum lily in one corner of a luscious mirror surround. "Please shoot the contents of this cabinet, and the towels on the rail. Thanks."

I suspected that the kitchen wouldn't be of much interest, but we checked it in any case; I was right, there was nothing of a personal nature in there, then we started on the main room.

"Okay, Pierre…I accept that I was wrong. I hadn't factored in that Églantine had a cleaner, and that people brought her food each day, so she really had no private, personal space in her home, which means we're as likely to find out the truth of the woman in here as anywhere. I'm going to start with the books on her shelves – which always offer the chance for huge insight – and you can shoot away to your heart's content. Okay if I open a few of them – if they're on the top of a pile, and I place them back exactly as I found them…once you've snapped them?"

Pierre considered my request, nodded, and we began.

The jumble of books made the hairs on the back of my neck stand on end. Books are precious, and should be treated with respect, handled gently, and allowed to rest upright…preferably in some sort of order that makes browsing a joy. But Églantine's idea of order had me sweating: books lay on their backs and fronts, with spines angled in every direction; some were balanced precariously on the edge of a shelf, and some were already on the floor. And…there was no order involved at all: author, size, title, topic, and even color of jacket had all been discounted as categorization methods, and I wondered how on earth she'd ever find a book she wanted. I reasoned that maybe rummaging was a delight in itself to her…then noticed that there was a short unit – just a couple of shelves tall – set against the wall but hidden by the side of a sofa, with its top acting as a sort of narrow side table. I kneeled down to try to get a look at the books on these shelves, and used the flashlight app on my phone to see better in the dimly lit corner.

I stood. "Okay – I'm reassessing. I thought that Églantine was a haphazard storer of books. Now I'm thinking that all these books might have been searched – by someone who didn't have the time, or maybe the will, to replace them in an organized manner. Pierre – take some shots of those two shelves down there, please. You'll see what I mean."

Pierre kneeled, snapped away with his tablet, then stood to show the photos to Bud.

Bud said, "They're all philosophy books, in alphabetical order, by author. This lot? A mess. You could be right, Cait. I'd suggest that someone was looking for something they thought might be hidden in a book, or between volumes.”

I added, “And…we've no way of knowing if they found it…though the extent of the disorganization suggests that, if they did, it wasn't easy to find. But surely Églantine's cleaner would be able to tell the police that this wasn't normal? Have the police interviewed the cleaner yet, Pierre?”

Pierre shrugged. “Sorry, not something the captain shared with me. We…you…can ask, when she arrives.”

I stepped away from the bookshelves. “Let me take this in, with the idea that this isn't Églantine's mess.”

I re-examined spines and titles, browsed inside a few accessible volumes, and bobbed about to get a better look at some covers. “Okay…now let's consider the rest of this room in light of the possibility that someone was in here searching for…something.”

My scan of the room suggested that nothing else had been disturbed. I asked Pierre to take photos of several items and areas: the peony-filled vases – a few were clearly by Gallé; the delicate decorative glass pieces on shelves – more by Gallé, as well as items crafted by Lalique, Kralik, Tiffany, and Loetz; several more vases holding peacock and ostrich feathers, and four side tables.

I noted, “These *objets d'art* are all worth a great deal of money, as are many of the other items that are still here – and they're clearly untouched.”

“Not theft, then,” said Bud.

“Theft has not, officially, been discounted,” noted Pierre.

I asked, “Does anything look out of place – or even just odd – to you? You're both experienced in assessing crime scenes.”

Both men shook their heads. Bud said, “Nothing obviously out of place except the books, and the only incongruity I can see is that modern heating pad on that chair.”

I'd noticed the pad, and also that it had some hairs on it. "Does Églantine have a cat, or a small dog?" I asked Pierre. I thought it unlikely, because I'd not seen anything else in the apartment to suggest that a pet lived there.

He shrugged. "No idea. No one's mentioned one, and I certainly haven't see one around…though I didn't even know there was an elevator."

Bud noted, "You'd be sneezing if she had a cat, Cait – your allergies would have been triggered. A small dog's more likely."

I replied, "But there are no water or food bowls, nor food or treats in the kitchen – or anywhere else. And you know what Marty's like, Bud – even if you don't allow for all the things he needs for sustenance, there are always signs that he lives in our home. And there's nothing here to suggest that an animal does – other than one slightly hairy heating mat. You'd better take some shots of that, too, Pierre, thanks. Anything else?"

Pierre offered, "The medicine cabinet in the bathroom had absolutely no medication in it, except for some over-the-counter pain pills…and a lot of creams and potions, of course. Isn't it unusual that an older person would not be taking any medication at all?"

Bud said, "Another one for your captain, I think, Pierre. Églantine might have been one of those people who won't go to a doctor so has no medications to take, or was as healthy as an ox."

Pierre reacted to a beep on his phone and checked a text. "The captain will be here soon, we'd better join the others, downstairs. Are you happy with what you've seen here, Cait? Do you think it's…helped?"

I nodded. "I am, and it has, thanks. Yes, let's go and meet Francine. I'm eager to hear any news she has about Lucienne's death, and – of course – any updates she has about the search for Églantine George."

Dix

When the three of us entered the meeting room, I was surprised to see that only Monique and Monica were sitting at the massive oval table. I assumed some sort of bathroom break on the part of the others.

Pierre looked horrified. "Where is everyone?"

Oh heck…of course, we're back to having to speak French again. Come on, Cait, you're not too tired to manage that.

Monica replied, "Gone home. Drifted off, one by one."

I saw Pierre's fists clench. "They can't have gone home. I told them to stay. The captain wanted them to stay. The officers at the entrance shouldn't have allowed them to pass…I told them about the captain's orders when I went to collect the forensic protection gear. They shouldn't have let them leave." As he spoke, his voice got higher and higher.

Bud reached out and touched the young man's arm. "Pierre, you made Captain de Gaulle's instructions quite clear to everyone here, and I dare say you did to whomever was posted outside the building. You're not to blame for this."

Monica said, "They took the elevator, so probably used the side door. Maybe there wasn't anyone posted there?"

Pierre was agog. "What side door? None of the officers here told me about a side door…but they didn't tell me there was an elevator, either – sometimes I feel like a real…outsider."

I suddenly realized that, when I'd been sitting at the table earlier on, I'd not really noticed the significance of the fact that behind me – instead of a row of windows like the ones I'd been facing – there was a paneled wall, with a door in it.

I asked, "Is there a corridor through there, leading to an elevator that goes all the way up to Églantine's apartment?"

The twins nodded and shrugged – in unison. I strode through the door, and found myself in a corridor as narrow as the one I'd seen on the sixth floor, with a row of windows on one side, and three doors along the inner wall. The first two on my left led to shallow, but wide washrooms; the next had a glass panel and a button – the door to the elevator; the final one, facing me, led into the anteroom. I realized I'd seen that door when I'd been in the anteroom itself but had believed it to be a cupboard. I tutted at my error.

Upon re-entering the meeting room I asked, "Does the elevator go all the way to the ground floor?"

Monica said, "Of course."

I muttered, "Yes, of course…there'd be no point, otherwise. Bud – you didn't see a door when you originally walked along that side of the building early this afternoon – you said that, right?"

Bud's shoulders fell. "I didn't say that, because I suspected there was one. It was almost exactly the same as all the other windows, but it had a hinge…though no handle, so I carried on until I found the main front entrance. I didn't mention it at the time, because…well, it wasn't going to help us, and then…well, we met Lucienne. It turns out that it was…significant."

I sighed, but smiled. "You weren't to know, and I dare say I'd have discounted it too, even if you'd told me about it then, because it wasn't what we were looking for at the time. Context – right?"

Bud nodded. "Always."

The thought of context sparked a thought. "Monica, Monique, while we have a few moments, what can you tell me about the amber necklace, or collar, that was worn by Églantine? I could see from her apartment that she had wonderful taste in décor and clothes – so why did she always wear the same item of jewelry? Was it special to her?"

The twins sighed, in unison, then Monica said, "Back in the 1970s, when we met her, she already had the necklace, and the voice. But she's never told anyone about what happened to her – not as far as we know, and certainly not us."

I asked, "What do you mean by 'the voice'?"

Looking at me as though I were from a different planet, Monica said, "What do you mean, what do I mean? Églantine's voice was unique – so hoarse that it sounded as though she were speaking and gargling at the same time…and it was incredibly deep, too."

I said, "Oh, thanks for that…I never met her, so had no idea, of course."

Monica continued, "We've always assumed that something happened to her voice box when she got burned. She had a scar…and that was why she covered her neck. Monique caught an accidental glimpse of the scar many years ago, but Églantine never removed her collar in public. Ever."

Monique added, "She was changing clothes before she went on stage at the end of a show – one of the early ones, where we all did pretty much everything ourselves. She'd had a mishap with some gold make-up she'd been slathering onto Avril's legs, so had to change her dress. I walked in on her. She didn't care that she was naked, just that she wasn't wearing her necklace. Her hands flew to cover her neck and chest, not her other parts. She had a scar – a dreadful one. I thought it looked like a burn, and Monica and I have always suspected she might have hurt herself when she was experimenting with acids."

Pierre – still white-knuckled – interrupted. "Why would Églantine have been experimenting with acids? I thought she designed clothes. What more have I missed?"

Monica replied, "She started out by painting her designs onto light-colored velvets with dyes. But then she began to paint with acid; it burns away the velvet until the backing fabric is exposed.

That's what *devoré* is. This process fascinated her – the way she could expose the backing, then alter the appearance of that layer by using different dyes in different areas of the reverse, while the velvet texture remained intact 'in front' of it."

Monique added, "She told us that it felt as though she were exposing the beauty and the possibilities that were hidden in the fabric – the way some sculptors say they have released figures trapped inside a piece of marble. Then she carved her own blocks and started to print acid onto fabrics, which was when she designed what's become the signature pattern for the Maison…and she went on from there."

Monica tapped her sister on the arm, and took over the explanation, the pair acting like a tag team. "Although the end result is glamorous, there are some nasty things used in textile creation, and even in the production of couture pieces. We've always suspected she'd had an accident with some sort of caustic material – she prided herself on mixing her own dyes, and we thought she might have been trying the same approach with acids, which is a dangerous undertaking."

Monique nudged Monica. "But that necklace she used to cover it up? That's got to be a one-of-a-kind piece. We've talked about it many times, haven't we?" Monica nodded. "She had it when we first met her, so we've never known her without it, as we said. In fact, I've stopped thinking of it as an item that exists independently of Madame – it is Madame, it is part of her body."

"Oh absolutely," agreed Monica. "And because she's never referred to it herself – it's just always there – there've been lots of theories in the business about where she'd got it, and what it was worth, of course."

Pierre was now on full alert. "It might have been valuable, you mean?"

The twins nodded, in synchronized fashion. Monica said, "And whatever it was worth intrinsically, it would be worth a great deal more because it had been hers for so long. There are some collectors who are…well, worryingly obsessive about certain things. You've no idea."

Pierre was now fully involved. "Please, tell me what you mean."

Monique smiled coyly. "I once had someone approach me after a show who offered me a thousand francs – when we still had them – to bring him a lock of Madame's hair. Just one lock. He said she wouldn't miss it, and that it would grow back in any case – but that it would mean the world to him. But that was a long time ago."

Monica added, "And there's the scarf woman, isn't there?"

Monique nodded.

Bud, Pierre, and I, all chorused, "Who's the scarf woman?"

The twins leaned in, and Monica whispered, "She has hundreds of the unique scarves that Madame has designed. She's never worn any of them. She just looks at them. Has a room for them. Offered Madame a huge amount of money to design a scarf just for her, based upon her own initials, and with Madame's signature etched into the velvet…which Madame did, of course. That one scarf got us through a tricky patch when *devoré* velvet was having a bit of a wobble. Odd woman."

"Rich, though," said Monique.

Pierre said, "Maybe we should be making a list of the people who had a special interest in Églantine and the Maison…maybe she's gone because someone wanted her amber collar."

"An interesting line of inquiry, Bertrand," said Francine de Gaulle when she entered the room, as though she were stepping onto a red carpet. "I overheard you as I came up the stairs, and can see we are…thin on the ground here. But don't concern yourselves – I'll need to interview everyone tomorrow, and will put calls through to ensure that each individual understands the gravity of their having chosen to ignore the…request…of a police captain. But it's late, and it's time that everyone saw their beds. You may all visit me at my office tomorrow. Someone will contact you with the details of a timed appointment. You may all leave."

Monica and Monique shot out of their seats. Monique said, "Thank you. We were here before seven this morning, and we have a long day tomorrow. We'll have our phones with us, but won't be here – we'll be at the exhibit, overseeing the installation, even though it's Sunday. Of course, we'll present ourselves at your office when required."

Nods were exchanged all round, and they scurried out of the room.

I hovered, unprepared to leave without the opportunity to receive any updates. I asked, "What news of Lucienne's death?"

Francine looked even more haggard than when she'd left us. "Toxicology results will be texted to me. Healthy corpse, except for the poison in his system…which he definitely ingested. Nothing was injected into him, for example. No trauma, except for that which he sustained when he fell to the ground. Time of death is placed at some point between two and six – hours before his body was recovered. Hours when good Parisians ignored a man lying dead on a side street…and didn't even report another human being in distress." She sounded exhausted.

I dared to place my hand on her arm; bright eyes blazed at me as she snatched it away and straightened her back.

Wrong move, Cait.

She said, "I imagine you'd like to get back to your hotel. A car will take you. But I should ask – did you learn anything from your sortie into the missing woman's apartment?" She looked at Pierre as she spoke, and he handed her his tablet.

He replied, "The evidence suggests that a search might have been made of all the books in the apartment – which I believe might be significant. You can see in some photos that one particular area escaped being ransacked."

He didn't quite bristle with pride, but he wasn't far short.

Francine flicked her gaze toward me and Bud, then scrolled through photographs. "I see what you mean," she said. Handing the tablet back to Pierre, she added, "I admit that, when I glanced around her apartment earlier today, I believed the woman was merely disorganized – but I shall take your observations into consideration. Anything else?"

Bud looked at me, and I said, "Quite a lot…want to hear it now?"

For the first time since we'd met her, I saw hesitation flicker in Francine's eyes…then it was gone. "Is it an urgent matter, or could it wait until tomorrow morning?"

I weighed my response. "I'm even more convinced that Églantine George is dead, and that I saw her being killed. I believe I could offer valuable insights into the woman's lifestyle, and her personality, that could be of use in the investigation into her death…once it becomes that – though I do understand that you're prioritizing the search for a person who is missing. Tomorrow morning would be fine, but earlier, rather than later, I'd say."

Francine sighed. "Let's say ten sharp at my office, which is in the building where we first met today. I have many tasks to complete prior to that. I will see you then. Pierre, please show Cait and Bud to the officer at the door, then return here. I've arranged for them to be driven to their hotel. Good night, or should that be good morning? Until…later."

Bud and I followed a silent, and tense, Pierre down the sweeping staircase and were handed off to an officer whose uniform looked so crisp that I suspected he'd just come on duty.

When we arrived at our hotel, the glass doors from the street were locked, and we had to buzz and identify ourselves to gain entry. As we shuffled our way toward reception, I remembered that the door that would give us access to the elevator needed a keycard to open it. I scrabbled in my bag, and Bud mumbled about…something or other.

"What did you say?" I asked, annoyed that I couldn't locate my keycard.

How does whatever I need always manage to disappear in my handbag?

He chuckled, "I can't believe it, but I'm hungry. I should have had more of those nibbles at *Maison Églantine*."

Dave, who'd checked us in, materialized beside us. "You've been to *Maison Églantine*? No one ever gets into that place…and we all thought you'd both been arrested for…well, I guessed espionage, but no one else thought that likely – so, what was it? Did the cops from Vancouver track you down here and make you pay all your parking tickets? And why were you at *Maison Églantine*? Do tell!"

Apart from Dave, we were the only people about. I didn't know what time the bar and restaurant closed, but it was clear that by – *good grief, a quarter to two* – all the customers, and other staff, had gone home. The hotel itself seemed to be asleep – except for we three.

Bud and I had enough experience under our belts to know that we shouldn't share any sensitive information, so I jumped in with: "Pierre – the detective in plain clothes who collected us – is an old friend, from Nice. He thought it would be a lark to 'strong-arm us' out of the place. And we were at *Maison Églantine* earlier today, so just…returned for another visit."

Dave rolled his eyes. "The place is out of bounds to all but the famous and ludicrously rich. Which are you? And how did you manage to get that past me when you arrived? My celebrity radar is usually spot on…it needs to be, here."

Bud and I couldn't help but chuckle. Bud said, "Not rich, not famous…just us. Your radar is safe, for now."

Dave smiled. "Now – did I hear you say you were hungry? We have snack bags – you could take a couple up to your room. And we open at seven for breakfast…which isn't that far off. Though you'll probably be having a bit of a late start, it being Sunday, I'd have thought."

We grunted our thanks and goodnights, grabbed a couple of the bags from the shelf behind us, and headed to our room. While I sat on the bed, with Bud on the chair beside the desk – both of us nibbling popcorn – I mumbled, "It's been quite a day, Bud…and I've been thinking things through."

Bud chuckled, "Of course you have. And do you have any observations?"

"I do. I'm wondering again about what I saw – exactly – in that window. I mean, yes, I'm sure that I saw what I did – but have I interpreted it correctly?"

Bud put down his popcorn and gave me his full attention. "Look, I'm fully aware that I have been known – occasionally – to accuse you of being…well, maybe a little too quick to judge, and we don't need to have that conversation again. But I totally trust that you saw what you say you did, so – now that we have that on the record – tell me what you mean about how you've interpreted what you saw. You're having doubts about it being a fatal attack? Despite the fact that the guy we met there this afternoon has already turned up dead?"

I mentally forced my brain to stop swirling, and pulled on a thread of a thought. "I saw someone with their hands around a person's neck. I'm sure that person was Églantine George. But…she wasn't struggling, and she was wearing what could be an incredibly valuable amber necklace. What if the person whose hands I saw was removing the necklace, not strangling her? I saw a split second of action…now, if you were to be reaching to remove a collar that had a clasp at the back of my neck, you'd probably reach forward with both hands to do that. Maybe that's what I saw. Maybe that's why she wasn't struggling…someone was helping her remove her necklace, for whatever reason, and then she simply wandered off, as people have suggested."

Bud raked his hand through his snowy hair. Eventually he said, "It could have been Lucienne up there helping her out, then he discovered she'd left the building and…followed her – saying he was sick? Then he ended up being poisoned by 'someone', for a reason we don't yet know about?"

I sighed. "Yes. Could be…though we both know you're clutching at theoretical straws there, Bud. Thank you. No, a strangulation is probably what I witnessed, but I am at least forcing myself to be open to different interpretations of what I saw. Trying to not be so…certain."

Bud hugged me. "It's good to be certain, when you are – but I'm really impressed that you're looking at this from a different perspective. It can't hurt, right?"

I stared at the bag of popcorn in my hand. "I don't think I'm going to be able to stay awake long enough to digest this."

Bud stood and gave me a popcorn-y kiss on the head. "Come on, madam, into the bathroom, then bed for you…we've got to be up early, and I reckon we're better off getting the best sleep we can then a proper breakfast, rather than stuffing ourselves with this junk and having indigestion all night. Not that there's much night left, of course."

I agreed, and was only annoyed that I hadn't left my toiletries in an easily accessible part of my suitcase. As it turned out, Bud had also managed to bury his toothbrush, so it took us a while to be able to clamber into what turned out to be a more delightfully comfy bed than either of us had dared hope…and we did so knowing we'd have to negotiate the obstacle course of two suitcases laying wide open on the floor – still fully packed, though now riffled through – if…*when*…we needed the loo during the night.

Onze

The alarm that I'd, thankfully, remembered to set on my phone woke me before I realized I was asleep. Bud and I agreed he'd unpack while I showered, then we swapped duties. We finally stumbled down to reception by eight, tired, but at least dressed in clean clothes, on clean – and theoretically refreshed – bodies. Dave wasn't around, but we were informed by a blue-haired young woman named Angelique that we could eat in the courtyard or the restaurant.

It was a dry, sunny morning, but the air was chilly, and the tall, triangular stainless-steel heaters dotted among the tables in the open-air courtyard were all glowing red. There were a few hardy souls sipping coffee and eating pastries, and two pairs of people with coffee and laptops were deep in animated conversation.

"The delights of breakfast meetings…on a Sunday," I said. "I'd hoped we could eat outside, but will you be too cold?"

Bud patted his jacket. "This, and my years as an RCMP officer in the snowy wastes of the Canadian north, are all I need to be able to cope with this weather. And if we might get stuck cooped up in offices and meetings with Francine, why not make the most of this?"

We chose a table beside a heater, and read through the menu.

A tall server with a blond ponytail, wearing a purple checked shirt and a cerise cravat, approached us immediately and addressed us in English. "Good morning, I'm Eustace. Can I bring you coffee, while you think about what you want to eat?"

His accent wasn't French.

I said, "Good morning, Eustace, I'm Cait, this is Bud. I'd like a cappuccino, please – by the bucket, if it comes that way."

Eustace smiled with confusion. "There is only one size of cappuccino."

I wondered if my slightly colloquial joke had been too much for his English and simply replied, "That'll be fine, thank you."

"Americano for me, please," said Bud.

Eustace smiled. "I shall return." He left.

"You appear to have developed quite a taste for cappuccinos since you got here," remarked Bud. "You've had two each day since I arrived. Are we going to have to get one of those fancy machines when we get home?"

"Nope – I like it here, but it would be too much for me, on an ongoing basis. In fact, the only reason I took to it was because the little break room nearest my office at the *Sorbonne* had a machine that created good cappuccinos but awful everything else." I nodded at the menu. "Know what you want yet?"

Bud smiled coyly. "When in Paris…so I'm having the Parisian breakfast. It sounds good. I like boiled eggs, and ham, and toast, and cheese…and a croissant is traditional, right? You?"

"Scrambled eggs and Parisian mushrooms – even though I have no idea what that means. I can't be outdone in terms of Parisian-ness by you, can I?"

Quick decisions by us, and swift service by Eustace – who turned out to be Argentinian – meant it wasn't long before we were both enjoying our meals, and second coffees. After quite a few "Mms" and "Ums", we were ready to talk about the considerable happenings of the previous day, and the prospect of the one ahead of us.

Bud said, "Francine's teams should have completed the local door-to-door by now, so, by the time we see her, she should have some idea if anyone in the vicinity spotted Églantine leaving the Maison yesterday. I also hope she'll tell us things like who was the last to see Églantine, and when that was…though, to be honest, I wouldn't tell people like us anything much, if this were my case."

"She won't give away anything she doesn't have to, Bud. Not the type."

Bud sat back, his plate empty, and his tummy full, I suspected, judging by the look on his face. "That was excellent. The ham tasted incredible – as it all did." I felt my multipurpose right eyebrow shoot up, and he hastily added, "Though not as good as the hams you roast at home, of course."

"My mushrooms were good, too. It seems that adding chives and possibly a pound of butter to mushrooms affords them the title of 'Parisian'. And the eggs were…well, I've never tasted such silky and yet simultaneously fluffy scrambled eggs, ever…not even when you've made them for me, Husband. Sorry." I added a cute smile, for good measure.

Bud sipped the remains of his coffee. "If Francine won't give up information easily, do we have anything worthwhile to trade with? You've been tight-lipped about what Églantine's apartment told you about her."

"Not 'tight-lipped', Bud – we've been doing other things, which is what I suggest we do now. Why don't we walk to the police station? It's just a block or two from the opera house, and that's only about a fifteen-minute walk from here. And it's a nice day…which we might miss due to 'meetings', like you said. Quick jaunt back to the room, then off?"

Our walk along *Boulevard Haussmann* was a delight, giving us the chance to size up restaurants and cafés for potential future use, peep into world-famous arcades – wishing we had the time to explore them, and promising ourselves we'd return – and revel in the architecture. We even got an amazing peek-a-boo view of the basilica of *Sacré-Cœur* which appeared closer than it really was, standing proud on its hill above the city surrounding it.

Once we reached the police station, we readied ourselves for the serious business of the day, and waited patiently, and silently, in the echoing rotunda area where we'd first seen Pierre.

Eventually collected by a uniformed female officer, we were led through heavy doors – which closed with an ominous clang behind us – along a series of gray corridors, then into what was, essentially, a gray cube of a room. Despite the fact we were in what was clearly a grand building, its interior had little character; it made me feel as though a series of modern, functional boxes had been dropped into a beautiful, but rather less functional, shell.

Once again we waited – this time less patiently – until Francine burst through the door, with Pierre in tow. She was wearing another silk shirt – *café au lait*, this time, and another dark suit – espresso-hued. Her perfect hair bounced around her still-haggard face as she entered, and Pierre was almost attached to her he was so close behind her…which I imagined was something he felt good about. He'd really stepped up his choice of a tie, and he'd nicked himself while shaving that morning, suggesting he'd been aiming for a close cut, but had probably still been half asleep at the time.

Both were grasping mugs of what I assumed was coffee, though none was offered to us. Francine placed a few folders stuffed with papers onto the table that sat between us, then pulled a tablet from her capacious handbag, which she placed beside Pierre's own, bulkier, tablet. They both woke up their devices at the exact same moment, with matching movements, which made me smile – thinking of the invisible connections between the Martin twins at the Maison.

When Francine looked up, there was…*hunger?*…in her eyes. I wondered for a moment about exactly how much stress this woman was under, but the broad smile she flashed at me the next instant made me realize that she was taking control. "We have results – Lucienne Durand died of strychnine poisoning. The post-mortem has concluded that he ate something laced with the poison, with…the expected results. The doctor suspected it immediately, which allowed for swift toxicological identification. And we know that the something he ate was a ham and cheese baguette. It had hardly been digested."

Bud said, "Lucienne seemed to be a pleasant man – hospitable, and proud of his association with *Maison Églantine*. Did he have a family?"

Francine replied, "No. He lived alone in a small apartment not too far from the *Gare de l'Est* in the *Strasbourg-Saint-Denis* district in the tenth *arrondissement*. It's not…the best of areas, and still has some of the alleyways and side streets that used to be the favorite haunts of cutpurses and thugs in the pre-Haussmann era. He was close to his building when he died, and – despite our original beliefs – his body wasn't visible from the street. A neighbor found him when they went to put out their garbage. It was…a sad end." Francine sat up even straighter. "We're doing our best to find out what we can about Monsieur Durand, but he had no driving license, no passport, and his only work records are with *Maison Églantine*, where he's been employed for more than forty years. He was sixty-four, single, and his home suggests he lived a simple life."

I jumped in. "Are you considering the possibility that his death is connected in some way to the…situation with Églantine herself?"

Francine mumbled, "I don't like coincidences."

Bud and I chorused, "Neither do we."

Pierre's eyebrows shot up and he dared a glance toward Francine – trying to work out what her reaction to our comment would be, I judged.

She smiled. "With your backgrounds, I'm not surprised. I've had a chat with a colleague about you, Bud, as I mentioned I would. You've got an impressive reputation in the world of international gang-busting, I must say. And one of my assistants, who has a sister living in the UK, has brought me up to speed on some interesting facts about your background, Cait. I understand you were arrested in Cambridge on suspicion of murder?"

I jumped in. "But completely exonerated – and cleared by many agencies in Canada to be able to work as a consultant to Bud's homicide teams."

Francine nodded. "As you say."

She paused and stared at the two of us for a few long moments. I grew concerned, because it appeared that Pierre was literally holding his breath as Francine considered what she'd say next.

Eventually, her micro-expressions told me she'd made her decision, then she relaxed back into her chair. "I'm a pragmatic person, and I've had to work in some less-than-standard ways to get where I am today. You two could be a valuable resource, and I'd rather have you helping me than…sticking your noses in and getting in the way – which I have a suspicion is exactly what you'd both do if I asked you to leave now and go about your vacationing with smiles on your faces. However, I cannot do that in any case, because of what you witnessed yesterday, Cait. So I have decided to bring you inside, and will rely upon you to not overstep, to not share the information that I am 'using you', and to report anything you discover or suspect to me directly – or to me through Pierre. He is the only person who will know about this arrangement, do you both…all…understand?"

I wondered if Pierre was going to faint: his color drained away completely, and he appeared to be hyperventilating, but he smiled, then nodded vigorously.

Careful, Pierre…this woman won't take kindly to a sycophant.

Bud said, "You have our word." I nodded.

Francine stood. "Good. And I'd like to add that I was sorry to hear about the death of your first wife, Bud. It's not easy to lose a loved one – under whatever circumstances – but to know they've been killed by someone who wished to do you harm because of the work you were doing, must be especially difficult. I'm glad to see that you and Cait have formed a good personal as well as professional relationship…especially given what Cait had to endure from the British tabloids when her ex-boyfriend was found dead at her home. You can both understand each other on many levels, I believe, which is an advantage, I'm sure. Right, come with me – we're all going back to *Maison Églantine*. Pierre will drive, and we shall talk. No more conversations here. I can smoke in the car…we'll take mine. You two aren't allowed to come to the car park with us, so we'll collect you at the main entrance."

As Bud and I stood on the street – avoiding being bumped into by people hurrying about their business, or visitors wandering along with their eyes on their phones – I said, "I don't know why we need a car. We walked from *Maison Églantine* to here yesterday in less than a quarter of an hour."

Bud said, "That's half an hour or more there and back. Francine can't waste that much time during an investigation, and you know how a car can become a moveable office, as well as a private space."

I knew he was right, but didn't fancy the idea of being stuck inside a car with Francine puffing away. Being an ex-smoker means I try to avoid situations where my craving can kick in, which means pretty much anywhere someone is smoking. I stuck my hand into my bag: yes, I had nicotine gum in there, which Bud reckons I should be over, by now, but I know it never hurts to be prepared. And Paris had already challenged me on so many occasions, because lighting up was second nature to such a huge swath of the population, especially among the student body, I'd found…though the vaping thing had caught on in a big way with that crowd. When I'd joined small groups from my classes, over the past weeks, to grab a lunch of sandwiches and soft drinks on a few occasions in the magnificent gardens surrounding the equally magnificent Luxembourg Palace, a few blocks from the university, they'd almost all sucked on their vapes, surrounding us with white, fruit-fragranced clouds – and I'd coped really well, I'd thought. But being in a car with someone smoking an actual cigarette? I felt anxious.

When Francine's gleaming, silent car slid alongside us, she was already puffing out of the window. Bud got in and shuffled across the back seat, and I stuffed myself in beside him. Then we were off, with the light attached to the roof flashing and the siren blaring through Francine's open window. She was juggling her tablet on her knees, and the part of Pierre's face that I could see told me he was concentrating on the traffic ahead of us…which was good, because we were going pretty fast, considering where we were. As we nudged across a pedestrian crossing, where cars had sort of parted for us, Francine clamped her phone to her ear, threw her cigarette out of the window, and closed it. "What? Repeat that. Right. We're coming."

Pierre shot a glance toward her. "What?"

She replied, "We're going to the *Petit Palais*, Bertrand. Get us there fast." She half-turned toward Bud and me in the back seat. "They've found Églantine George. She's dead."

Douze

The journey across Paris was hair-raising, to say the least. Bud and I had buckled our seatbelts when we'd got in, and we needed them, otherwise we'd have slithered across the back seat like two eggs rolling around, loose in a box. We slalomed through traffic that, thankfully, at least paused to let us pass as we navigated the massive *Place de la Concorde*. I couldn't help but imagine the sound of tires squealing as we swerved past the obelisk that more than three thousand years earlier had stood proudly in Luxor, Egypt. Now it marked the spot where Louis XIV and Marie-Antoinette had lost their heads to the guillotine. History was careening past me, and all I could do was hold on, and hope we'd all reach our destination safely.

Shuddering to a halt outside the imposing façade of the museum, the police presence was evident, as was Francine's importance: we all simply abandoned the car, and two officers rushed to her side – both speaking at once – as we mounted the wide stone steps that led us to an entrance of massive proportions, that really put the portico at *Maison Églantine* to shame…and that was saying something.

I felt a creeping sense of unreality when Bud and I were treated with the same respect and deference being shown to Francine as we bypassed the significant number of members of the public who were standing respectfully in a line on the steps. We entered the magnificent golden doors flanked by officers, who saluted. It felt especially odd to me because the *Petit Palais* had been on the list of places I'd wanted Bud and me to visit, so I'd done my research and had been looking forward to seeing it. However, I hadn't imagined for one minute that our arrival there would have been under such extraordinary circumstances.

The doors designed by the architect himself, Charles Girault – when the building was created for the Universal Exhibition in 1900 – literally blurred as we rushed through them, and the spiral staircase for which he'd designed a delicate balustrade also became no more than an obstacle that had to be overcome as Francine and Pierre romped up ahead of Bud, with me – once again – bringing up the rear, except that, on this staircase, I had three police officers following me.

Another officer greeted us at the top of the stairs and directed us through an area where the third of three massive banners was being suspended from the ceiling by two men, using an alarmingly tall ladder. Each banner displayed a photograph of a gown of such dazzling perfection that I had to pause for a moment to take them all in…and catch my breath. One showed an intricately patterned, form-fitting gown by Worth – the "inventor" of the couture fashion house back in the 1800s; another was a photograph of a simple, drop-waisted black gown – Coco Chanel's original "little black dress" of the 1920s; the third was from the controversial collection for Maison Margiela's 2024 Artisanal collection by Galliano, which appeared to be little more than a corset with an impossibly cinched waist, surrounded by translucent gauze, which would provide little coverage for whomever might be brave enough to wear it. The Worth piece was, by far, my favorite.

Before any of us could enter what appeared to be one of the wings of the building – which was cordoned off with crime scene tape, as well as a host of officers, and had, presumably, been set aside for this specific temporary exhibition – we all had to get suited and booted, which took a while. Then we paused at the entrance.

Francine spoke through her mask. "I want you to tell me if this is the woman you saw in that window, Cait. Bud – you're an expert pair of eyes. Pierre – you're my second on this – get the notes and photos I want, not just what the forensics people are after, got it?"

We all nodded, but, before we had a chance to enter, a tall, almost emaciated man rushed toward us. He had long hair, was dressed like a 1960s cool cat in a black, clinging polo neck sweater and trousers, and bore an agonized expression that suggested he might age from his current mid-forties to about ninety before the day was out. He cried out, "Please…please — if you're the one in charge, tell them I need my space back. We must continue to set up the exhibits. It's a matter of life and death."

Francine paused, turned, and approached the man. She pulled down her mask. "You are Monsieur Valli, the organizer of this exhibition?"

The man almost bowed to kiss her hand. "I am…indeed I am. And we have our private opening tomorrow night…tomorrow night! And everyone is coming…everyone! The entire fashion world will be here…here!"

I saw Francine grow an inch, despite her paper suit. "Monsieur Valli, not even the President of France will be here tomorrow night, if I say he cannot be. Your *soirée* might have to wait. We must do our work. You might think that *canapés* and champagne are a matter of 'life and death', but a woman has lost her life — a woman I would have imagined you'd have thought of as a significant figure in your world — and I am the one responsible for discovering how she met her end. *That* is a matter of life and death, sir. Now, please, allow us to continue our work uninterrupted. One of my officers will take your statement. This will be a grave matter…after all, you are the one with responsibility for the scene of the crime."

She gestured to an officer to escort the babbling Valli, who looked more panicked than before; I suspected it was on behalf of himself, rather than his exhibits or his opening evening.

Returning to our group, Francine said, "Finally…now we shall enter. I shall lead. Be alert."

The entryway was bounded by tall partition walls bearing large panels of text printed in French and English, plus several oil-on-canvas framed portraits and photographs of fashion designers…including one of Églantine George. I paused. This was a photograph taken of her when she was probably in her thirties; her hairstyle of a corkscrew, plum-colored frizz cut in a Cleopatra style, and her heavy make-up – which also had a touch of the Elizabeth Taylor-version of the Egyptian Queen about it – made it hard to discern the woman's features…but it was her. The full-length portrait showcased the woman's clothing rather than the person. And what clothing it was: tight velvet trousers with wide flares where you could see an intricate design painted onto the cloth; a loose, velvet top – also bearing what looked like a hand-painted design; above that was her amber collar; a kimono-style over-garment that had all the jewel tones you could imagine, upon a base of her very own emerald green, and featuring what I now realized was her signature paisley, *fleur-de-lys*, and tattered peonies house-design, finished the look. The portrait's lighting had been expertly managed to show that all her clothing was velvet, and she stood – barefoot, with her head held high – staring into the camera with what could only be described as defiance. It was a magnificent portrait.

Is that the real Églantine, or a piece of performance art?

Bud reappeared. "Cait? You coming?"

I gestured toward the picture. "She was quite a woman."

Bud held out his gloved hand. "She was. But now? Now you need to take a look at what's in here."

The crinkles around his eyes – which were the only visible part of his face – told me he was smiling…sadly.

I braced myself, because I've seen…far too many corpses. Of course I've seen them laid out in morgues as part of my studies as a criminal psychologist, and I've even visited a body farm, but my ex-boyfriend Angus was the first person whose body I'd seen exactly where it had expired, which – unfortunately for me – had been on the floor of my home in Cambridge. Every corpse I've seen *in situ* since then has reminded me of that instance, and, necessarily, of him.

As I took Bud's hand, and followed him into the large room beyond the entrance cubby, I told myself that at least I was expecting this…that I wasn't going to be surprised by someone dropping dead beside me – as had happened when I'd first met Pierre in Nice, nor suddenly appearing behind me – as had happened most recently in Tahiti.

Francine was standing beside one of a large number of wooden crates – all of which looked like utilitarian, rectangular coffins. The one she was hovering beside was also surrounded by mounds of air-filled plastic pockets, some of which were being placed into large bags by people wearing paper onesies – I assumed for forensic examination. This meant that I had to approach the crate slowly, and with caution, which I was happy to do.

Since the photograph of her that I'd just been admiring had been taken, Églantine George had withered. I looked down to see a small, wizened figure nestled on top of a layer of the plastic bubble things that covered the bottom of the crate; her expression was surprisingly serene. Due to the thick make-up on her face, Églantine didn't have the deathly pallor one might have expected, which was off-putting, to say the least; her pink lipstick was still vivid, though a little smeared, and her foundation made her look as though she were sleeping, not dead. Swathed in a velvet garment that was so dark I could only just tell that it was green, not black, a striking feature of the woman was that her amber collar wasn't there – exposing a massive, livid scar that ran across, and possibly around the back of, her neck and down onto the top of her chest. I understood what had made the twins believe that this might be an acid burn: the scar tissue still looked almost glossily molten, and it really did give the impression that something caustic had been poured onto the woman when she was on her back or maybe sitting up a little.

I heard myself gasp, and felt a little foolish when Pierre whispered, "We're sorry to ask you to do this – we know it's upsetting. But…is this the woman you saw through the window?"

I nodded. "It is. Same hair, might be the same clothing, missing an amber collar. It's her. And this is definitely Églantine, right?"

Francine nodded.

As if on cue, I heard crying; I turned to see Monica and Monique in each other's arms, far across the room, at what appeared to be the entrance to another area.

Francine followed my gaze. "They opened the crate and were removing these…packing bubble things…then mayhem ensued, apparently, until they'd completely revealed the remains. Not what I'd have wanted them to do, of course, but to be expected, I suppose."

Bud noted, "The impression I got last evening was that Monique and Monica were truly close to Églantine, and had been for many years. I expect they're devastated."

Francine shrugged. "I'll speak to them soon, then we'll see. Meanwhile…they formally identified the deceased as Églantine George, and you've now confirmed her to be the woman you witnessed being attacked, Cait. As we can all see, there might be some slight bruising around the general neck area, though that scar tissue makes it almost impossible to be certain. If, as you say, she was strangled while wearing her famous amber collar, that would also have diffused any markings. We can all see she's not wearing her necklace, however, it may be inside the packing case, beneath her body…or it might have come off during the attack, or afterwards, when her body was being disposed of."

I dared, "Or its theft might have been the reason she died. I recognized, late last night, that what I saw at that window might have been someone removing Églantine's necklace, not strangling her…but, now? Well, now I'm back to believing my previous interpretation…though, if the necklace has gone, then maybe that's what someone was after. Maybe even Lucienne? I'm guessing that no one found the necklace on his body? Not a planned theft, leading to an accidental killing, then…he took his own life?"

Pierre stared at me, with his mouth making a small "O"; I wondered why he appeared to be so shocked.

Francine's tone when she responded to my observations suggested a reason. "Thank you so much for your suggestions, but I am quite capable of doing my job, Cait, and we're already investigating every angle you've mentioned…or will be, now that I've seen what we have here."

I knew I could have backed down at that point, but believed I owed it to myself to add, "Her fingernails aren't broken. One of the things I thought odd when I saw her at the window was that the victim wasn't struggling at all – she was simply sitting there, passively. I also can't see signs of any restraints on her wrists, so maybe we can assume she wasn't bound to a chair…but why, then, wouldn't she have put up some sort of fight? Whether she was being strangled…or robbed."

Pierre glanced at Francine, she nodded curtly at him, and he said, "Maybe her attacker was so large and powerful that she knew she couldn't win?"

I said, "That would fit with me having seen large hands at her throat. Though, now that I can see the woman herself, I have to admit that the hands might have been smaller than I'd thought. Her neck is tiny, and even with the collar on it, it wouldn't have been much bigger. I'd think that some tests would help with that, Francine, because it's going to be important to know if a woman's hands could have looked big when they were around that neck. And all of us here know that, while it would be a statistically unusual method for a female to employ, it would probably have been possible for a fit woman to have overcome someone this…frail."

A quiet, "Note that, Bertrand," came from the senior officer, who appeared lost in thought.

I continued, "Now we're faced with the question of how Églantine could have been killed in a room that was supposedly being used by other people at the time, then bundled into a packing case that was – what? – simply carried out of the building…all without anyone seeing anything that raised any suspicions. It beggars belief, to be honest. Oh no…wait…the people bringing the exhibits here would have been up and down in that elevator all morning – Lucienne told us that, Bud. Remember – he said that the caterers complained that they had to use the stairs?"

Bud nodded. "Perhaps Lucienne saw or did something, and then he was killed because of what he saw or did. It's…a theory. Fits the facts, as far as we know them."

Francine was still in another world, then appeared to snap out of it. "Let's leave this area so the body can be properly examined and removed. I want to talk to Monica and Monique. They told my officer that they oversaw the packing of all the garments at the Maison – they should know something. Come."

We left the tragic sight of the grim box in the middle of a room where some magnificent gowns had already been placed on mannequins within glass display cabinets. I couldn't help but feel they were watching over the remains of one of their own, and maybe mourning her; I'd never even met the woman, and yet I already felt the loss of what I believed had been her vibrant spirit…if the clothes she'd designed, and what I'd learned about her from her home, were anything to go by.

We found the twins in the next room of the exhibition, which had progressed much further than the first in terms of being ready to be seen by the public. They were seated close together, on a bench, wrapped in each other's arms, and both were sobbing like small children; it was clear they were taking comfort from each other's presence. Monica spotted our arrival over her sister's shoulder, and wiped her eyes, pulling away. Monique turned, her face red and blotchy, her eyes even redder. She, too, wiped her face with a large handkerchief, then stuffed it into a pocket in the dark green smock she was wearing over a simple gray shift. I wondered if they actually wore the clothes they did as a sort of uniform, then realized that might be a good idea; if a person needed access to pins and threads, and so forth, on a daily basis, they'd spend forever transferring them…and the lower half of each smock appeared to be almost entirely covered with pockets.

Pockets are handy.

Before Francine could say a word, Monica blurted out, "We did it. We killed her." Then the twins dissolved into tears again.

Treize

Francine paused, then moved to stand in front of the two sobbing women. She gestured that the rest of us should remain where we were, which we all did, of course. Then she squatted down, and…became a different person. Reaching out to pat each woman on a leg, she said quietly, "There, there…cry it out. It'll be alright…just let the tears come. Then you can tell me all about it."

You've got children, was what I thought; "Shift in tactics," was what I whispered.

Bud nodded, as did Pierre, who appeared to be completely entranced by the way his boss's sort-of boss was acting.

Standing again, Francine said, "I'll get someone to bring some water – or maybe a hot drink?"

Monica looked up, pitifully, and squeaked, "Cognac, maybe? For the shock?"

Francine flicked a finger at Pierre, who scampered off. Returning her attention to the pair, she spoke softly, with warmth in her voice. "You've lost an old friend, as well as an employer. I understand that you must grieve…but I must find out who took her from you. Will you help me do that?"

Both women nodded, silently.

Francine smiled warmly. "So what do you mean by telling me you killed her?"

"As good as," sniffed Monica. "We should have been better at looking after her. She was our responsibility."

Francine nodded. "In what way?"

Monique replied, "We were like her little sisters…she always looked after us when we were younger, and we promised we'd look after her when she was older. But now…she's gone."

Francine cooed, "I understand. Now – you were probably the last people to see Églantine alive, yesterday morning. Her cleaner had been, and left, and you said in your statements that she called you to her apartment to discuss this exhibit around ten, is that correct?"

More nodding.

"And you were both with her at that time?" They agreed. "And, when you left her, she seemed in good health?" Nods. "And did she mention that she was due to meet with anyone after that – or do you know if she was maybe due to speak to anyone on the phone, for example?"

Glances were exchanged, and there was a shaking of heads.

Monica said, "She was her usual self, but she had no meetings planned, and didn't tell us of anyone she might call."

"Good. That's helpful. And can you confirm what time it was when you left her? Either of you?"

Monique said, "We were back at our workbenches by ten twenty, where we had a meeting with Jacques about a piece he wants embroidered by next weekend, even though he knows that's physically impossible. We explained that to him. He left us to speak to the client, he said. The movers arrived at ten thirty."

Monica said, "No, they didn't – they were almost ten minutes late. Remember? Said Lucienne had been 'obstructive', which he would never be…he's only ever efficient, and firm. That's the soldier in him. They didn't have the correct paperwork – that was the problem, he said."

I saw Francine's back stiffen, and realized mine had done the same: people arriving with packing materials, but improper paperwork? A glimmer of something…maybe? And what was that about Lucienne being a soldier?

There are so many things I want to ask you, was what I thought; "A soldier? Francine said his only work record was for the Maison," was what I hissed.

Bud whispered back, "She said 'work record'. I believe that military conscription only ended here in 2001. Probably most men his age did some service time…unless they were let off because they were at university, or something. Not sure how it worked here."

Had I noticed any military bearing in Lucienne? Not really – but if he'd been at the Maison for forty years or more, he could easily have lost whatever he'd gained during his time in a uniform…that wasn't made of green velvet.

Francine was still hovering in front of the two women when Pierre materialized. He was carrying a silver tray with two large crystal tumblers balanced upon it, which he carefully offered to the twins. They each accepted a drink.

He said, "Monsieur Valli apologizes that he doesn't have access to the correct glassware."

It didn't look to me as though either Monica or Monique would have cared if the cognac had been served in jam jars; they both gulped, then replaced the empty glasses onto the tray, surprising Pierre.

Smiling at her twin, Monica said, "Another like that wouldn't go amiss, would it, Monique?"

Monique smiled sweetly at Pierre. "My sister's quite right. Is there any chance?"

Pierre stared at Francine, his eyes wide, eyebrows twitching.

She said gently, "Maybe later, ladies – for now, that'll be all we need of that cognac, thank you, Bertrand."

As the twins deflated, Pierre backed away – as though leaving royalty – and disappeared around the corner of the opening again.

Francine said, "There – that'll help, I'm sure. Now, I wonder if you could both tell me exactly what you did between the time you left Églantine and the time you joined the others for lunch, in the meeting room, yesterday?"

The twins exchanged a glance, then Monica spoke. "Like we said in our statements, we were both in our *atelier* the whole time. We had a great deal to do. We had some tasks to catch up with – Saturday being the day we like to do that – and we also had to make sure that the garments being taken away were correctly packed, labelled, and then removed with care."

Francine nodded elegantly, and smiled graciously. "Could you explain how that all happened, please? I'm not aware of how these sorts of events are arranged, you see. I'm sure that exhibiting garments is work that requires great attention to detail."

You're laying it on a bit thick, was what I thought; "Softly, softly," was what I hissed to Bud.

"Honey not vinegar," he observed.

Just then Pierre – sans tray – rejoined us. Waking up his tablet, he asked, "Did I miss anything?"

"Lucienne was in the army," I whispered.

"Of course, it's being looked into," was his laconic reply, and he stood rigidly, like a Pointer – with a digital pen.

Monica said, "We had the issue with the embroidery, and there was another challenge with some beading we're having done at the moment; the girl we have working on it just isn't up to the job, we fear. Those matters engaged us, of course, then the men arrived from the moving company. As far as I could see, all their paperwork was, in fact, in order…and, to be fair to him, the man in charge seemed to know what he was doing. We'd already prepared the garments, some of which had to be brought from our facility, which is a portion of a place that's been specially designed to store valuable, and archival, garments of all types in the optimum conditions. It was set up by Madame Églantine herself, in fact, when she realized that smaller houses, like ours, couldn't afford the sort of facilities that the big ones had. It was established as a cooperative, back in the 1980s, and is run by a committee of people from all the companies that use it, who volunteer their time. We represent *Maison Églantine*, of course, and it's our honor and pleasure to lend our expertise, and to be able to mix with people from other houses. We've made good friends through it, haven't we, Monique?"

Monique perked up. "Indeed." She finally looked a bit more composed. "Though that's not why we do it…and we're not conservation specialists, by any means. We hire real experts to guide us, and learn as we go, so maybe we've picked up more than we think we have, over the years. In this instance, a few of our fellow houses were bringing out garments for this exhibit, though we had the opportunity to display the most, which is gratifying for such an important exhibition. The pieces were selected last year, in collaboration with Monsieur Valli, who has curated the exhibit, and who needed photography to be done some months ago – so they could print the book that will accompany it. That in itself was a major undertaking. He couldn't make up his mind about the final pieces until right before he wanted them. Madame was cross about that, but we assured her we could accommodate him, and did…though he didn't seem to understand how time-consuming it would be for us to get the items ready for photography."

Her sister butted in. "Exactly – you can't get something out of a box that it's been in for thirty years and expect it to look good. It has to be relaxed, prepared, examined, then…presented properly. It's not something that can be done overnight. But…we managed it – then each garment was carefully packed away again, until we needed it, now. We brought all the items to the Maison, prepared them, then packed them again for this short transportation period, and now we're bringing them back to life, here, for the public to admire, and study."

The sisters stared at each other at the realization of what Monica had said.

She sobbed, "We'll never be able to bring her back to life, will we? Oh no…" And they were off again.

Francine's shoulders hunched, and I suspected her patience was wearing thin. "So you were with the people moving the boxes at all times? Did you check the contents, seal up the packages, then send them on their way?"

The sisters nodded. Monica sniffed. "They took them down in the elevator, and we only saw them again here, this morning."

"You didn't notice that there was an extra crate?" For the first time, Francine's tone had a slight edge to it.

Both sisters shook their heads miserably. Monique said, "There wasn't an extra crate. We checked them all against a list when we got here first thing – we had the right number, all labelled correctly. Other deliveries had been made, too, you see, for other houses, and we all had to sort out our own crates. The men who were here with trolleys helped us do that, then they left, once we'd all made sure our crates were in the correct rooms, and we'd reached the unboxing stage. The one…that one…was the penultimate box we opened. The label said it was a piece from 1979 called 'One Night In Luxor' – an incredible dark-blue, silk-velvet evening gown, with draping, bell-shaped sleeves, and a body embellished with seed pearls, sewn in the shape of the constellations of the sky at Luxor on Midsummer's Night. We packed the gown, together, yesterday, and the label I wrote was still on the crate – you can see it for yourself. But instead of the gown, we found…Madame."

Francine asked, "Why such a large crate for one gown?"

Thank you, I've been wondering that myself.

The brows of both sisters furrowed – in unison. Monica replied, "Well, like we said, we'd prepared the gown, so we wouldn't fold it, after that. It was stuffed with those balloon things, and they were placed all around it, too – so that it was held safely inside the large crate…sort of suspended within the balloons, and filled with them. The crates all have to be large enough to accommodate the gowns that way…as though bodies were inside them."

A gasp from both sisters led to another bout of the sniffles, though less so, this time.

Francine mused, "So someone swapped the dress for the body – at some point after you'd packed it, but before it arrived here. Right – I know that one of my officers took the details of the moving company from you yesterday, and went to get their statements…and I'm due to speak to them, personally, today. Thank you, ladies. One more thing – did anything at all seem…off…about any of the removal people? I shouldn't assume, so were they, in fact, all men?"

Monica nodded. "They were all men…and large ones, at that; the only way the crates would fit in the elevator was upright – and the men had to send them down on their own, so to speak, because they couldn't fit inside with them. That's why the whole thing took so long. That elevator is old, and cranky – it pauses between floors for no reason at all sometimes and you have to jiggle the buttons, but there wasn't anyone in there to do any jiggling, so they had to wait until it decided to start again…which it does, usually, also for no reason. We hardly ever use it – it's not worth the trouble, and it's healthier to use the stairs in any case."

Francine nodded. "Got it. Anything else…anything odd at all? Unusual people about the place? Unexpected arrivals?"

Monique said, "There were the removal men, the caterers, everyone being there for the board meeting…it was an unusually busy Saturday at the Maison. That was enough."

Francine nodded. "Thanks for your time. My people will be busy in the other room for quite a while, so I suggest you follow this officer to the place where all your colleagues from the other fashion houses are giving their statements, and you'll be asked to repeat all of this for it to be noted, and then you'll sign it, and you'll be free to leave. I realize that your Monsieur Valli is anxious to have us all out of his hair, but I can't hurry my forensics team. If it turns out that it is, in fact, possible for the opening to be able to go ahead tomorrow, you might find yourselves working through the night, so I'd suggest you get what rest you can, when you can. Meanwhile, as I said, thank you, and I'm sorry that you've lost a friend."

As the twins rose, I moved forward and hissed at Francine, "Can I ask a question, please?"

She turned back. "Cait wanted to ask you something. Is that acceptable?"

The twins nodded, and I asked, "What was the board meeting yesterday due to be about? Anything special? Was there an agenda, for example?"

The twins actually giggled, though they didn't look particularly gleeful. Monica said, "It was about the usual boring things…money, profits, losses, all that stuff. Gustav could tell you properly – we just pass things, and sign things. We have to, because poor Madame made us accept shares in the company, so that we can have a say in how it's run…though we always agree that whatever Gustav says is best for the Maison really is usually best for the Maison."

I pressed. "So Églantine hadn't mentioned anything to you about any topics she was planning to bring to the board's attention?"

The twins shrugged. Monique replied, "She'd probably have mentioned the archives, because she always does – the paper archives, not the garments. Drawings, designs, patterns and so forth…she's kept them all, forever, and keeps suggesting they should be published. But Gustav is against it…says we have to preserve the mystique of the brand, which we think is silly, don't we, Monica?"

Monica nodded. "We think that if people could see what she'd been designing in the early 1970s – and her sketches from the 1960s even – they'd realize the extent to which she drove mainstream fashion in the direction it went. So, yes, I agree that she'd probably have brought that up. She always does."

I thanked the twins, Bud and I commiserated with them again, then they went on their way with the officer Francine had assigned to them. The captain was already speaking into her phone, finally disconnected, then said, "Right, back to the station, Pierre…Bertrand. There's nothing more for us here at the moment, and the Maison can wait. I've got the caterers and removal men who worked at *Maison Églantine* yesterday being brought to the station now." She looked at me and Bud. "Happy to take you both back there, but these interviews are no place for either of you. Let's go, Bertrand."

Quatorze

We didn't retrace our route back to the station, because Pierre had discovered that there was an accident he needed to avoid. This time our pace was slightly less petrifying, so I took the chance of a little time with Francine to ask a long list of questions, but all her answers were: "I don't know", or, "I can't say", which was irritating.

Eventually she countered with: "You said you learned things about the victim – Églantine – last night, when you visited her apartment. Tell me."

I gathered myself, and began. "No sign of a special partner ever having been in her life, no obvious sign of past love affairs even – in fact, no photos at all. I'd say that suggests a woman who looked forward, not back. Her income allowed her to indulge her tastes in art and décor at the highest level, and she had a clear esthetic – which I would say she fully embraced and actually lived, rather than it being something she added into or onto her life. In fact – I'd say that would be an overall observation – Églantine George lived what she believed in…and I suggest she'd have acted this way in every single area of her life. Some might have seen that as obsession, others as the understandable drive of a creative spirit to seek perfection. I'd say that her entire living space – taken as a whole – suggests she had extremely well-rooted ideas about what she wanted, and then did whatever she needed to, to have it…her way."

Francine asked, "Selfishly so, would you say?"

I considered my answer. "It could easily have been perceived that way – which might account for the lack of a significant other in her life, I suppose…but I didn't get the sense that she was crowing that she was special. Her home wasn't a way for her to show off, it was simply her…domain. Her persona, externalized, in a way…and I saw different aspects of her personality showing – for example, her bedroom was relatively spartan, a sort of sanctuary. Her one public space was designed for entertaining, which she no longer did. Rather more mundanely, there were side tables with ashtrays, lighters, and some incredibly ornate *art nouveau* silver cigarette cases that were being used for their intended purpose – so I'm guessing she was a cigarette smoker. However, there were also ashtrays dotted along her outdoor terrace – I believe it's called a *balcon filant*…the balcony garden that extends around her apartment – so it might be that most of the smoking took place out there, because I couldn't smell cigarettes in the apartment. But there was definitely a smell of cigar smoke in the lounge, which is quite distinct from cigarettes – though no sign of any actual cigars, or cigar-smoking paraphernalia."

Pierre added, "I have photographs of the tables and items Cait's talking about."

Francine thanked him, as she puffed out of her window, then said, "Continue."

I did. "Someone came to visit her that day who has either a cat or a small dog – and I'm favoring the small dog. I'm saying they'd been there that day, but it might have been the day before and her cleaner missed removing the hair from the pad that was on a chair…though I'd say that's unlikely, because, in all other respects, her cleaner does a marvelous job. As does her florist. Vases contained peonies that looked as though they'd been there for at least two days – they were fully open, which is never how peonies are delivered – and the fact that no petals had dropped from them tells me that whomever it was that searched through Églantine's books didn't disturb anything else…those petals fall at the slightest nudge of the vase."

Francine asked, "What of the woman herself?"

I weighed my response. "Her reading tastes ran to the eclectic. Despite the fact that her books had been disarranged, I could see there were many titles relating to the history of fashion and other types of art and design, which one would expect. Beyond the areas that would have directly fed into her career, she read widely in terms of general history – especially of France and Europe, was keen on pre-1970s cinema on a global basis, and had a good many biographies on her shelves ranging from politicians to rock stars. She had a surprisingly wide range of books about philosophy. I say 'surprisingly wide' because, unless one's following a set course of study, most readers tend to delve deeply into one part of such a topic…following their preferences. But Églantine read across the topic…almost as though she were a student of philosophical thinking. Though it might be worth noting that she'd annotated her copy of Arendt's *The Human Condition* quite heavily, especially in the sections where the concept of 'natality', the ability to 'start again', is concerned. I'd say this ties in with the lack of photos – she was always moving on, starting afresh…an aspect of her persona that would have found an outlet in her creativity. She also had a great number of true crime books – all relating to French crimes, not global ones. Speaking as a psychologist, I was surprised to see how many psychology textbooks she had, and I mean that in the literal sense – they were books that are set texts on courses covering general, and criminal, psychology…which I found interesting. Taken together, I'd say this all suggests she wanted to understand how to move on after some sort of criminal trauma…but that's only my interpretation."

Francine turned as far as she could in her seat, and our eyes met. "Explain."

I hesitated, then dived in. "The way Bud used my skill set – back in the days when I built victim profiles to help his homicide teams better focus their efforts – was to allow me to take what

I'd seen, apply my experience, and then…take a stab at theories that he and his team would discuss. On this occasion, I think you should consider the possibility that Églantine George not only had more than a passing interest in true crime and criminal psychopathy, but that she herself had been a victim of traumatic crime, and was trying to…understand why whatever had happened to her had happened…to *her*…and how to 'move on' from it. That scar on her neck? I would suggest you consider that it might have been the result of a criminal act, not just an 'accident' she caused while experimenting with acid treatments for fabrics…as the twins have suggested."

Francine returned her attention to the road ahead, as Pierre drove on. "Now that we know she's a murder victim, I shall be looking into Églantine's background more deeply, of course. As Pierre is always telling us – in his presentations to our teams – understanding the victim's life can bring you one step closer to understanding their death…isn't that right, Pierre?"

I saw the young officer's neck flush scarlet. "It was something Cait herself wrote to me, in an email, once," he said, with a nervous grin, "and it's what underpins her entire discipline…our discipline."

"Is there more, Cait?" Francine sounded her usual calm self.

I replied, "Well, there's one final point about her reading materials which might be significant. She had a copy of Yalom's book *Existential Psychotherapy*, which was extremely well thumbed. It tackles the intersection between philosophy and psychology, and is an example of the level to which her reading had taken her. Interestingly – and I would suggest, significantly – one of the areas Yalom addresses is the fear of death…alongside freedom, isolation, and meaninglessness. Now I can tell that this woman was truly 'free', chose isolation, and don't believe that her life was in any way meaningless, so I wondered if Églantine feared she might be dying soon…and I don't mean that in the way that someone who's in their early eighties might do, in terms of a natural acceptance of the likelihood of a shorter, rather than longer, future life. I'd be interested to know if she maybe had a…life-threatening condition or disease. No one's mentioned any such thing to us, but there's a chance they might know, but haven't told me and Bud…which would be completely understandable. Or maybe she'd not told anyone. You see, absolutely everything I saw in that apartment told me she was a woman who had a meaningful inner life, as opposed to being someone who shared her life with a large number of people."

Francine said, "The post-mortem might shed light on any diseases."

I concluded. "Finally, and obviously, her dressing room was an intimate space for her. Unsurprisingly she had a lot of clothes, and shoes, and accessories, but – to be honest – not as much as one might imagine a fashion designer of almost sixty years' standing to possess. Her make-up table was completely covered with high-end products, and well lit – she regularly used heavy make-up on her face, which I noted on her remains. There was also a wide range of hair-fixing paraphernalia – modern, and expensive. She paid a great deal of attention to her personal appearance – which would probably be something she'd always 'had to do', given her role in the world of fashion, but I believe she did it for herself. She didn't mix much, but her supplies suggest she had an ongoing routine in these matters. On that same make-up table there was a large pewter platter with a couple of worn-looking sets of rosary beads on it. They didn't look as though they'd been handled recently, because they were tangled up in each other, but maybe they point to a Roman Catholic upbringing, or they might have been family pieces. Quick cultural question for you two in the front seats there, please. How unusual is it for a French woman in her eighties to own a couple of sets of rosary beads? I know that France has a strong Roman Catholic heritage – but do only people who are practicing Catholics have them these days?"

Pierre mumbled, "I have a set, given to me on my first communion by my grandmother."

Francine replied, "I don't have any, but my mother had at least three rosaries that I know of, and she didn't set foot inside a church between her wedding, my baptism, and her funeral. Sometimes they're things that people and families just…have."

I said, "Thanks for that, so I'll set those to one side in terms of their ability to inform me about Églantine's lifestyle, or beliefs, for now. All of that being said, her dressing room is an area I'd welcome the chance to explore more thoroughly. As requested, I didn't move things about, but I believe that space – of any within her apartment – might provide us with more insights into the woman."

I could tell we were closing in on the police station. "In conclusion, then, her home was elaborate, but that was because of her design aesthetic…she wasn't flashy. I would suggest she came from humble roots, and understood the value of money. The fact that outside service providers came into her home suggests to me that her dressing room would be her most personal space. She was a woman who knew her own mind, yet sought to improve it, and she was facing the impending reality of her own mortality."

Francine asked, "Anything else?"

I looked at Bud, then he added, "There was the comment about Lucienne having been another of Églantine's 'stray dogs'. It was something Gustav mentioned. I think it would be worth finding out how Lucienne came to be employed by Églantine. If she did gather people about her who needed help, maybe the reason they needed that help – possibly to escape a bad situation – followed them to her door."

"Thank you. You should both get out now," said Francine as we pulled up outside the police station. "I will be in touch – I want to keep you on hand. Pierre will be our liaison. Goodbye for now."

When the car left us standing on the pavement, I said, "That's twice she's called him Pierre."

Bud stared at me. "That's what you've got to say after the morning we've had?"

I had to laugh. "It's not all I'm going to say about our morning…but I have to think it's unusual for a superior officer to call someone under their control by their first name. It's not something you ever did, I know that much."

Bud kissed me. "I always called you 'Cait', and there was nothing between us except for a professional respect…at that time."

I nodded. "I know, but, still. 'Pierre', not 'Bertrand'…twice."

Bud said, "Let it go, Cait. Now…I could do with something to eat, how about you?"

I agreed. "How about we head back toward the opera house, and find a bistro, or brasserie…or something? At least we'd have a great view as we ate, even if the places there might be a little more expensive, and touristy."

We agreed it was a good plan, and fifteen minutes later we managed to grab the last table of the outer row at a brasserie opposite the side of the *Opéra Garnier*, that not only had a great view of the stunning building itself, but also of the performers doing their best to entertain the dozens of people sitting on the steps of the grand old building enjoying the sunshine, and their lunch…and the traffic, which mesmerized us both.

As Bud tucked into a relatively exotic – for him – dish of poached salmon with a spring salad and artichokes, he mused, "I don't know how anybody gets anywhere on time here. The traffic is unpredictable, to say the least."

"Maybe everyone plans in buffer time," I suggested, enjoying my smoked duck salad, with its zingy raspberry vinaigrette dressing. "Good grief, how did those two cars miss each other?"

"I know," said Bud. "I thought you had to be brave to ride a bicycle around Downtown Vancouver…that's nothing compared with this mayhem. At least there are traffic lights here, but that area when the bus was nosing its way across traffic down near the *Comédie-Française* was just nuts."

I sat back in my typical rattan brasserie seat. "Such a lot has happened since yesterday morning, Bud. Are you ready to talk about it, now?"

Bud also sat back. We ordered coffees.

He began, "Two deaths, both murders, of a woman and one of her employees. Two significantly different methods. Hers by strangulation, so up close, personal, and truly violent. His by poison, so more…remote. Strangulation might mean a spur of the moment decision. Poison suggests planning, and intent. Are the deaths connected? My cop instincts say yes. Did one person kill both victims? My cop instincts say…if so, why such different methods?"

I nodded. "Okay…I believe they're connected too. And as for the two different methods? The strangulation wasn't planned, though the possible use of gloves shows some intent. The poisoning was planned, because the…second victim – no names, here in public – would have been less likely to have been overcome by the killer."

We accepted our coffees from our waiter, and Bud said, "That could fit the facts…as could two different killers. But…why? And that's your thing. Any ideas, yet?"

"Anger, hate, and jealousy are the main drivers for impulsive killings. A desire to not get caught for killing the first time might have led to the second death. Maybe the second victim saw, or even heard, something that could have implicated the killer in the first victim's murder, and thus their life was taken to protect the guilty party? The second victim was well placed to have become a witness to the first death – even if they might not have known or understood the implications of what they'd seen or heard at the time. In fact, they might not even have known it before they died…but the killer couldn't take that risk, so they killed again."

Bud sipped his coffee. "Good point – I've seen that be the case…a witness is killed to protect the guilty, but we were never able to establish if the witness even realized they possessed critical information. But I've also worked cases where they did, and then tried to use that knowledge to get something they wanted from the guilty party – usually money. Might the victim of poisoning have become so because they threatened to expose the strangler?"

I sighed. "Look, we know the killer of the first victim had to be in that room when I saw them there. We don't know how the killer managed to get the second victim to ingest that poison, or when they might have done that. From the point of view of establishing an alibi, the killer only needs to prove they weren't in that anteroom at noon-ish, but there's no way to pin anyone down for the timeline of the second killing."

Bud said, "I concur. So I'll ask the classic question…beyond your motives for an unplanned crime of passion – who benefits from the death of the first victim? The necklace was gone, so maybe it was a theft gone awry, witnessed by the second victim – or maybe there was some other sort of 'benefit'?"

I mused, "A crime of passion – a moment of anger that results in the death of another person – doesn't necessarily provide a 'benefit' for the perpetrator that goes beyond releasing their rage in the moment, so let's not forget that. Though, again…the gloves – if there were gloves – suggest that there was at least some level of premeditation. So, yes…who benefits?

Well, we don't know, do we? I'm sure it's something that Francine will be establishing. It was mentioned that everyone at the board meeting owns shares in the Maison…I wonder if she'll be looking into the dead woman's will. Surely she'd do that."

Bud nodded. "I'd have already been in touch with the person who could tell me about that, and I don't think Francine's any slouch, so I dare say she's all over that angle. Probably along with anything else we can come up with."

I mused, "But if…the woman…was murdered so someone could gain more control over the company, that wouldn't suggest such a passionate way of killing."

Bud made the universally understood action of drawing squiggles in the air to request our bill, which arrived almost instantly; I got the impression they were keen to turn tables as quickly as possible.

"What do you fancy, Wife? A stroll? Or should we take the Metro to…somewhere? Or…what?"

I clearly surprised Bud when I said, "*Galeries Lafayette*, please. It's only around the corner, so no Metro required, which is fine by me because I'd rather be above-ground and see…all this. And, yes, I know it's 'just' a department store, but it's also a work of art itself — especially the glass dome they have, and there's a rooftop terrace with fabulous views of the whole city. Fancy that?"

Bud smiled. "The weather's wonderful, and seeing Paris laid out in front of me would be delightful…great idea. But — to be clear — you don't want to do any actual shopping, right?"

I laughed as I stood. "Go shopping with you? Oh Bud, I do know you a bit better than that. No actual shopping, okay? Besides, I'm pretty sure that if there's a store that'll be full of designer label this and that, it'll be *Galeries Lafayette*. You're safe."

We wandered happily for a block or two, tried not to laugh at the beefy security guards in smart suits standing inside the main entrance to the store, then ooh-ed and ah-ed at the magnificent stained glass of the dome at the center of the main building. Bud even walked out onto the Perspex catwalk that protruded above the sales floor to be able to get a better look and take some photos, which was not something that appealed to me – due to my fear of heights. Then we took the elevator to the roof, which was surprisingly quiet; we were able to get out there right away – apparently there are often long waiting times – and the views were even more spectacular than I could have imagined. I stayed well back from the insecure-looking glass panels that allowed an unobstructed vista of the city, of course, and looked out, not down, while Bud – doing it half to turn my tummy, I reckoned – ventured right to the edge. It was much chillier up on top of the building; the wind battered us, and we ended up being glad to get back into the warmth of the elevator and rub our noses – mine was quite pink.

We were back on the ground floor, among the groups of tourists who were wandering between the sales pods bearing globally famous high-end brand names as they looked up and around, rather than in the direction in which they were moving, when a ping told me I had a text message on my phone. I shoved it in front of Bud's face. "There can't have been reception up on the roof – which is weird – but here's a message just come in. It sounds…urgent."

Bud checked his phone. "I've got one too. Alright then – since Pierre has instructed us both to phone him 'immediately' – who's going to do it? You, or me?"

I said, "I tell you what…you phone him, because there's a scarf over there that's just caught my eye. Meet me at that counter."

I pointed toward a brand name that made Bud guffaw. "Just keep that credit card where it is, Wife."

I blew him a kiss.

Quinze

Bud decided it wasn't worth trying to get a taxi outside *Galeries Lafayette* at three in the afternoon. "Let's just walk to the Maison, Cait…it's not far – ten minutes, no more. We could walk off a bit of that lunch."

I knew he was right, and was looking forward to what we'd been promised: a chance to be there when Francine interviewed a certain Anne-Marie Lefebvre, who'd been Églantine George's cleaner for – apparently – the past thirty years.

As we walked, I observed, "Églantine surrounded herself with people who stayed within her circle for unusually long periods of time. It seems as though everyone we've met so far has stuck with her for decades. I'm going to say that suggests she was not only a good employer, but also a woman people enjoyed working for…maybe even a good woman."

Bud agreed. "Staying at a job for a long time is something that folks used to expect, but someone like a cleaner would probably work for more than one client and – if they're any good – I dare say they could move on if they thought they'd be better treated elsewhere, or if they didn't like the person they were working for. So, yes, maybe that suggests that Églantine was a good employer, and person. Something we can maybe assess when we're with Francine and this Anne-Marie. Pierre did make it clear that we're expected to stay in the background, though. You'll be okay with that – right?"

I might manage to sneak in the odd question or two, if Francine doesn't ask all the right ones, was what I thought; "Of course – that's to be expected," was what I said.

Bud paused. "Cait, we're being offered a great deal of access by Francine…which is just as well, because, otherwise, you wouldn't be able to talk or think about anything else – so let's not bite the hand that's feeding us, eh?"

As we were waved into the Maison by a police officer at the door, I nodded to Bud that I understood what he meant, which I did, even though I knew I'd be prepared to steer things my way, if needed. Once we were inside the building, another officer directed us to a door that was cut into the wall beneath the grand staircase; I hadn't noticed it before, because it had been designed to be invisible, though now it stood open, and obvious. We entered a corridor, passed the door to a W.C. then the elevator – with another door in the outer wall facing it – then walked into a small, triangular-shaped room set in the point of the building, which had obviously been Lucienne's area. It had been set up with a sofa, a small television set, a kitchenette, and with a table and chairs that looked as though they'd come from a pavement café. The windows that filled almost the entire height of the room allowed an extraordinarily good view of the bustling *Avenue de l'Opéra* beyond them, as well as both streets that ran along each side of the building – though I knew it was impossible to see into the room from outside.

It was clear that the place had been tackled by forensic specialists, because there were daubs of fingerprint powder all over the place, and all the shelves and surfaces were completely bare. I suspected that the small refrigerator in the corner had also been emptied of its contents.

Francine looked up from her tablet when we arrived. "Good, you're here. I'll be interviewing the elusive Anne-Marie in the meeting room upstairs, but I wanted you both to have the chance to see where Lucienne Durand spent whatever little 'leisure time' he had while he was here at the Maison. He was the only doorman, and worked a twelve-hour shift, starting at seven in the morning, five days a week. The main doors were locked when he had to leave his post, and at weekends –

although this weekend was different, of course, with the upcoming exhibition and board meeting. It was an arrangement that suited all parties, I'm told, though I can't imagine how it worked…well. Anything that he might have ingested has been removed, as you'd imagine, and you're free to touch what you choose, though I would ask you to wear these gloves, and beware of the powder, which can ruin clothing…which I'm sure is something of which you're only too well aware. Églantine's cleaner is being driven here. I shall send word when she arrives, and you can join us. Meanwhile, this place is yours."

I'd initially liked Francine's no-nonsense approach to her job, but now I was beginning to wonder if the total lack of niceties and small talk suggested that she was lacking in empathy – despite what Pierre had initially told us about her. That she was professionally driven was a given, or she wouldn't have managed to get as far up the ladder as she had done by her age, and being a woman – but maybe there was just nothing else in there?

Or…maybe there is, but she isn't allowing it to show? She'd be good at masking her true self.

Bud and I donned our gloves, and I stood in the middle of the room, taking in my surroundings. "He's got a fabulous set-up here, Bud. Just look…we can literally see everyone outside, but they can't see us. It's…well, it's making me feel a bit peculiar, because I'm watching people without their knowledge, which is a bit creepy, don't you think? And the fact that there's a deadness to all the colors out there is off-putting too. Mirrored glass, but with some sort of light-filtering treatment?"

Bud stood next to one of the windows and peered at it. "Not my field, though I know there are lots of products available to allow one-way vision, of course. We know the outer view is of mirrored glass, so I dare say Lucienne witnessed quite a few oddities, if people took the opportunity to fix their hair, or whatever."

I mused, "I wonder if he witnessed something from inside here that got him killed. He wouldn't have missed anything, would he? The side door leading from the elevator is just beyond that door. I bet if he'd been looking out of here at the right moment, he might have seen the crate with Églantine's body inside it being removed."

Bud countered with: "But how would he have known her body was inside it, Cait? All he'd have known was that it was one crate among many that left here yesterday. It's not as though it was marked in any special way, and there was no sign there was a corpse inside it…no blood, or anything like that."

I conceded that my husband made a good point as I checked a few books I'd pulled out of a pocket in the arm of the sofa. "Another devotee of true crime – and crime fiction, this time. These are old books, well worn…probably from a used bookstore, definitely not a library. There's little else here that's personal though…which is odd, given that he spent most of his waking hours here at the Maison."

Bud replied, "Not really, Cait – think about your office at the University of Vancouver, or of what mine was like, when I had one. Both impersonal spaces…neither filled with items that we were, or are, emotionally connected to, right?"

"True. I feel suffocated when I visit some of my colleagues' offices – they're full of mementos, and knickknacks that mean something to them, but look as though they're there to just gather dust from an outsider's perspective. So, yes, you're right – not so unusual. Oh, Bud, look – here's a photograph."

Stuffed beside the books in the pocket in the sofa's armrest was a square photograph, laminated in hard plastic, that showed a group of young men lounging beneath a tree. The black and white photo suggested they were seeking shade from strong sunshine; they'd taken off what were obviously military uniform jackets, and were passing a water bottle.

I gasped. "Is that a young Lucienne – without a beard?"

Bud took the picture from me and peered at it. "It's hard to say. We could barely see anything of the man's face yesterday, with the beard and the top hat, but yes…it could be. Let me take a photo of that, then we can enlarge his face."

The screen on Bud's phone was soon filled by the face of the man in question.

I said, "The teeth. That's him. Let's take the original to Francine. Maybe she's found out which part of the army he was involved with, and might be able to match the uniform to confirm, or deny, this is him. Though I'm convinced."

Bud asked, "Anything else in that pocket – which seems to be the only thing revealing anything about the guy at all."

I pulled out a lump of fluff. "Nope, that's it in here. Is there another one at the other end?" Bud shook his head. "Okay – anywhere else that things might be tucked away?"

Bud pulled open the tiny cupboard beneath the sink, which served to do little more than hide the pipework, as well as both drawers above it. "Nothing of interest. Oh, hang on – there's a rosary wound around a fork here, but goodness knows why. I'll take a photo, and leave it where it is. Anything you've spotted?"

The officer who'd directed us from the front door appeared. "Captain de Gaulle wants you, upstairs, now." He disappeared.

Bud and I exchanged a glance. I said, "There's nothing like abruptness to make a person feel wanted, is there?"

My husband took my hand. "I expect he feels he could be doing something more useful, elsewhere in this teeming city, Cait. The back-up officers for crime scenes do an awful lot of standing about, you know. We need them to do what they do, but I know it can grate on them, sometimes. Let's get going, so he knows we took notice of him, eh? So that he knows he matters."

Seize

As we exited the room, I said, "Let's use the elevator – I want to get a feel for it…see if it's noisy, that sort of thing." I pushed the button, and we waited. It didn't sound as though anything was happening, then the floor of the lift passed in front of the little glass panel. With a slight thumping noise, the lift stopped. I pulled at the door, which opened silently to reveal an expanding iron grille gate, which slid back easily, allowing us to enter the tiny compartment that accommodated the two of us – just about. When I pressed the button with "*2eme*" on it, there was a slight jerk as the mechanism moved. I pulled my phone out of my bag and said, "I want to find out what this means." I snapped a shot of the control panel.

Bud gave it his attention. "Oh, I see – there's no button for the sixth floor, though there's a keyhole thing where it would be. Controlled access to Églantine's apartment? You're right, we should check that out."

The ride up was smooth and silent, and there was no more than a slight jolt when we arrived at our destination. Stepping into the corridor outside the meeting room, I commented, "It felt as though it was in good working order to me, but maybe it has one of those annoying 'intermittent faults' if what the twins said was true…that it conks out without warning now and again."

Bud shrugged. "Maybe…or maybe they wanted us to think it was less reliable than it is…for some reason."

We entered the meeting room to see Pierre and Francine standing toe to toe; he had his hand on her arm. It was an interesting tableau, which lasted for about half a second, whereupon they all but leapt back from each other, though

Pierre's hand was still on Francine's arm which meant they then bumped back into each other again, and both laughed. Awkwardly.

"May I be of service?" Bud strode forward. "You seem to be attached to each other."

Pierre stammered, "There was ash on the captain's sleeve, and I was brushing it off, but my watch somehow caught on a button on her cuff and…" Bud unhooked them from each other and Pierre stopped babbling.

Francine said, "Thank you, Bud, Bertrand. Now – before we meet the victim's cleaner – do you have any observations, or questions, about Lucienne's staffroom?"

Bud handed over the snap we'd brought from the sofa, and showed her the enlarged photo on his phone – explaining that we believed it to be of the young Lucienne. He then emailed the photo to Pierre.

I showed her the shot of the elevator's control panel.

"We know about this aspect," she said. "Indeed, as you might imagine, we have gathered a great deal of general information that I have not passed to you. My people have spoken to the four people who catered the lunch, for example, and are checking their backgrounds…again – though it appears they didn't interact with anyone except Lucienne when they arrived at twelve fifteen, and then two servers attended to the needs of those at the lunch, while two more worked on prep in the anteroom. It was, by all accounts, an informal affair, with people popping in and out of the meeting room. For example, I understand that Gustav went to see Lucienne, to whom he gave permission to leave. Most people were in the meeting room for most of the time, though each attendee left for some reason, at some point."

I said, "That's not right. Lucienne told Bud and me that the caterers had arrived at eleven thirty – that they complained about not being able to use the elevator because the moving people were using it."

"Check your information, Bertrand," snapped Francine – rather too harshly, I thought.

Pierre scrolled madly on his tablet. "You are correct, Captain. All four caterers independently said they arrived in their van just before twelve fifteen. They used a credit card to park at a meter outside the building for twenty minutes from twelve ten onwards while they unloaded, then one of them drove their vehicle to the underground parking, where it remained until they collected it again after our people had interviewed them all, here, yesterday afternoon. We have the credit card information for the meter, and the parking garage. It is correct. It is proof."

I turned to Bud. "Lucienne definitely said the caterers had been on the premises since eleven thirty, which made us think that the anteroom had been in use when I saw Églantine being strangled around noon."

Bud nodded and said to Francine, "Correct. Even I remember that, because it was one of our major sticking points when we were discussing what Cait had seen."

Francine hooked her bottom lip up over her top one. "Interesting."

I waited until it became clear that was all she was going to say, then asked, "Anything of any note you can share?"

Francine muttered, "There was the scar, of course."

Bud said, "The one on Églantine's neck? Any idea what it was – when it might have happened? Was it acid?"

Francine appeared to snap out of a trance. "The medical examiner has seen her body, though the post-mortem hasn't happened yet, of course. But I was speaking of another scar – one the doctor saw when she was preparing the remains for examination. Églantine had a scar that suggests she'd had a child delivered by cesarean section."

Bud and I chorused, "A child?"

That's a turn up for the books, was what I thought; "Do we know when?" was what I said.

Francine's head snapped around. "When? No, we do not know when…ah, here she is. Do come in and make yourself comfortable Madame Lefebvre, or may I call you Anne-Marie? I am Captain de Gaulle – no relation – Francine, please."

A small, plump woman – possibly in her mid-seventies? – bustled into the room, ushered by a police officer. Dressed entirely in black, and wearing a dilapidated black "pleather" crossbody handbag that looked as though it might contain a boulder, she was in obvious distress, seemed almost incapable of breathing let alone speaking, and looked as though she might have a heart attack at any moment. She had a handful of limp paper tissues that were doing nothing to dry her tears, and she peered – almost blindly – around the room.

I rushed to the washroom, grabbed a long length of toilet paper and then rushed back in again – by which time Bud was helping the elderly woman to settle on a chair at the meeting table, and Pierre was re-entering from the anteroom with a bottle of water. It took a few minutes for the poor woman to gain some composure, and I thought we'd all done a good job of helping her feel at ease, so was surprised when Francine loomed over her and gave her what I could only characterize as a death stare.

The captain's voice held no warmth when she said, "When my officers spoke with you last evening – when we believed that your employer, Madame Églantine George was missing – it was made clear to you that you would need to remain accessible to us. You disappeared this morning, and didn't respond to any phone calls or text messages. Why did you do that? And where did you go? I understand you haven't given that information to the officers who brought you here. I need to know. Tell me."

Anne-Marie Lefebvre didn't flinch.

Bud and I managed to exchange the briefest of glances, as I wondered how this approach would work on the distraught woman.

Having been taken aback by Francine's choice of approach, I was equally surprised when the cleaner took one huge, gulping sob, then stopped crying altogether. She looked up at Francine as though she'd been slapped in the face, then said, "I was in church, of course. It's Sunday. I heard that Madame was dead when I came out of Holy Mass, then I went back inside again, because I had to pray for her soul."

"How did you hear the news?"

"Monica called me. Or was it Monique? One of them. They knew I'd want to know."

Francine's nostrils flared, then she continued, "So you chose not to help the police who are trying to find out who killed Églantine George, but, rather, you ignored us and remained at the church?"

Anne-Marie still seemed surprised that this didn't seem to be a natural course of action to Francine. "Of course I did. I could help her soul more than I could help you. I don't know who killed her. How could I?"

Francine stepped back from the woman's chair and took a seat herself. "I needed you to come here to be able to tell me if anything's been stolen from your employer's apartment. I needed you to come here to tell me if you saw anything out of the ordinary when you were in that apartment yesterday morning. I needed you to be available to answer my questions when I needed them answered, not when you'd finished lighting candles and waving incense about the place."

Anne-Marie reached out and placed her hand on top of one of Francine's. "My child, this anger inside you will not help you – not in your career, nor in your home life. If you want to ask me things, ask me now – I am here, beside you, and will do all I can to help. But I had to tend to Églantine's soul first…it was my duty, and my honor. You must see that."

The soothing nature of Anne-Marie's tone was disarming, and she made me feel as calm as she appeared to be.

Odd.

It appeared that Francine felt wrong-footed, too, because she hesitated, then said, "Tell me about your relationship with Églantine. You were close?"

I knew that was what I'd have asked at that moment, too, because Anne-Marie's words suggested to me there was a deep connection between the two women.

Anne-Marie replied, "We were. She gave me work here, connected me with other clients, helped me make my new life."

"Your 'new' life?"

I noticed that Anne-Marie's right hand was deep inside her handbag, and she was…fiddling about with something in there.

She looked up. "I stepped away from my calling almost thirty years ago. I believed I would serve my Lord as his bride for my whole life, but…I was wrong. I belonged to an Order that provided for the sick, and the dying. I did not suffer any crisis of faith, but I felt I could better live the life the Lord had planned for me outside the Order. Of course, when I left, I had nothing. My ring, my crucifix, my habit…they all belonged to the Order, though Mother Superior allowed me to keep my prayer book. Églantine found me a place to stay, furniture, clothes…and gave me a job. I owe her…everything."

Pierre sounded in awe of the woman when he all but whispered, "You were a nun?"

"I was a Bride of Christ, alongside my fellow Sisters…yes. I was a foundling, raised by the Sisters, and maybe that is why I believed – wanted to believe – that I had been called to a life within the Order. But it was not…correct, for me. I am better living as I do now."

I wonder how you met Églantine, was what I thought; "The rosaries," was what I hissed at Bud. He nodded.

Francine asked, "How did you first meet Églantine George?"

Thank you!

"I was never a trained nurse, but I helped those who were. About sixty-five years ago, Églantine was brought to our convent's hospital in the countryside close to Buguet-sur-Marne outside Paris. Two women had found her on the side of a road, half-drowned in a water-filled ditch. The police were called that very night, of course, but Églantine was in a coma, so couldn't answer any questions, and there was no way for anyone to identify her. Her neck and chest were horribly burned. It was assumed that she'd been the victim of some sort of attack with acid, and that she'd been left for dead. The police suggested she might have been thrown from a car, and had rolled into the ditch – both her legs, and one arm, were badly broken. The doctors said that falling into a ditch full of water had prevented the acid from actually killing her. Our Order offered to care for her as she either recovered, or failed. The police and the doctors agreed this between them, because no one knew what would happen…if she would even survive. She was in a coma for almost a year. During that time, I spent many hours with her. You see, she was not much more than a girl…no one knew how old, of course, but they said maybe she was fourteen or fifteen. About my own age. I practiced my reading with her each day – reading aloud to her, even though she was asleep. And I watched as she…grew. Eight months later, the doctor removed her child – because it might not have thrived inside her body any longer, he said. The birth was a safe one. The child was given for adoption. It wasn't until a couple of months later that Églantine regained consciousness – but she could not speak, because of the injuries to her throat. She remained with our Order for a total of three years, and gradually recuperated enough that she was able to walk, and feed herself and…eventually, she spoke. I was there when she said her first word. She loved art, and I found as many books about art for her to read and look at as possible. One day she pointed to a picture in a book, a poster created by Toulouse-Lautrec, and she said 'Églantine' – the name of…well, a rather questionable woman who ran a troupe of can-can dancers, as it happens. It took another year for her to learn how to speak properly. It broke my heart that, one day, she simply walked away from us. No word, no note – just walked off in the clothes she was wearing."

Francine asked, "And did she tell you, before she left, what had happened to her? How exactly she'd been injured? Had she been raped? Was that what had led to her pregnancy?"

Anne-Marie sat back in the chair, and finally folded her hands on her lap. "The Lord was merciful to her in at least that respect. She never remembered what had happened to her – and she had no idea about having had a child at all. The doctors thought it best to tell her that the scar they'd made on her had been among her initial injuries."

Francine leaned forward. "So Églantine George didn't know she'd had a child?"

Anne-Marie shook her head. "And…well, I suppose I should tell you that Églantine wasn't her real name."

Francine sat back, her eyes narrowing. "What was her real name?"

Anne-Marrie shrugged. "No one knew. You see, the girl had no memory of who she was or where she came from, let alone what had happened to her. The police said that no girl of her approximate age had been reported missing in the area. Of course this was a long time ago, and maybe the police in Paris did not connect with the police outside Paris about missing girls, but that wasn't our business – our business was to help her become whole again. However, I know at least that George was not her family name, because that was my name, and she asked if she could take it…and she said she liked the 'look' of Églantine, so she chose that."

"Your family name used to be George?"

Anne-Marie smiled. "No, I was Sister George. We choose our new name when we marry into the Order, and there was much discussion about my choice, because the grand church of Saint George in Paris is an Anglican church, but I have always admired Saint George for his bravery, so they let me have it. As I said, I spent a great deal of time with her – we became friends. We were contemporaries among adults. I was happy she chose to take my name."

You're over eighty…yet you're still working as a cleaner? was what I thought; "Good skin care?" was what I whispered to Bud.

Francine said, "So how did you two…reconnect?"

"As I said, I left the Order, and the first thing I did was go to church to pray for guidance. This was almost twenty-nine years ago. It was winter. My Sisters had given me a coat, and a woolen dress – neither fitted me, though I was a thinner woman in those days. Afterwards, I walked in the streets, and I found some newspapers to tuck inside my coat, to help me stay warm. On one newspaper was a photograph of a beautiful woman – who I now know to be Mademoiselle Avril – and an article that spoke of Églantine George. I came to *Maison Églantine* that day, and that is when she started to help me. That newspaper? It was many years old, and had been placed outside on the street by someone whose hand was guided by the Lord."

Knowing how efficiently Anne-Marie had cleaned Églantine's apartment, I wondered not only how the woman remained so obviously nimble and capable at her advanced age, but why Églantine "allowed" her to still work.

Francine said, "If you'll forgive me, Anne-Marie, you're of an age when one might expect you to be enjoying your retirement."

Anne-Marie nodded her head graciously. "When I left the Order I was a non-person. I had never had a life outside the walls of the convent, you see. The State did not care about me – no one except the Sisters had cared about me, or for me, since I was an infant. As a 'new' person, it was difficult to navigate everything the government asked me to do. Églantine helped me, and paid me well for my work, and I have the minimum pension, now. But I must live, as well as eat. Her needs are not onerous – she is a clean woman. And she lets me bring my companion with me. I do not like to leave him alone. He is old, now, too, so I cycle here usually, with him in my basket. She enjoys spoiling Guillermo. He is a dog from the street – like me…like her."

The silence that followed Anne-Marie's statement allowed me a moment to reassess what Gustav had said about Églantine gathering "stray dogs" to herself; the idea took on new meaning.

I want to ask you so many questions, was what I thought…but I said nothing.

Francine continued. "Now we come to questions you have been asked before, Anne-Marie, and we have your answers, but I must ask them again…because now we know that Églantine George, and Lucienne Durand, are both dead. That they were murdered is beyond question – what I need to know from you, is whether you saw anyone or anything unusual here, at the Maison, yesterday morning. Please tell us about all your movements, and about everything you saw, and did, here then."

Anne-Marie sipped some water, settled her shoulders, then said, "I have already told the woman you sent to my home last evening. I arrived at Madame's apartment at eight thirty, which is my usual time for a Saturday. On weekdays I come earlier. As always, by the time I arrived, Madame had taken her coffee and breakfast, and she always cleans the kitchen after herself, as she does the bathroom. All I do is gather the rubbish, and remove it when I leave, which I did. I made up her bed, and gave her fresh towels, as always. I take the laundry away with me, too. The rubbish goes to the ground floor. The laundry goes there too, and is collected, and returned, every three days. She sat with Guillermo inside the apartment, then on her balcony with a fresh cup of coffee, smoking, as always. On Saturdays I clean the bookshelves, and I did so yesterday. The main room I tackle in parts, throughout the week. I do not work on a Sunday, of course. I sweep each day, I wash one floor each day. On Saturday it is the floor in the bathroom. I did my usual jobs. It takes no more than an hour. Then I make more coffee, and we sit together for a time. Sometimes we talk, sometimes we do not. Yesterday we did, a little. She talked about the board meeting, and her plan to – once again – put her proposals to Gustav and the others. She has control of the Maison, but doesn't want to act against the wishes of the others, and – in this matter – she could not, in any case, because her wishes would have to be enacted by the others, who are against her idea."

I wondered how the potential publication of the archives of the Maison – which the twins had mentioned as being one of the topics likely to be raised at the meeting – would need to include the others.

Francine asked, "This topic would be?"

Anne-Marie replied evenly, "That Églantine believes the Maison should begin a ready-to-wear line. Jacques, Avril, Monica, and Monique are against it. Gustav is for it. Joanne goes back and forth."

I whispered to Bud, "The twins kept that quiet." He nodded.

Francine asked, "What did Églantine say – specifically – about this topic?"

Anne-Marie shrugged. "I'm sorry, I'm not a business person, so all I can remember is that Églantine said she'd been spending more time than she'd ever done going through the financial records of the Maison, and that she was going to make an argument to the board that none of them would be able to refuse, because now she knew how to get people to agree with her. I didn't know what she meant, but didn't ask, because I didn't think I'd understand the answer. But she said it was going to lead to fireworks…which, I suppose, is…worrying."

Francine nodded. "Indeed. Anything else?"

"She noted that Guillermo has put on a little weight, and said she wished she could do the same – but her appetite has not been what it once was."

"What do you know about her arrangements regarding other…service providers, or even friends, who came into her apartment?"

"No friends, any longer. She says they are all dead, now…except for those she knew as clients, who were acquaintances, not friends. Of these, many are still alive. There's a brasserie across the circle, and they used to bring linens and food each day, at dinnertime, and would cater for her *soirées* and parties. Her server there was always Marco. He'd been doing it for a long time. A man with a Portuguese father, his entire life had been spent as a waiter – it was his career. But he died a year or so ago. Since then, the food is left with Lucienne on weekdays, and he brings it up before he leaves. Madame enjoyed seeing him every evening, she said. At the weekends she would give a person access to the side door using a panel in her apartment which allows her to do that. They would place the food in the elevator, and she would call that up, and serve herself. On Mondays I would remove the rubbish and the leftovers. Her florist comes twice a week, usually, always with peonies – even in the winter. Madame calls them her 'indulgence'. There have been several times over the years when there has been a special problem and she has not had them – bad weather, or some disease – but, otherwise, she always has peonies here, though, recently, she's asked for more than one vase of them – says they don't smell as much nowadays as they used to…but so many things are not as good now as they once were. I know she deals directly with a cooperative in Amsterdam, and they send the flowers to a florist who is not far from here. The woman who brings them is new. Madame was happy to have her as she loves peonies, too. She has pink at the moment – which she prefers – but she has other colors, sometimes."

Francine replied, "We've interviewed the woman from the florist. She was here on Thursday afternoon and was due to return on Tuesday morning, though she has been told not to come, of course."

Anne-Marie's eyes welled up with tears again. "Oh dear – Guillermo will miss her so. He loved his special heating pad and chair. We would lift him onto it together – two old women and an old dog. I shall miss her in my heart. She was a good woman – even if she didn't know who she really was. She was generous, and so talented, and worked so hard, even now. The evil person who killed her must be found. You must make them answer to the court. The Lord will make them answer to Him, when it is their time."

So Lucienne lied about the time when the caterers arrived, and he said he hardly ever saw Églantine?

I must have made some sort of noise as I was thinking, because Bud nudged me, and Francine said, "Something you want to add, Cait? Anne-Marie, this is a…colleague, visiting from Canada. She might have a question for you – of an informal nature. Do you mind?"

For the first time since she'd arrived, Anne-Marie Lefebvre squinted in my general direction.

I wonder how good your distance vision is, was what I thought; "Thank you, yes – Anne-Marie, do you think that Églantine ever remembered anything about what happened to her when she was attacked as a teen? And did you ever tell her she'd had a child?" was what I said.

The color drained from Anne-Marie's slightly florid face. She looked back at Francine, who nodded, and then stuck her hand into her handbag again, where she fiddled about as she said, "I did tell her about the child. She'd been so kind to me that I felt I owed her that much. But – it was strange – when I told her, I got the feeling she already knew."

I said, "Maybe, as an adult, she'd worked out that she carried the scar of a cesarean birth."

Anne-Marie pulled her hand out of her bag quite sharply, and a rosary fell out. She scrabbled about on the floor to pick it up, then shoved it into her coat pocket. "The way they took the child from her body was…brutal, by all accounts. The doctor said that was the normal way, but the Sisters said…well, they said it didn't look right to them. He was the doctor who cared for the unmarried mothers we looked after. He wasn't a kind man. He seemed especially upset by Églantine. Though at that time, before she claimed that name for herself, we all called her Mademoiselle Durand."

I jumped in. "Like Lucienne Durand?"

Francine said, "It's like your 'Jane Doe'. 'Mademoiselle X', 'Mademoiselle Dupont', or 'Durand', are commonly used this way. 'Jane Doe' is from English common law back in the 1700s, where it was used to refer to an unknown plaintiff. Durand is a common name in France."

Yes, I know about the origin of Doe, but I didn't know about Durand, was what I thought; "Thanks," was what I said…feeling a bit miffed, but trying to be gracious.

Francine didn't seem to notice my magnanimity, but simply asked Anne-Marie, "At what time did you leave on Saturday?"

"I was gone before ten – I usually am on a Saturday. I have most of the day to myself. I saw Lucienne with the rubbish bag, which he took from me in reception, then I left. It was a pleasant day, for the time of year, so Guillermo and I cycled back to our apartment slowly, avoiding the main roads – though there are so many roadworks at the moment that it's busy everywhere. Goodness knows what it'll be like when all the tourists arrive…but I won't have to be coming here, then, will I? Oh dear…oh dear."

Francine continued. "Now that you know what's happened, is there anything you saw, or heard, or…felt…yesterday that you might not have mentioned that now occurs to you as out of place, or unusual?"

Anne-Marie breathed in deeply, and I could tell by the way she rubbed her thumb, as well as the way she was nibbling her lip, that she was trying to control her emotions and refocus her thoughts. Her eyes darted about the room – though I still wasn't sure how much she could see, which made we wonder about how safe she might be, in traffic, on a bicycle.

Eventually she said, "I wish I could think of something. But everything was normal – well, not exactly normal for a Saturday because I'd heard the twins squabbling, and Lucienne told me they were on the fourth, fussing about with giant boxes. And Jacques was here too. He swanned through reception while I was there – and he's never here on a Saturday…he's usually off doing something with one of his many, many friends. And Lucienne seemed to be…not himself. He's normally quiet, a little aloof – though he's a good man underneath it all – but he even tried to engage me in conversation on Saturday. Something about…it was about Guillermo and his treats, which I always bring with me. That was it. He said he'd met someone with a dog, and wanted to give them a gift for the dog, so I told him the name of the treats that Guillermo likes. I thought at the time it sounded good that he'd made a friend – not that we usually chatted, as I said. He struck me as a…solitary person."

Francine pressed on. "Anything else? No strange people lurking about the place?"

Anne-Marie straightened her back. "If there had been, Lucienne would have seen them off – he was good at that. It was his job to greet people, yes, but it was also his job to generally keep an eye on the place."

Francine cooed, "Thank you, and if you think of anything else at all, please phone me. Here's my personal card."

Anne-Marie took the card, and placed it carefully into her handbag. "I shall."

Francine stood. "Now, if you'd be so kind, this officer will ensure that one of his colleagues will accompany you to Églantine's apartment. We believe that…certain articles…have been moved about. I won't say more than that, because I don't want to sway your honest opinion. Please wear the protective gear that the officer will give you, and make a full and thorough assessment of the apartment. My officer will take notes. I'd appreciate any information you can give him about anything that's been moved – and in what way – or is missing from the apartment."

Anne-Marie was slower to get to her feet than the more youthful captain, but did so with relative ease for a woman of her years. "Articles have been moved, you say? Well, I know that place as well as I know my own home – possibly better – and Madame believed that everything had its place, so I'll certainly be able to tell what's been moved, and what – if anything – isn't there that should be. But she had a lot of…articles, so it might take some time."

"We appreciate your help. You'll be driven home, of course, and I hope Guillermo is managing well without you."

"He'll have to wait for his walk – though I could telephone a neighbor to ask them to take him out. Would that be alright?"

Francine smiled. "Please do. Do you need a phone?"

Anne-Marie pulled a massive phone from her bag. "I have this – it's old, but it serves my purposes. I can't cope with those 'smart' ones, which aren't 'smart' at all, if you ask me…or else they're too smart by half. Oh – goodbye everyone…I'm off to do my bit to help catch this devil."

She waved above her head as she headed toward the elevator, calling, "I have my elevator key, and your policeman can get himself back down – but anyone else will have to walk up…as I dare say you've all worked out, by now."

Pierre flashed us a nervous smile as he shot out of the room, heading after the woman.

Turning to us, Francine said, "So?"

Bud replied, "A truthful statement, I'd say. Likely rape and attempted murder of a possibly fourteen- or fifteen-year-old girl, approximately sixty-five years ago, possibly just outside Paris, or maybe the attack was inside Paris and the dump site in the countryside, to cause confusion and mean the victim couldn't be identified…which appears to have been successful. I have no idea about the state of your records, Francine, so you might be able to find out who Églantine was before she 'became' Églantine, given what you now know. But I would suggest it might be difficult to work out who might have attacked her back then. In any case, that's likely to be a blind alley as far as her murder is concerned, and therefore not fruitful."

I piped up with: "I agree that I believe Anne-Marie was being truthful. Lucienne Durand lied to us about the arrival time of the caterers – which suggests to me that…'something' had happened before we arrived here that he didn't want to share with us. It could have been something not connected to the case in any way, of course…or it might have been something significant. Unfortunately, we have no way of knowing, at this time. Interestingly, it appears he also lied about the frequency with which he interacted with Églantine – which I suppose he might have done on the basis that such insight was none of our business."

Bud said, "How so?"

I replied, "It's clear to me that Églantine was an incredibly private person, and I believe that Lucienne was someone who would have respected that. Upon reflection, I believe it's likely that he saw his employer's dinner-delivery arrangements as something two compete strangers didn't need to know about."

Francine nodded. "I'd agree. Not a lie…an omission. Probably an innocent one."

I continued, "Let's not forget, though, that the twins also lied, or at least omitted information – possibly less innocently – about the agenda for the board meeting. I believe Anne-Marie will be able to tell us if anything's missing from Églantine's apartment, and that might be illuminating. Her information also bolsters some of my own conclusions about the dead woman, and answers some questions I had about her. I'd say that the desire to introduce a ready-to-wear line might have been a Big Deal for those set against it – which might point to a motive. It needs more meat on the bones, though."

Francine nodded. "I agree. If the twins lied about the agenda, do we trust them when it comes to their estimates of the timing of the arrival and departure of the moving people? That's an important one – and I'm still waiting to hear back from my team at the station who are conducting those key interviews, which I had to hand over. Give me a few moments, alone, please."

Bud and I left the meeting room, and I whispered, "Fancy a quick peek at those sewing rooms?"

Dix-sept

It didn't take more than a glance from me for Bud to follow me up the stairs. For once, I beat him to our destination, and pushed open the double doors on the fourth floor landing to what I expected to be a wide-open area with some sort of organized workspace within it. What I saw surprised me: Monica and Monique were engaged in hand-to-hand combat. A few dressmakers' mannequins had already taken a hit and were lying on the floor; there was a jumble of rolls of tapes and fabrics surrounding the mêlée, with one particular bolt of fabric threatening to topple over and crush the two short women.

Bud stepped forward and used his calming voice. "Ladies, let's be civil, shall we? I know that siblings can get under each other's skin, but we don't need it to come to blows."

As he spoke, he batted what little air there was between the two elderly sisters, until they each pulled back, and skulked off to opposite sides of the room; the farther away they got from each other, the better I felt about the situation. The bolt of fabric toppled, and Bud caught it – just about. He stood it upright, and stepped back.

"Now then, ladies, what seems to be the problem – and let's remain calm, shall we?"

With both women in a state of disarray, I couldn't be sure which was which any longer because their hairdos were all over the place, and I'd been relying upon hair-length to tell them apart.

One of them said, "She started it – she always does. Just because she's the oldest by ten minutes, she thinks she can tell me what to do."

"And 'she' is?"

Thank you, Bud.

"I'm Monica, not 'she', and Monique started it, not me. I don't boss you around. You said I couldn't have that fabric after all, and you know I've had my eye on it for months. I thought we'd agreed I could have the remnants."

I found it hard to believe that the sisters had come to blows over a bit of material.

Bud said, "Now then – where's the fabric you're talking about."

The twins scanned the room. Monica sobbed, "Oh no, there it is…ruined. It was exquisite, now you've gone and trampled all over it. It's of no use to anyone. I was going to make it into a hat. On Monique – why did you do that to it?"

Monique spat, "I didn't do it, sister dearest. You did it yourself. You've caught it with your foot and ripped it, right in the middle. Serves you right."

Knowing that my sister Siân and I have had some really bitter arguments over the years – often started by something that's really nothing at all – I had at least some insight into how the twins had reached the point of fisticuffs…though the damage they'd managed to do to their working environment made me suspect they were going to regret their actions quite soon.

They both surveyed the devastation, their expressions suggesting they understood the gravity, and pointlessness, of what they'd allowed themselves to do.

Monica said quietly, "We'd better clear this all up, I suppose."

Monique agreed, "I suppose you're right."

Bud and I looked at each other, and he said, "Would you like a hand?"

The twins smiled at us. "Yes, please," they said in unison – and it felt for all the world as though a derailed train was back on the tracks, and that the journey would go smoothly from that moment onward.

I bent to pick up a ball of yellow velvet ribbon, which I wound and wound, pulling it from within a tangle of other ribbons until it knotted, whereupon I had to pick up a whole nest of the stuff to try to sort it out. Meanwhile, Bud moved furniture that had toppled, and placed larger items back onto an array of high tables, with tall chairs; I assumed the tables were high to allow people to stand to work at them. I swore silently as I wrestled with the mess of ribbons, and used one of the tables to lay it all as flat as possible, to be able to thread various pieces in and out of others; the similarity between what I was trying to achieve with the ribbons, and what I was trying to do with regard to the deaths of Églantine and Lucienne, wasn't lost on me.

Around me, Monica and Monique moved silently, restoring order within their workspace, and – presumably – within their relationship.

I dared, "So Églantine wanted the Maison to start making a line of ready-to-wear clothes, and you were both against the idea. Why is that?"

Both women stopped what they were doing, their hands full of the fabrics, doodads, and thingumabobs that were a part of their daily life.

Monique snapped, "Who told you that?"

I said, "It doesn't matter."

Monica said sullenly, "She mentioned it once, a few months ago, at our last quarterly board meeting. We – and Jacques and Avril – didn't think it was a good idea because we felt it would undermine the brand's promise of exclusivity."

Bud paused in his tasks and added, "Wouldn't it mean that the business would grow? Selling a lot more garments – so making a lot more garments, and, presumably, making more money. Isn't that a good thing?"

The twins pouted. I tried not to smile; they looked like two slightly wrinkled small children.

Monica said, "Not if one of the main things you have on your side is that you have a waiting list for exclusive pieces. If anyone can just go out and buy your designs as they wish, at any old place, then the people who currently pay for the right to say, 'Yes, this is an Églantine,' won't want to do it any longer, because all sorts will be able to say it."

Monique agreed. "Part of owning an Églantine piece is the fact you have to come here – to the room through there – to be fitted. By us." She waved toward the door at the end of the room which I knew, by now, would lead to a triangular space with impressive views of the avenue beyond it.

I said, "But other houses do it – I know at least that much. Dior and Chanel have made it work wonderfully well for them…haven't they?"

Both women snorted, in unison. Monique sniped, "They sold out long ago, once Bohan and Lagerfeld came along, in fact. Gold tweed? Whatever next? For them, it's all about the perfumes, and make-up, and those handbags of theirs, these days. They don't do it the way they should. We keep it…pure. That's that."

I suspected that Monica and Monique could be quite stubborn…well, more than suspected it, actually.

I stopped trying to unravel what I was beginning to believe was a twenty-first-century version of the Gordian knot, and said, "You two said that Églantine wanted to publish her archives – why didn't you tell us about the ready-to-wear proposal?"

The twins looked puzzled. Monica said, "It's not relevant."

Bud said, "Anything might be relevant. We don't know who killed Églantine, and we don't know why they did it."

As the twins patted down their hair, and straightened their green smocks, they began to look more like their usual selves.

Monique said, "No one knew about it but us. Do you honestly think that one of us killed Églantine just because she wanted to do either of those things? Maybe people would do that in Canada, but not here. Paris is a civilized place."

I dropped the annoying tangle of ribbony…stuff…and jumped in with: "You know what – we're only trying to help, but if you can't see why being honest and open with us, and the police, is critical, then maybe we're wasting our time. Bud, let's get back to the captain. She might have finished by now. There's nothing more for us here."

I stomped out of the *atelier* feeling myself getting warmer by the minute…and feared a hot flash was to blame. As we started down the stairs, I said to Bud, "I need to splash some water on my face, Husband. Let's go down to the second floor, and I'll get myself sorted while you check when we can talk to Francine, okay?"

Bud's eyes crinkled with concern. "You look a bit pink around the gills – I hope this one doesn't last too long, Wife."

We hugged and went our separate ways – Bud into the meeting room, and me to the washroom. I moistened loo paper with cold water, and patted the back of my neck, allowing my eyes to wander as I felt the cooling effects help my body to stop feeling as though it were going to burn up. The previous night, I'd merely stuck my head through the door to discover what was behind it; now that I had the chance to take in the details, I could see that the washroom was – of course – incredibly well appointed. It boasted an intricately tiled floor, patterned with Paris green mosaic tulips that swirled around its outer edges; the shape of all the porcelainware was voluptuous and soft-edged, with sinuous brass hardware in the shape of stylized lilies; the lighting was dim, because it was all jewel-toned stained glass, and the place was a bit…stuffy.

I flushed the wet loo paper away and stepped into the corridor, allowing the air there – which at least had a little movement in it – to play on my damp neck, continuing the cooling. If I'd still been in the washroom, I'd probably have missed it: a keening wail sliced through the air. I dashed along the corridor, and met up on the landing with Bud, Francine, and Pierre who all appeared from the meeting room.

Each of us had an unspoken "What was that?" expression on our face.

The scream came again – this time in duplicate.

"It's the twins," I said. "We only left them moments ago, on the fourth floor. They'd been fighting, and…oh heck…there were so many pairs of scissors in that room."

Francine nodded. "Bud told us. Pierre – you're the youngest and fittest – get going up those stairs and find out what's set them off this time."

Pierre did as he was told, and we all followed, but at a slower pace.

Just as we were approaching the fourth floor, Pierre's voice called down from above. "We're up here, on the fifth."

We trudged on up; he was standing outside one of two separate doors let into the wall, where there was only one set of double doors on each of the floors below. Monica and Monique were there too – one standing either side of him. Their green smocks were smeared with black marks; their hands were smeared with dark…*blood?*

Monica jabbered, "We came to see if we could find any clues about Madame's death. We thought he might know something…or have something in his office that would be useful."

Monique took a deep breath and added, "We were trying to be helpful. Really we were. The door was open. Honestly – it was open…well…unlocked."

Then, in unison they whined, "We didn't do it."

Dix-huit

Pierre mumbled, "Inside, Captain. At the desk. There's…a lot of blood."

"We didn't do it," squealed the twins. Again.

Francine snapped, "Be quiet," then grabbed a pair of gloves from a pocket and pulled them on. "Pierre – Bertrand – get those two down to that meeting room, and don't let them touch anything. Get an officer up from downstairs to watch them at all times. Get another one to secure this scene, and get medics and forensics here. Now."

She pushed the door with the toe of her elegant shoe; it swung open easily, and silently. Gustav Sutter's desk had been set up so that he could look out to the street through a large window, in front of which sat a green velvet Chesterfield sofa and walnut coffee table. But he'd never see that sight again, because it looked to me as though someone had slit his throat from behind, while he'd been seated, and he'd fallen forward – or had maybe been pushed forward – so that his head lay on his desk, his lifeless, milky eyes staring toward us.

Bud grabbed my arm and pulled me back. "Let's allow Francine to do what she needs to do. We'll wait here until your officer arrives, Francine, then wait on the second floor, until you know if we can be of more use."

Francine barked, "Don't go anywhere – you're both gloving up and walking this room with me. Now. Take these, put them on. Obvious rules apply. Best observations. Come."

We did as we'd been "requested" to do. As I took in the minutiae of the scene, I felt the loss of the man…and suspected his daughter Joanne would, too, even if his sniping ex-wife Avril might be less devastated.

Bud walked carefully around the desk, then pointed. "Possible, or I'd say probable, murder weapon on the floor, behind the desk, far side. Knife with a hooked blade. Bloodied. Looks…old, but sharp. Staying well back. Taking photos. Establishing if that belonged to the victim, and if it would have normally been here, in this room – and therefore readily to hand – would be one of the first things you'll be aiming to establish, Francine…I imagine."

Francine said, "Of course," then swore under her breath; it sounded intriguing in French, rather than angry…or hopeless. "This man's been dead for some time. Look at the eyes, and the blood on the desk. The outer edges are completely dried, and even the pooled parts are congealed. I thought we knew that everyone had left here last night, but it looks to me as though he might have been here, like this, since then. They'll have me for this. This shows disgraceful management of an existing crime scene. Not only have I lost my husband and my child for this job, but now I'll lose the job, too."

I froze: had Francine's remarks earlier in the day about Bud's loss of his first wife been made because she, too, had lost a husband – and child? – to a violent crime, connected somehow to her job? I didn't know quite what to say, but knew that saying nothing was wrong.

I ventured, "I'm so sorry, Francine. That must feel…awful."

The venom in the woman's eyes when she turned around shocked me. "Awful? You could say that. I discover that my husband has been having an affair for five years, and when he tells me his mistress is pregnant and he wants a divorce so he can marry her, I play nice, and say yes…because, by then, I certainly don't want him anymore. Then, two minutes after he's married her – and he and she are cooing over their baby like it's the first one that's ever been born, and organizing the most lavish event surrounding a christening that's ever been held – he goes back to the court to say that I am not present enough as a mother, because of my career. His lawyer bleats on for hours about how my ex-husband and his new wife, and my son's half-sibling, will make a much better, more settled and devoted, family for my son to grow up with. And the judge agrees! So here I am – a captain who gets to see her son every couple of weeks. And now? Now I could lose my job over this massive…cock-up."

She said "cock-up" in English, making it sound like "cook-up", which made me want to smile, so I literally bit both of my lips together, because she deserved sympathy, not a smirk.

An officer presented himself at the door, did his best to hide his surprise when he saw Bud and me, then said, "Captain, Officer Bertrand said to tell you that the medics and forensics team have been notified and will be here as soon as possible, and that the witnesses are in the meeting room with him. Shall I remain here?"

Francine nodded – and any possibility of sharing more personal moments evaporated. I silently wished I'd had the chance to say so many things to her; I hoped I might have another opportunity in the future.

Her tone had shifted from incandescent to chilly when she said, "Yes, stay there. Cait – anything you can offer to tell me about this man from what you've seen here, or have come to know about him?"

I'd had a good look around the office – without touching anything, of course, which was starting to feel like my specialty. "Seven photographs of his daughter at various ages, but none of his ex-wife. Having met him yesterday, I'd say that tallies with my impressions of him then – a solid, loving relationship with an adult daughter, and a poor, but resigned one, with an ex-wife. I'm assuming the woman in the photo on his desk, draped around his shoulders, is his second wife. She appears to have a similar overall appearance to Avril – long, lean, slightly haughty expression – so maybe he had 'a type'…which a lot of people do and it's not a gender-specific thing. That photo looks recent, judging by how he appears in it and how he looked last evening, and she appears to be about twenty years younger than Avril. A smoker of cigars – you can smell it in here, even though there's no stub or ash in that massive crystal ashtray, and a drinker of scotch – he has an impressive variety of bottles. He was also a man with a sweet tooth – see the bonbons in that jar? His desk is a luxurious antique, as is his chair. He told us he spent little time here, often working from home, and I'd say that chair suggests that to be the case – it wouldn't be good for a person's back if they needed to sit in it for long periods. The rest of the furnishings in here are also mainly decorative, and of the highest quality, giving an impression of importance rather than functionality. I'd say he's earned that right, and that the rest of his life was lived at the same level. He's wearing the same ruinously expensive clothes he had on last evening, so I think you're right, Francine…he never left the Maison. I wonder why his wife didn't raise the alarm? I'm sure that checking his phone will tell you if she's been phoning or texting him repeatedly…or maybe she didn't worry because he'd told her he was staying here at the request of the police. Then…there's that."

Francine paused beside the painting on the wall to which I was pointing. She said, "That's…not in keeping with the rest of the room."

Bud and I both agreed, and Bud said, "Maybe it's there because it's the right size, rather than because he liked it. It's out of his normal eyeline. A hidden safe?"

Francine nodded and took a photo with her phone. "I'll let forensics get to it first, then take a look."

I noted, "The shelves behind his desk were probably originally designed to hold books, or even files and folders, though, as you can see, they've been replaced with *objets d'art* which suggest he possessed similar taste to Églantine…if he chose them, rather than them maybe belonging to the Maison, and its head. However, I can't see a computer, tablet, or laptop anywhere. There might be something in a desk drawer, I suppose…there's an electrical outlet behind his desk, in the wall – not conveniently placed, but it was probably intended for a lamp, not to cater to today's needs."

Bud noted, "He's got a cut on his left hand – it's deep. Defensive, I'd say."

Francine and I peered from a distance, then both of us copied Bud and used our own phone's zoom functions to take a better look.

Francine asked, "Did either of you happen to notice if he was left- or right-handed?"

I replied, "Give me a second." I closed my eyes to the fuzzy stage and recalled Gustav offering drinks, then pouring them, the previous evening. "Dominant left hand."

Francine asked, "What did you just do?"

I didn't see any point in beating about the bush, so simply replied, "Eidetic memory."

She chuckled. "I bet that's handy…though, maybe remembering everything isn't all I might imagine it is." She gazed at the corpse in front of us, as did I…and nodded.

Bud asked, "May I open this door?" He pointed to the door set into the room's oak paneling, at the end of the office farthest from the door though which we'd entered.

Francine replied, "Let me do it. Stand back."

She drew her weapon – which I thought a bit extreme – then tried the handle, but it seemed that the door was locked.

Bud offered, "I could pick that lock, it you want."

Francine arched an eyebrow toward him. "I think not, Bud – maybe we should try less extreme measures first."

I said, "On each floor, there's a corridor at the far right, which leads to the toilets and the elevator. It might also lead to a triangular room beyond this one, like the anteroom on the second floor. Do you think that's worth a try?"

Francine nodded. "I'm aware, and I do. But let's take this in before we leave – we won't get another chance until the medics and forensic folks have been and gone."

We all stood still…and turned, and bobbed up and down, as we stared. I said, "What's that?"

Francine bent to peer under the desk. She said, "Beside his foot?" I nodded. "Something…shiny. It's catching the light now that someone across the way has opened a window that's reflecting the sun. I think…I think it's a paperclip."

I heard the disappointment in her voice, and felt it in my tummy. "I don't see anything else of note," I said.

Bud agreed. "Me neither. How about we try to get to the other side of that door – or would you rather do that alone, Francine? Would that be breaking some sort of protocol?"

Francine chuckled. "Oh Bud…I've got a dead body in a box at a national museum, where the President of France – and his wife, of course – are due to be schmoozing with the best of the best from the world of French fashion tomorrow night. To say that it's a high-profile case would, therefore, be understating it somewhat. I'm also using huge resources to try to discern via cameras across the city, where exactly – at some point between here and his home, across a period of some hours – a fairly non-descript, bearded man was given, or purchased, a baguette that was somehow laced with strychnine…a man who then lay dead on the street for hours, unnoticed. I shall not allow his death to be ignored, just because he wasn't a fashion icon. Now? Now we have a prominent businessman who died right here, in the Maison – which was already a crime scene – and possibly when my officers were still in the building. Certainly when they were supposedly keeping it secure. I'll admit that all I know about this man is that he drove himself here in his own car and entered the car park at ten twenty yesterday morning…and that he told my officers he had no idea why anyone would want to kidnap Églantine. He admitted that he'd be the one to gather together the funds required to pay any ransom that might be demanded, and that the Maison would be able to get its hands on quite a bit, quickly, which suggests a relatively liquid organization, with good cashflow. But – and here's a nice additional nail in my career's coffin – he was one of two people I wasn't able to reach on the phone when I started calling people at seven this morning. I should have followed up…but didn't."

She paused, swore, then sighed. "And then, of course, you two have been allowed the sort of access that could be a career-wrecker all on its own – except for the fact that I do believe your skills are valuable, and have always believed that collaboration leads to strength. So – to answer your question, Bud – yes, I'll be breaking protocol if you come with me, but no more than I have done by allowing you to 'trample all over a significant crime scene' which is how anyone who choses to speak against me could easily characterize my most recent actions."

I took my chance. "The best way to stop anyone from daring to speak out against you is to crack the case…and I can promise you that Bud and I will do everything within our power to help you do that. So let's find out if there's an interesting reason for that door being locked, shall we?"

Sadly, there wasn't: the door – and another, the same – simply formed a part of a wall within a triangular room that housed three neat workspaces. They all looked as though they might operate as hot desks – devoid of anything except the electronic connections needed for a laptop, and chargers.

"Gustav's door must be locked so that it offered him privacy, and merely acts as a wall within this office," said Bud.

I agreed. "This other door is locked too, probably for the same reason. The name plate on the second office at the top of the stairs said it's Jacques', so, if that's unlocked, should we take a look in there? Just to make sure…"

Francine tutted and said, "What…that we've not got another body to deal with?"

We returned to the open door to Gustav's office, being guarded by the officer, where Francine said, "We're checking this other one, and I might need you to break it down."

She tried the handle. "Locked."

Bud jumped in. "Captain, you said you needed to show this officer the location of the other door to Gustav's office that we just checked, because he has to be clear about where all points of entry to the crime scene are located. Why don't you do that, and we'll wait here?"

Francine's eyes narrowed, then she said, "I shall. Come."

She marched off toward the corridor with the officer trailing behind her, and Bud started to work on the lock with something he'd pulled from his pocket. He hissed, "I can't let them go wrecking a perfectly good – and magnificent – door."

I whispered, "They're coming back."

Bud made a show of pushing his weight against the door, which opened. He announced proudly, "There you go – just stuck, not locked, after all."

"Thank you very much, Bud," said Francine, then she peered into the office. "What a mess!"

We all looked inside: this office was a mirror image of Gustav's and had a small desk with its back to the shared wall, behind which shelves were stacked with files and sample books. There were swatches of fabric hanging off, or pinned to, almost every surface, including the walls; two dressmakers' mannequins stood draped with fabrics; a high drafting-type table was set in front of the window…and it looked as though someone had tossed dozens of rolls of fabric, trim, and sketches around the room, letting them land…everywhere; several arch-lever files were also laying, open, on the floor, and one mannequin was on its side, under the desk.

Francine sighed. "Someone's been searching for something in here. Those forensics people are going to love me. I suppose…I suppose I'd better find out if Jacques himself is still in good health, at home."

Dix-neuf

We left the rather bemused officer to oversee both crime scenes, and made our way down to the meeting room on the second floor. The staircase I'd seen as a designer's dream made manifest on Saturday afternoon – *was that really just over a day ago?* – was now beginning to lose its charms for me.

We paused on the landing. Francine sounded tired when she said, "Of course, I'll lead the questioning of the twins, but I need to do a few other things first…so why don't you two have a bit of an informal chat with them, while I brief Pierre?"

Bud replied, "As in 'we're all in this together, twins'?"

Francine smiled. "See? We'd have worked well as a team, Bud."

Bud grinned. "Isn't that what we're doing?"

Francine entered the room. "Bertrand, I need you. Bud, Cait, wait in there."

When Pierre passed us as he left, with a weak smile – his phone in one hand, his tablet in the other – I whispered, "Have they said anything?"

He replied, "No, but they've had a large cognac each."

He left us, and I gathered my thoughts.

When I started shaking out my hands to help me focus, Bud said, "Are you okay?"

I sighed. "Yes, but…twins have always made me feel a little…overwhelmed. Maybe it's because, as a psychologist, I'm firmly of the belief that we're all absolute individuals…then I see an undeniable, yet invisible, connection between twins, and I'm forced to challenge my thinking. Of course, there's been a great deal of research using twins, especially when it comes to the field of the balance between how our genetic make-up, as opposed to our upbringing, might impact our psyche and personality, and the preponderance of results show a clear influence of genetics upon behavior. Though there's still a lot of work to be done on how that balance works upon what I'm, personally, always interested in – not just what people do, but why they do it. So…well, maybe it's natural that being with twins always puts me on an even higher than usual level of alertness…because I'm always trying to understand why they do what they do, especially when they're doing the same as each other. I need to understand more about these two women. I mean – are they really almost just one person, as they appear to be? And, if not, then where are the differences between them? Might one act without the other knowing? Or would they always operate as a pair?"

Bud hugged me. "Don't ask me, I'm not the psychologist in this marriage – and I clearly recall how our past close encounter with twins, in London, turned out. But I can tell you that in my policing career I actually got to know some sets of twins, though not as colleagues, you understand. The result of 'were they both good, or not' was a fifty-fifty split – two sets were just about as low on the scumbag scale as you'd ever care to go…and they pretty much egged each other on. The other couple of sets? One upstanding, one definitely not in each case. So – I guess I'm no help, eh?"

"You're always a great help. I need to face my own challenges, and focus on the Martin twins and this case…right?"

"Right."

When Bud and I joined Monica and Monique in the meeting room, they'd shoved two chairs as close to each other as possible, and each was holding the other's hand. Both were wearing blue latex gloves – which I assumed was an inventive attempt on Pierre's part to keep the blood they'd managed to get onto themselves where it was, pending forensic examination. Two empty tumblers sat on the table in front of them.

Monica asked, "Is he really…dead?"

Good grief, how could you imagine anyone surviving that much blood loss, was what I thought; "Sadly, yes. It must have been a great shock for you, finding him like…that," was what I said.

Both sisters wailed, almost as though they'd rehearsed it – same pitch, same level, same up, then down…same cut-off point.

Monica said, "Neither of us has ever seen a dead body before – and now two, in just one day."

Monique chimed in with: "Exactly. Though he did look a lot worse than her. We were just saying that might have been because Madame was still wearing make-up, whereas Gustav didn't wear any, not even a little bit, like Jacques does."

Monica broke across her sister with: "What about the exhibition…will it be able to open tomorrow night, do you know?"

Bud and I shared a glance that told me he was as surprised by the change in topic as I was.

He said, "There's a lot to be worked out before that can happen."

Monique snapped, "But you said that Madame was killed here, Cait. The fact that she ended up in a crate at the *Petit Palace* isn't important – surely they can just take her to the hospital, or whatever, and then we could all get back to our staging."

I didn't quite know what to say, but decided to follow their lead, so asked, "Do you both think you'd be ready to go back and continue with the set-up in the morning, if they'd let you?"

The twins didn't even blink. "We'd go tonight," they chorused.

Monica added, "We know that might sound heartless, but you've no idea how much this exhibition meant to Madame. She cried so much when they invited her to be part of it, and said it was the greatest honor of her life to have the chance to show so many pieces. This will be the exhibition the whole world remembers, you see – the one that puts all the greats up there, on display. And her work will be there. Our work will be there. And she was so excited about it. She was due to be at the ceremony tomorrow night, you know, and she hasn't attended anything except her own shows…oh, for years."

I jumped in. "So she truly rarely left the Maison?" The twins shook their heads. I continued, "But didn't someone say they thought she might have gone wandering off…before we knew what had happened to her, I mean. Why would she wander – if she never went out?"

I know it was you, Monica – but what will you say now?

Monique said, "I think I mentioned that, or maybe it was Monica, but we'd talked about it before all…you lot arrived, and we agreed that she was getting quite forgetful, recently. And quite…confused, sometimes. Lucienne mentioned that she'd called him 'Papa' and had also referred to him as her son – both on the same day – a few weeks back. And she mixed us up a few times recently – and she'd never done that before. Ever."

Monica took up the refrain. "And, although she didn't leave the Maison, she did leave her apartment. She'd frequently visit us in the *atelier*, either to look at something in particular that we were doing, or just to see what we were up to, in general. Once, she looked surprised that she was there, when she'd been chatting to us for five or ten minutes…that sort of thing. She went for a nap after that episode – in fact, she'd talked about how much she was enjoying napping. Not like her. She always used to be a powerhouse."

Monique added, "And there was the book thing, wasn't there?"

I asked, "The book thing?"

The sisters smiled. Monica said, "A couple of times she came into our space and shouted about someone taking her book…that it was an important book — there was something in it that she needed. Avril was with us one time, and she tried to help…tried to work out which book Madame meant. You see — in our business — there are lots of sorts of books, and even more things that look like books, and she never explained what book she thought she'd lost. Monique once handed her a book of samples of silk — which we use for linings — and she was like a child with a new toy…delighted she was, wasn't she? She almost skipped away, telling us how happy she was that she'd found her book."

Monique added, "That's a good way to describe it, Monica, sometimes…more often these days…she looked like a child would when they're happy or sad. Not the way an adult expresses their emotions, in a way that society expects, but rather in a more…full-blooded, or innocent way, I suppose. Though, no, she didn't skip — she was getting a bit stilted in her movements of late — you know, not as flexible as she'd been? Shuffled a lot more these days, but she was a good age, and none of us is getting any younger. Sometimes I can't recall ever having been able to get out of a chair without needing to groan."

Monica nodded. "Well said."

Not the way I need this chat to go, was what I thought; "Your desire to respect Églantine's enthusiasm for the exhibition, and to ensure that her work is seen, and admired, is wonderful," was what I said.

The twins sat a little more upright in their chairs, and Bud added, "I dare say your long careers mean you know most of the other people who do what you do in this business. Did a lot of you setting up at the *Petit Palais* today know each other?"

The twins nodded: four beady eyes staring though glinting spectacles, two noses bobbing in time with each other.

He continued, "And did a lot of fashion houses use the same movers? I mean, is what those movers do a…specialized task?"

The twins shook their heads as one. Monica replied. "Not now. It used to be the case, but now we use general companies, or else the same sort of system that the public uses for ride-sharing, but we use it for delivery-sharing. However, for this particular exhibition, we made plans to use a moving company for one large collection, yesterday, and they'd been booked to collect the entire display cabinet from the reception area this afternoon – but that didn't happen, of course. Once all the other garments, that were taken yesterday, had been prepared, and stuffed – ready for transportation – we packed them into their crates, and the movers just…moved them."

Bud pressed on. "So you didn't know, or recognize, any of the people who moved those crates yesterday?"

Monique said, "Everyone keeps asking us that, and the answer is the same – neither of us had ever seen any of the four of them before."

"They were all very polite," added Monica.

"Oh yes, very polite. And clean."

"Yes, and clean. Very serviceable overalls."

Oh, heck – they might begin to critique the stitching of said overalls soon, was what I thought; "Why, after all these years, do you still refer to Églantine as Madame?" was what I said.

Suddenly both twins found their latex-encased hands to be interesting, then what they were looking at appeared to register, and they both lifted their heads at the same time.

Monica spoke proudly. "She gave us work when no one else would. She allowed us to do what we were good at, and get better at it. She gave us a chance when no one wanted two very young, inexperienced country girls anywhere – at any *atelier* – in Paris, not even as apprentices. She was always Madame to us, and always will be."

Monique added, "Yes, we country girls have to stick together, and us, her, and Avril – we're all the same."

Monica added, "Well, sort of – though we come from Marnesse, which is quite a big provincial town, though only a little way from the village of Montlyon, where Avril was from. But…we took over the big city, between us. That meant something to all of us – still does."

I pounced. "Églantine was from the countryside? Do you know where?"

Two perfectly timed shrugs.

Monica glanced at Monique, then said, "She never told us where she was from, but you can always tell a country girl…we have our ways. And have you seen what she did with her terrace upstairs? If that doesn't show a green thumb, I don't know what does. And look at the brand color of the Maison – it's not just Paris green, or emerald green…the green of countryside trees that is, and her love of nature came from living in green surroundings. That's what we think, isn't it, Monique?"

"It is. Definitely a country girl. Avril is, too, though she's developed in ways that make you think she's never been anywhere the Metro can't take you…except on a holiday, or for a show. When Madame and Avril met us for the first time, we all knew that we fitted together very well. There was something…unspoken. An ease we had when sharing each other's company. We, and Avril, are country girls through and through…so Madame must have been, too."

The thin mouths showing satisfied smiles signified to me that the twins felt the topic had been fully dealt with; I was disappointed, having hoped for a glimpse into Églantine's roots.

I almost shouted, "Welcome back, Captain," when Francine re-entered the room, then I blustered on. "Monica and Monique were just saying they'd never met any of the four removal men who were here yesterday, shifting those crates."

The twins nodded – like two bobbleheads, each still with blood on their hands, each still smiling with satisfaction.

I'm getting flashbacks to those twins in Kubrick's version of The Shining…*but it's like I'm seeing them when they're old, and bloodstained.*

Francine had clearly been about to say something, but she shut her mouth, blinked and said, "There weren't four removal men, there were only three."

Monica said quite firmly, "No, there were four."

Francine called, "Bertrand, check the files, how many removal men?"

Pierre's voice floated from outside. "Um…just a moment, Captain, I'm checking. There were three: two shifters, and a driver who also helped with the shifting work."

The twins chorused, "But there were four."

Francine sat down and said, "Now that's interesting. At last, something that doesn't fit. If I showed you photographs, could you identify them all?"

The twins nodded. Up, down, up, down.

Francine called out, "In here, Bertrand…with your tablet."

Pierre rushed in, his tablet held out in front of him.

Francine said, "Show them the photos of the removal men."

The twins agreed that the three men in question had, indeed, been three of the four removal men who'd taken the crates away.

Then Francine said, "Please describe the other one. Tall or short? Fat or thin? Broad or weedy? What about hair color?"

Monica said, "He was normal height, but broad-ish…filled his overalls – which were tan, not brown like the others wore. And he had a moustache that I didn't care for…one of those twirly ones they have these days."

Monique added, "Don't forget the beard, dear. He had a beard, too. Not unlike poor Lucienne's."

"And dark hair – thick dark hair. It poked out all around his cap…or hat."

"Oh yes, he wore that funny hat – like the sort they wear when they watch football…a bucket hat."

"Now that was the only thing was even slightly grubby about any of them, wasn't it? That was an old hat, that was. Sweat-stained. Not pleasant."

Francine tried again. "So you couldn't really see much of his face?"

Monica said, "Not with the hat, and the beard, and the moustache…and the glasses. I thought he had something wrong with his eyes, because his glasses were pinkish, like the logo thing on his hat. The lenses were pink, not the frames…which were thick and black, you know?"

Francine let out air until I thought she might completely implode. "So…a normal-sized man, with a full facial disguise, tan – not brown – overalls, and a slightly grubby hat. Great."

Monique added, "And he whistled. Out of tune. '*Clair de Lune*'."

Monica snapped, "It wasn't out of tune, it was lovely."

Monique tutted. "And you'd know? You do not have one musical bone in your body."

Monica sighed. "And you can only manage 'Hello' and 'Thank you' in anything other than French."

Monique gushed, "I can say more than that in Italian. I have to with those three new girls from Italy joining us in the *atelier*. And I am working on my English, as you know. That new Norwegian apprentice, Emma Kraft, is going to do great things – her attention to detail is excellent, and she's taken to our requirements extremely well. I know she'll develop quickly…once I can work out how to instruct her properly. Though, I have to say, I think her French is coming along faster than my English, and I freely admit that Norwegian is…well, wouldn't it be beyond most people?"

At last…some real differences between you two.

Francine snapped, "The extra moving man in question had no wooden leg?"

Monica clapped her blue and bloody hands together. "No – but he did have a limp, didn't he?"

Monique's mouth fell open. "He did. How did you know, Captain?"

Francine rolled her eyes and muttered, "Experience."

The twins looked confused.

Vingt

Francine slammed the table, making us all jump. "Bertrand – in here!"

Pierre was standing right behind her, so said quietly, "I'm here, Captain, what do you want?"

Francine stood, turned, and said, "So much, Pierre, so very much…but for now, firstly, I want everyone – who's still alive – who was here yesterday back here, in this room, as soon as possible. Note this everyone – no one is to mention the death of Gustav Sutter to a single soul. Do you understand that, ladies? No texts, no phone calls. Got it? I understand you were the ones who got in touch with Anne-Marie Lefebvre to tell her about the death of Églantine George?"

The twins nodded in perfect time with each other – like two metronomes.

Monica said, "We didn't know we shouldn't, and we knew she'd want to know. They were always close…though we never knew why. Oh, that's another thing – Anne-Marie's another country girl, like us."

Francine's flaring nostrils told me she was working hard to control her anger. "It wasn't the best idea to spread such news – these things need to be handled with delicacy. So this time, not a word. And when people arrive here, not even a look, or a tear – got it?"

The twins nodded. *Tick, tock, tick, tock.*

Francine returned her attention to Pierre. "Check on Anne-Marie's progress up in the apartment – I'll want her here, too, but I want her to be certain about anything that's missing, which, given how much stuff is up there, I do recognize might take some time to determine."

Pierre offered, "I understand that our officer is helping her to replace all the books in their correct order – which she said she needed to do to work out if anything had been taken. It is, indeed, taking a long time."

Francine sighed. "A sensible approach. Cait – you said you wanted more time in the dressing room up there, didn't you?" I nodded. "Our lot have done what they can in there, so why not join Anne-Marie and learn whatever you can about Églantine by being able to touch and move her stuff around as you want. We need…something…more."

I felt as though I were being dismissed, but didn't move. "Thanks, Captain, I'd be glad of the chance."

Francine concluded, "We need supplies of coffee and some snacks here, Pierre. It's getting on, and I know I'm famished, so I dare say everyone could do with something…but no more cognac, please, ladies. I need you to be alert, to be able to answer some more questions. Oh, and get the forensics people in here to deal with these two as soon as they arrive, please, Pierre. Don't worry, ladies, we'll get you out of those smocks as soon as possible, and we'll rustle up something else for you to wear."

The twins glanced at each other in horror. Monica said, "What do you mean? We can't give you our smocks. They're our…our…they have everything we use every day in them."

Francine's jaw firmed up. "I'm afraid you'll have to manage without them for a while, ladies – probably forever. If you'd just walked away when you saw the body, and hadn't gone pawing all over it, you could have kept them, but now they're evidence in a murder case and must be held…until they're no longer needed."

For the first time since I'd met them, I saw true devastation in the twins' eyes.

Francine nodded toward Bud. "Feel free to accompany Cait, or wait here."

I could tell that a major shift in the case was taking place, and was desperate to find out everything that Francine knew.

Just do it, Cait, was what I thought; "I wonder if Bud and I could have a quick word before I join Anne-Marie?" was what I said.

"Talk as you walk with me," said Francine, so we did.

I spoke quietly, and quickly. "The eidetic memory thing, Francine – really useful when it comes to large quantities of data. So could I have access to everything you've got, from all sources…please? It won't take me forever to get through it – speed-reading, too – and I could be useful." I used my "pretty-please" face.

Francine turned to Bud, just as we reached the door to the washroom.

Ah…

She looked me up and down, then did the same to Bud. She also spoke quietly, "So Monsieur Gangbuster, what do you say? Is your wife up to it?"

Bud patted me on the back…a bit like he does to Marty, when he's been a 'good boy'. "More than up to it – she's even better than she thinks, sometimes. Trust me – and trust her. You won't be sorry."

Francine pushed open the door to the washroom. "I'm not sure about that last point, Bud, as I might already be sorry – but I'll text Pierre to let him know he can share what's on his tablet with you, but you can access only that, Cait. No database or live-camera access."

I asked, "But I can use it to look up anything…else?"

Francine nodded. "Goodbye for a moment."

I want to be in two places at once, doing two things at once, was what I thought; "Bud, could you go and have a good poke about in Églantine's dressing room and take lots of photos of anything interesting, or out of place, that you find?" was what I said.

Bud sighed. "You know I'll do my best, though I'm a bit less familiar than you with what might be expected to be 'normal' when searching the closet of a woman who's been a fashion designer known around the world for fifty years or so. However, I dare say I'll find a decade or two of my own experience as a detective to call upon, Wife."

I grinned. "Thank you, Husband. You're good, and you know it, so let's drop the false modesty, shall we?" I gave him a wink, then a peck on the cheek. "Right, I'm off to try to get Pierre to surrender that tablet of his – which he holds onto as though it might contain his life force – then I'll find myself a quiet corner and work through it."

"How about the anteroom?"

We kissed again, and Bud headed off upstairs, while I tracked down Pierre – who was hovering on the landing outside the meeting room, half peering over the banister, and half keeping an eye on the twins through the open door.

I asked, "Any sign of the forensics team, or the medics, yet?"

Pierre shook his head. "The last I heard was a text saying they were five minutes away, but that was ten minutes ago."

I chuckled, "We had a ride-share car like that a few days ago…oh no, yesterday afternoon, actually. Good grief, time's taken on a whole new meaning over the past day or so. Anyway – did you get a text from Francine about me being allowed to read through everything you've got about this case on that tablet?"

Pierre looked down at the device he was cradling, as though it were his firstborn. "I did…but you can't go far with it. I might need it at any moment."

I promised, "I'll only be through there, in the anteroom, and I won't delete anything, or alter anything. But just take a moment to show me how information is organized on there, would you? That'll save me some time. And then I'll be as fast as I can be."

Pierre flicked and scrolled and clicked, and it all made sense.

I thanked him and noted, "Good titles, good division and collation of information, and it looks like…a lot."

Pierre explained, "Several files in that folder are video files – which take up a lot of space. They were sent to me by the team trying to put together a timeline of Lucienne's movements after he left the Maison yesterday afternoon. They've got their hands full with it, because, as you'll see, he kept changing his appearance as he moved around the city, so they keep losing him. It's almost complete – they've been tackling it from both ends…from where and when his body was found, and then backward in time, as well as from when he left here, and forward in time. Now there's just a bit in the middle that's missing – and I've been told to expect that soon, so let me know if anything comes in, please."

"Wouldn't they text you to let you know it's been sent?"

Pierre smiled. "They should. But…"

I patted his hand, then curled my fingers around the tablet. "I promise I'll let you know if anything pops up on the screen. So…may I take it now?"

Pierre gazed at the device with a mixture of terror, and longing. "I'll be in here, making sure the forensics people deal with the twins. You can just shout if you need me."

I promised I would, then headed off before Pierre had a chance to snatch back his precious computer.

Once I was alone in the anteroom, I was surprised to discover I could hear hardly any noise from the *Avenue de l'Opéra*. Examination informed me that the windows – which looked as though they were original Haussmann fixtures – were, in fact, modern and triple-glazed, which meant that the anteroom was almost freakishly quiet, given all the activity I could see outside.

I grabbed one of the folding chairs that had been stacked in front of the shelf units, and sat myself at the worktable, facing the point of the room. The window didn't give me the incredible view of Napoleon's column that Églantine's bedroom did, but the building in my eyeline was beautiful, its corner topped with a dome covered in fish-scale tiles, that shone in the sharp, late-afternoon sunlight.

I settled my body, settled my brain, opened the first of Pierre's folders, and began.

I worked through interviews, crime scene photos, more interviews – Francine's teams had been busy back at the station – and then I worked through the videos following Lucienne across Paris. I saw what Pierre had meant about the man changing his appearance, but it didn't seem to be as suspicious as it had first sounded: Lucienne began his journey on his bicycle – which he wheeled through the side door of the Maison – not, of course, wearing his green velvet coat and top hat, but in jeans and a tan jacket. Some time later he'd removed his jacket and was wearing a gray jerkin over a white shirt, and – at some point – he must have removed his jerkin, because he was wearing only the shirt when his body was found. Interestingly, no bicycle or helmet had been found with his body. I wondered if some officer – probably in a basement bunker somewhere – was currently trying to locate that bike somewhere in Paris. Possibly, if it had already been found, they were going through the same tracking process for that as they were for Lucienne himself.

As usual, for me, the more I viewed and read, the faster I got…and time really did disappear. I was jolted from my focused state by Bud, whose gentle, "Cait – I need to talk to you about something I saw up in Églantine's dressing room," brought me back into the anteroom.

I looked up. "What did you find?"

Bud held his phone in front of my face, just as Pierre's tablet pinged, and a small rectangle popped up in the top, right-hand corner of the screen. I moved Bud's phone and said, "Quick, let's take a look at this – then I must let Pierre know it's come in. It might be the missing video."

I knew that Bud had no idea what I meant, but it didn't matter. I clicked on the icon, and the little rectangle grew to fill the entire screen. Bud and I stared as Lucienne Durand sat beneath a shady tree, beside his bicycle, in his shirt sleeves, chatting happily with someone from whom he accepted…half a baguette.

Bud leaned in. "Who's that with him? Come on…turn to face the camera."

We watched. And watched.

I said, "Lucienne knows the person, is happy to – literally – break bread with them. Look – he's relaxed…this is someone he feels completely comfortable with. But that could be a man, or a woman – baggy clothing, a unisex hat on their head, not enough resolution to see their hands as they passed the baguette, which could help determine gender, and all we have is the view of their top half, from the back. And now Lucienne is moving away, on his bike, and they…rats – I wonder if they knew there was a camera there? But look, Bud, they're passing that window – might there be a useful reflection of their face, or even just of a side view of their face, here?"

Bud looked at me as though I'd lost my mind. "What ludicrous movies have you been watching? You know that sort of software is so expensive that it's really only available to the top international agencies. Trust me – I know how hard it is to get funds allocated to that sort of ID process and, even when you get a grainy shot, unless you already know the person, you'll never find them on any of those oh-so-handy global databases of photos of every single driver's license in the world."

I laughed aloud. "Oh Bud, I do love you. What I meant was that maybe you could play around with this image in case we recognized someone. Just a thought."

Bud's smile creased his face. "I see what you mean, and there is a reflection; how about I do a bit of grabbing, blowing up, then grabbing again until we – maybe – get…something?"

He snapped photos of the tablet with his phone as I kissed his cheek. "But I interrupted you, Husband – show me the photo of what you found upstairs."

Once again, Bud held out his phone: I was looking at a jumble of bits and pieces on top of a cabinet I knew I hadn't seen in the apartment. I asked, "Where was that?"

"Behind one of the lower racks of clothes which turned out to be a double rack. It was hidden, but not hidden-hidden. I reckon it was just a convenient spot to keep an old cabinet, and a pile of stuff Églantine didn't want cluttering up the place – though it was, generally speaking, nothing but clutter in there…even if the clothing was color-coded clutter."

I nodded. "Let's give this tablet back to Pierre, and I'll tell him he's got a video to watch, then I'll come upstairs with you. I'd like to see that for myself…it could turn out to be a treasure trove of clues about the woman."

Vingt-et-un

Pausing outside the loo, before getting into the elevator, I announced, "Bud, I'm just popping in here while I've got the chance."

"Good idea. I'm going to grab some coffee. Want one?"

I realized that my smoked duck salad was no more than a distant memory. "Yes, please – and if there's something I could graze on, I'd be grateful. I'm completely empty…well, you know what I mean."

"I do, and I will. Back soon."

The water shot out of the tap more quickly than I'd anticipated – it had barely dribbled when I'd moistened the loo paper earlier on – and I ended up having to hold my vivid orange shirt under the hand dryer, which was disguised by a fancy flip-down cover, painted with stylized lilies. My blouse was still patchy when I met Bud at the door to the elevator, where I noted he had four cardboard cups of coffee on a tray, and large, interesting bulges in each of his jacket pockets.

"Four coffees?"

"Me and you, Anne-Marie and the officer who's still up there with her, who oddly – or maybe not – is another Pierre."

"Very kind of you, Husband. And sweet or savory treats?" I asked as I summoned the elevator, pulled open the outer door, then the inner accordion gate.

"For you, Wife, both, of course. But we'll have to wait until we're in the apartment. And I suggest we eat on the balcony, because things are bound to get flakey, and crumbly, which isn't what Francine would want, I'm sure."

It was difficult for me to join Bud in the little cabin, so he had to hold the coffee tray up high to accommodate it, and us. I stared at the control panel. "Of course – we need a special key to be able to get up to the apartment. Oh bother – we'll have to walk up."

Bud winked. "No worries. Use my phone – it's in my right-hand pants pocket – and text the number for Anne-Marie that's in there. She'll call the elevator up to the top floor. I made an arrangement with her."

"Clever Husband." Unfortunately, I couldn't get a signal to be able to send a text while I was actually inside the elevator, so had to step out into the corridor to be able to do it, then I leaped back inside so that the thing would work when it was called.

Anne-Marie welcomed us by pulling open the door, while I grappled with the gate.

She grinned when she saw Bud. "Ah, coffee. You are my savior." She crossed herself, then giggled.

Bud handed around coffees, packets of sugar, and stir-sticks, and offered snacks. The other Pierre declined the snacks, but agreed that it made sense if the three of us took ours onto the balcony, to avoid messing up a crime scene, even though it had been cleared by forensics.

Once we stepped outside, away from the officer's presence, Anne-Marie switched into hostess mode, offering seats – several metal-framed chairs and tables were folded and hung on hooks along the roof wall itself – and then she magically produced cushions from a long box that sat against the low outer wall of the balcony, below the decorative balustrade. I made sure that I sat with my back to the railing, at an angle which allowed me to look out across the city, rather than down to the street.

Bud plonked the bags from his pockets onto the table. We had no plates, so he tore them open to reveal sugar-encrusted, swirling *palmiers*, quite a few tiny *madeleines* – with their signature shell-like pattern – and slices of something that looked like a cross between bread and cake, studded with what appeared to be bits of olive, cheese, and ham, or else nuts and bits of greenish…something.

Anne-Marie grinned and clapped her small hands. "It's like *le goûter*, but for adults," she said, referring to what I knew was the French term for a child's teatime snack.

Familiar with the tooth-achingly sweet *palmiers*, and the less dentally challenging *madeleines*, I asked, "What's that?"

Anne-Marie picked up a slice of the nutty version of the cakey-bread and said, "It's called *Cake Salé*. It's an unsweetened quick bread dough base that allows you to use up leftover bits of savory…anything, really. I make it often, because I hate waste. This will be good, though it's a shame there aren't any *macarons*. I like *macarons*, though I never make them – no patience – and they have become horribly expensive in the *patisseries*."

I tried the savory slice with the olives, and it was delicious, making me realize just how hungry I was. We all ate, and sipped our coffee, and allowed ourselves just a few moments to take in the sights and sounds around us; it felt wonderful to be outdoors, even if it was just for a little while. I happened to be looking toward the point of the building – getting much the same view as Églantine would have done from her bed – and reveled in the shift from Golden Hour to twilight, as the floodlights illuminating Napoleon III on top of his column kicked in, and the birds went berserk with their final feed of the day. As the light faded, I realized that – from this angle – I could also see the top of the Eiffel Tower, on the horizon. If it hadn't been for the specific circumstances, it would have been idyllic, and I was less surprised than I had been to know that Églantine had hardly ever felt the need to leave the Maison.

I could get used to this, was what I thought; "It's a beautiful evening," was what I said.

"Spring will soon be summer," said Anne-Marie wistfully. "The birds will nest, eggs will hatch, and the circle of life will begin again…for some, though not for all. I shall miss my old friend. Even if she was my employer, we were friends before that."

I tried to visualize Anne-Marie as a young nun, in her habit, and her face fitted that vision extremely well; unadorned, rounded – almost cherubic – and amazingly unlined, for her age.

As though she were reading my mind, she said quietly, "It is having a good soul and living a clean life that keeps me looking young, as I told Madame…Églantine." She chuckled. "Everywhere but here, at her apartment, she was Madame. Here? Always Églantine…so I shall continue that way. Églantine did not live a clean life when she was young, she told me – though in the past thirty years or so, her life was less…chaotic, I know. In my youth I lived a small, inward-looking life of study, reflection, prayer, and devotion. She – so she told me – lived life to the fullest. We agreed that we had each changed our path…for the better."

I dared, "Why did you leave the Order, Anne-Marie?"

The old woman set down her slice of cake and said, "That's a deceptively small question, which would require a…big answer."

Bud encouraged her. "We've all got coffee, and these treats…try us."

Anne-Marie's eyes darted between our faces, sharp and inquisitive. She picked up her coffee. "I didn't lose my faith in the Lord. However, my faith in the ability of human beings to live the life He wanted for us…wavered, when it came to light that some members of our Order – in a certain part of the world – had not been honest about the deaths of children born to unmarried mothers. It broke my heart, then…my faith in humanity, though never – as I said – in the Lord. I couldn't…be there any longer. Couldn't be proud to be associated with…any of that. I explained myself, and was allowed to leave."

I decided to focus on Anne-Marie's relationship with the dead woman. "And Églantine basically took you in, once you'd found her?"

"She was easy to find, once I read that article about the Maison, because, by then, she was so famous and successful…and my life was set because of her. I don't need much, but when you have nothing at all, even a little is a great deal. As she knew for herself. You see…we shared that – we had both left the same convent with, truly, absolutely nothing. She…they said she 'ran away', but I believed she was running toward the person she would become. I walked away…not knowing what would happen to me. She comforted me, found me a place to live, gave me work, and a way to make a living. That was all I needed."

I decided to challenge her. "And what did you give her?"

Anne-Marie smiled knowingly. "Ah, you seek the transactional element. Well, I dare say I gave her back a remembrance of how far she had come – from the girl with no name, and no possessions…to the woman who was leading the world with her wonderful designs. Though we never spoke, directly, of such things, she was herself in this. She was never haughty, but once she decided the way it had to be, she would not allow anyone to prevent her from having it so. It was this way for her designs, and for her home, and – eventually – for her life…though her idea of what the right way was for her life to be lived had changed over the years."

"How did she react when you told her that she had a child."

Anne-Marie's eyes darkened. "She was grateful that I had told her."

Bud asked, "Did she ever try to find her child – as far as you know?"

Anne-Marie put down her coffee. "As I told you, when I confessed to her that I knew she'd had a child, she seemed…at peace with the idea, in some way. I'm sorry, I cannot say if she ever looked for, or found, her child." Anne-Marie bowed her head and crossed herself.

A male or female, now sixty-four years of age – if their correct date of birth were used – and located 'somewhere in France'…possibly? How could Églantine have made any headway with such a dreadful lack of information?

Bud said, "I suppose that child would be Églantine's next of kin…might even stand to inherit her empire – if they knew she were their mother."

Anne-Marie gasped, "Oh, but that's not true. Well, it would be, except that we all know that Églantine has a will, and we all know what's in it. Her shares get divided between those who already have them – proportionately – and she told me she would leave me a little something too…though I don't know what. But, yes, if she didn't have a will, I suppose her child would be well off, though only if they sold the business. And what would it be worth without Églantine herself? I mean – she's the one who's always designed everything, though I know Jacques does some of that now. So…whoever owned it would have to sell the business – the name – and him. Can you sell a person like that? Or would you bring in someone new? It's…well, I never thought of it before."

I was impressed by the way Anne-Marie's quick mind had grasped the key elements of the situation, and looked at her with fresh eyes: a foundling, a nurses' aide, a nun, a cleaner, a good friend…and a woman with a truly sunny disposition. But she was more than that; she was razor sharp, valued the simple things in life, and she'd followed her conscience to leave the security of the only world she'd ever known, which must have taken a tremendous depth of commitment and grit…or disillusionment with her fellow Order members.

I decided that Anne-Marie Lefebvre would be someone I'd want on my side in any sort of undertaking, which led me to say,

"We believe that the murders of Lucienne and Gustav have flowed from the murder of Églantine – please help us to work out who killed her."

Anne-Marie rolled her shoulders. "I understand. When Bud told me, in deepest confidence, earlier on about this new death…I prayed, didn't I?" Bud nodded. "I knew Monsieur Gustav a little. I always knew when he'd been up here with Églantine because of his cigars. He was even sucking on one of those horrible things before eight in the morning when he was here last week. I couldn't believe it. He was in the salon, not even out on the terrace. Him being here threw out my whole schedule."

Bud asked, "So Gustav had some time alone with Églantine last week?"

Anne-Marie nodded. "It was Thursday, just gone. I arrived at eight and he was already here. I heard them shouting at each other when I got out of the elevator."

I tried to keep my excitement down to a dull roar when I asked, "Did you hear what they were shouting about?"

Anne-Marie tutted loudly. "It was all gibberish. He said she couldn't expose anyone, because it would ruin the family, and probably the business."

I checked, "Ruin 'the' family – meaning his own family?"

Anne-Marie looked puzzled, then said, "Oh yes – part of what he said was something like, umm…'but you can't know it's true, and if you tell anyone about it, you'll ruin my family, and probably the Maison…' That was it, essentially."

Bud asked, "And how did Églantine react?"

Anne-Marie nibbled her lip, then said, "Well, she's gone now, bless her soul, so I dare say it can't hurt to tell you. She said something like, 'I have a photograph that will prove it, and I've kept the secret long enough, Gustav. They deserve to know…' but I don't know who 'they' were, or are, because then they heard me – when the elevator door closed – and they stopped talking. When I walked into the room he was puffing away like a train and Églantine looked…so old. For the first time ever, I couldn't see the light in her eyes. That's a terrible thing…once that light goes, it's a bad sign. I saw it when I was working with patients in the Order. It's why…well, it's why I wasn't surprised to hear that she'd disappeared. I thought she might have just…gone. Though I do believe she had some faith left in her – whatever she might have said – so I never thought she'd take her own life, of course. But to be killed? It's too awful to think about. She must have been so scared at the end. And that shouldn't happen to anyone."

Bud and I exchanged a glance, and I said, "We both agree – it shouldn't. In fact, it's that belief that drives us to do all we can to speak up on behalf of victims of crime…especially those who can no longer speak for themselves, because someone's taken their life."

As the knowledge that so much tragedy had impacted so many over such a short time settled heavily upon us, we all sat quietly for a few moments, each of us contemplating our own, private thoughts.

Eventually, I said, "I wonder if you'd mind if I just went inside quickly to check on something Bud drew my attention to? Why don't you two hang on here – I won't be long."

I beetled off into the dressing room and carefully parted the clothing on a rack, above where Bud had left a pair of blue latex gloves on the floor as a signal for me. As I'd seen in the photos he'd shown me on his phone, a small – yet beautiful – cabinet sat almost entirely covered with bits and bobs, some of which appeared to be pieces of precious jewelry made with gold, silver, and gems, whereas others were no more than half-used match books, and there were even a few beer mats. Everything was coated with a film of dust, and I reckoned they'd been tucked away for quite some time – possibly forgotten about. *Mementos from Églantine's more reckless days?*

Underneath the layers of detritus there was an envelope – yellow and brittle with age. There was no name on it, and it had never been sealed…though there was something inside it. I opened it carefully and pulled out a piece of newspaper with no date. One side had a lot of personal ads on it – none of which were circled or marked in any way. Turning it over, it became obvious that the clipping had been taken because of a photo and its caption: it was the same photo I'd found in Lucienne's room, but this caption told me that I was looking at the winning shot in an amateur photography competition, over forty years ago. It was entitled "A Well-Earned Break", had been taken by a man named Henri Plank who lived in a northern suburb of Paris, and featured "Some of our well-trained soldiers taking the chance to enjoy a cool drink". He'd won a prize of fifty francs…and I felt as though I'd hit the jackpot.

I was tempted to rush out to Bud holding the clipping aloft, claiming that I'd found something fascinating in the pile he'd spotted in Églantine's dressing room, but I didn't want to air my thoughts in front of Anne-Marie, so I took a photo of what I believed to be Lucienne's face with my phone and blew it up. It wasn't as good a resolution as the original snap we'd found in Lucienne's room, because of the newsprint, but I was even more convinced that this was the man I'd only met in a bearded state…who now lay dead, in a morgue, somewhere in Paris.

I stuffed my phone into my pocket, then took a little more time to check around the dressing room, and allowed myself a few moments to pull out some of the garments I assumed Églantine had once worn. They were exquisite. As I studied the intricate patterns and felt the luxuriousness of the cloth through thin latex, I couldn't ignore the largely invisible details that were a part of the garments: richly embellished linings; buttonholes finished with gold or silver thread; clasps, buttons, and even zipper-pulls that were miniature works of art. It was clear that the type of garment created by a couture house was as far from the sort of thing I was wearing – a serviceable, if jolly, cotton shirt over a bouncy shell – as a normal vehicle on the road was from a Formula One car: two completely different sets of standards. And Églantine's obvious search for perfection had clearly been realized over and over again, judging by her collection.

That attention to detail, and the ability to follow that through, was also apparent in the fact that the woman had – unsurprisingly – taken good care of her clothes: everything was clean, and without creases; not only were the hangers padded, so that shoulders didn't mark, but sleeves were stuffed with tissue paper to ensure they didn't collapse; also, any item that could be, was buttoned to the collar. As I moved items, I realized that the dressing room was lined with cedar panels, and there were little cedar blocks hanging on the rails at intervals; I was familiar with those, because we have them at home, back in Canada – all you have to do is give them a light sanding every now and again to refresh the moth-repellent properties of the cedar wood.

One of the *armoires* beside the door was filled with hats of all shapes and styles; I've never had what's commonly referred to as a "hat head", though my sister can put on any sort of hat and look good in it, which is a bit annoying. I assumed that Églantine must have been blessed with a head like my sister's, and had made the most of it, by the looks of it.

The other *armoire* told me that the woman had also been blessed with normal-sized feet, not tiny ones like mine, though her shoes looked so exquisite that I wouldn't have been surprised if they'd all been handmade for her, so size would never have been an issue. They were made of some extraordinary fabrics, including velvet – and there were very few pairs of plain leather ones I noted. The shoes also confirmed for me that Églantine hadn't ever met an item of clothing that she didn't want to embellish – the buckles on some of them were extraordinarily beautiful.

The contents of the dressing room were so wonderful that I could have spent the next hour or so just admiring it all…but I knew I had to get on, and – other than the fact that Églantine George had been, unsurprisingly, blessed with amazing taste – I wasn't learning anything more about the woman. Just as my hand moved to turn out the lights, I realized how incredibly quiet the dressing room was. No noises from outside managed to get in there, and – when I exited and returned to the main salon – I realized that it, too, was incredibly quiet. I checked – yes, the same modern triple-glazed windows had been installed here as those I'd seen on the second floor. It made for a completely peaceful apartment, though I couldn't help but feel that it was just a bit too quiet.

I recalled that there hadn't been a TV, radio or, indeed, anything that looked to be a piece of modern technology, in the bedroom – which wasn't terribly surprising. Then I rationalized that the fact that I couldn't spot a television in the main room either was something that could be said of many elderly people who, clearly, enjoyed reading. But what about music?

Anne-Marie and Bud came in from the terrace, having stowed away all the furniture we'd used. Bud said, "It's getting a bit nippy out there now – and there's quite a breeze, being this high up."

Anne-Marie agreed. "Should we go back downstairs now? I've just been telling Bud that I can't spot that anything of Églantine's has been taken. Nothing. She knew all her books as though they were old friends, as do I. Ask her for something on almost any subject, and she'd have one."

I said, "I can see she had no television, but did Églantine listen to music at all? I haven't seen anything in the apartment that could play music."

Anne-Marie clapped her hands. "Oh she was so proud of that – she had a system put in a few years back that's completely invisible. Look – here in this bookcase, there's a hidden cupboard, and inside that is this tiny little thing – no more than a box, really. She had all her music put into it – digitally – and she had a tablet in a drawer in that table over there, that allowed her to play whatever she wanted. Let me show you."

Anne-Marie did, and I was impressed by the set up.

Bud asked, "So where are the speakers? Are they invisible too?"

Anne-Marie pointed to the cornice, which was as sinuously decorated as the rest of the apartment, and painted in several colors. "Along there – can you just make out those cross-hatched bits? Those are the speakers. All wireless. I know I told you that Églantine referred to her peonies as her indulgence – well, that was just one of them. This system was the other. She loved Ravel, Debussy, Saint-Saëns, Fauré, and Satie…we'd listen together, sometimes, though I admit I prefer religious works."

Why am I not surprised?

I looked at the electronic pad in the drawer that Anne-Marie had indicated. "Do you know how it works? I mean, could we find out what she was listening to last and – maybe even when that was?"

Anne-Marie took the tablet, woke it up, and swiped a few things. "At ten forty-three yesterday morning, she played this."

She swiped again and the entire room rang with clear, soothing piano music.

Anne-Marie smiled broadly. "I know it's not at all religious – because that poor man Debussy was a little obsessed with the way Pierrot yearned for Columbine – but I do love this piece.

We'd listen to it often. Églantine said it soothed her, and made her happy. We agreed it was the most perfect musical interpretation of moonlight ever created."

I couldn't resist. "There's a fair bit of research that suggests that listening to music you enjoy releases dopamine, which is a crucial neurotransmitter for humans' emotional and cognitive functioning. Though why a person specifically enjoys one piece or type of music more than another is – I believe – much more tied up with complex behavioral patterns, rather than simple chemistry. But it's always nice when the biochemists and neurologists come up with something useful, too."

Anne-Marie smiled awkwardly. "We thought it was a lovely short piece – just long enough for us to enjoy while she smoked a cigarette on the terrace. Oh Églantine…I shall miss her so much."

Anne-Marie began to cry again, so I reached out and held her; I felt it was the least I could do.

Vingt-deux

Bud leaned in and whispered, "Text from Pierre. Joanne's arrived. We should pop downstairs as soon as we can, he says. Well, Francine says."

I nodded, but continued to soothe poor Anne-Marie, who was clearly grieving the loss of her old friend quite bitterly. I couldn't help but wonder how she'd cope without the structure that cleaning Églantine's apartment had given her life. As her sobbing eased a little, I pulled back and said, "We should probably join the others as they arrive in the meeting room – but I know that Captain de Gaulle is keen that we don't let anyone know that Gustav is dead. Do you think you can manage that?"

Anne-Marie nodded dumbly.

She turned off the music and said, "I'll listen to that piece whenever I want to remember her."

I replied, "I hope it helps comfort you, and that you're able to smile about the remembrance of her soon."

Anne-Marie managed a wry chuckle. "Best I do – I'm no spring chicken."

My heart went out to her, but I knew that we needed to get going, so I called the elevator, while Bud headed down the stairs – and the other Pierre checked whether he was supposed to remain on guard at the apartment even if no one was there.

Inside the elevator – which proved to be a snugger fit than it had been when Bud and I had shared it – I pushed the button to take us to the second floor.

Anne-Marie was wiping her face when she said, "I've hardly ever been on the second, and now I get to wander in and out as I please. It's odd."

"Who cleans the other floors?" I thought I should check.

"A company sends people in overnight. On a contract basis, you know? But not at the weekend, of course."

Of course…so no contract cleaners to find a corpse sitting at its desk last night, was what I thought; "It makes sense," was what I said.

We discovered that Joanne had, indeed, arrived, and she was sitting at the meeting room's grand table alone – sipping coffee and nibbling a *madeleine*; we had no idea where Francine – or our Pierre – might have got to, so joined her. There was an amicable and mutual consolation about the loss of Églantine and Lucienne between Anne-Marie and Joanne, though it was clear the pair didn't know each other well. Within moments, Anne-Marie excused herself, and popped to the washroom; I wondered if she felt more comfortable using the "public" one on the second floor than she'd have felt using the bathroom in her late friend's apartment…or if she felt the need to get away from a woman about whose father she knew a terrible truth that she couldn't share.

Once we were alone with her, I dared to say to Joanne, "You didn't mix with Anne-Marie as much as you did with Lucienne when you were younger?"

Joanne gave me an upside-down smile. "No. I was aware of her, of course – always have been, since she arrived when I was about ten – but Lucienne was always there, right when I'd come into the place. And I was here a great deal, as I believe I mentioned. And not just when Avril thought I might blossom and be useful to her – before that, when I was really young. Being just across the road – and with Avril and Papa always coming here – I spent a lot of time playing in the reception area downstairs, or, when I was older, sitting in the little park outside, reading."

I asked, "How do you mean, you were 'across the road'?"

Joanne put down her coffee. "Oh, I don't live there any longer, of course, but when Avril and Papa were married, our family apartment was in the building across the road." She waved an arm toward the paneled wall behind her. "When they got divorced, Avril kept it, and Papa took a smaller apartment a couple of floors up – so that he and I could easily spend time with each other. I was away at school for most of the time, but I'd spend the holidays bouncing between their places. Papa kept his *pied-à-terre*, as he now calls it – which is handy if he needs to stay in the city – and he's always kept my room there for me. It's been mine since he bought the place and it's still full of stuff from when I was young, which amuses me when I stay there now, and he loves it, of course. I'll always be his little princess."

She sighed, and I felt her – as yet unknown – loss in my heart…though I hoped my expression didn't give anything away.

She continued, "Avril's turned what was once my room at her place into an extra dressing room for herself, so I could use the normal guest bedroom if I ever wanted to stay with her – not that I would, because I prefer to be with Papa. I have my own key to his place, whereas 'arrangements would have to be made' if I wanted to stay over at Avril's." She looked at her watch. "Given that she's – literally – only got to cross the road, where is Avril? She's habitually late for everything, and the captain said this was urgent. Papa might be stuck in traffic. I expect he went out to his country house last night – though I'd have thought his apartment would have been handier. But, no, he'd want to be with Sylvia – his wife. She's quite nice, and it's good to see him happy. They have a lovely home outside the city, and she's done a good job of making it welcoming for me, too, which is nice of her."

Hmm…that's two 'nice' comments about your mother's replacement; are you damning with faint praise?

Bud jumped in. "Do you live far away?"

Joanne did the weird smile thing again. "I live close to where I work, which…well, it's not the best area, as Papa keeps mentioning, but it means less time wasted trying to get from A to B. I'm on *Boulevard de Magenta*, not far from the *Gare du Nord*, and our laboratories are in a building close to the *Hôpital Lariboisière*, just a few streets away."

I asked, "Isn't that quite close to the *Gare d'Est*, too?"

Joanne shrugged. "Not so far – the stations are close to each other, though I rarely take the train. I prefer to walk, when I can, or cycle."

Another one taking their life in their hands, was what I thought; "So did you ever run into Lucienne socially? He lived out that way, too, I believe," was what I said.

Joanne looked…*wistful?* "I don't go out a great deal…not much of a mixer, I suppose. Though I do enjoy using Paris for the wealth of culture it offers, and that's something that a lot of people here do alone. Églantine and I used to listen to classical music together, when I was younger – though her taste ran to the romanticism of the turn of the last century, whereas I enjoy a wide range of music, from Bach to jazz. And I adore the theater. Paris has so many…from tiny performance spaces to the classic, large ones, and then there's the *Opéra Garnier* itself, of course. Avril took me there a lot when I was young – more to show herself off than to enjoy the performance, of course – but I got a lot out of that, in my own way."

Our little *tête-à-tête* for three was interrupted by the arrival of Jacques Novello, who swooshed through the double doors wearing cowboy boots made of purple python skin, a pair of jeans where tattered holes had been backed with a variety of velvet pieces, and sporting a shirt that used gold piping to emulate the look of a classic American Western shirt that, itself, was made of what appeared to be almost translucent blue silk.

All bold choices, Jacques…and you look amazing.

He hailed us with a booming, "What's going on here? I've had to prove my identity three times, and they won't let me go anywhere near my office. Do you know what's happening? Since I've been summoned here anyway, I wanted to collect some samples from there, but a nasty little policemen said that the fifth is off limits. I mean, why?"

Bud and I remained silent, and shrugged.

Jacques turned toward the sideboard, then Joanne. "Are you drinking the coffee from that? Is it any good?"

Joanne rolled her eyes. "No, but it's warm and wet, and the *Cake Salé* is excellent – I had a piece earlier – though the *madeleines* are dry…which they would be by this time of night. Where did they haul you in from? I was on my way to a comedy club over in the Second."

Jacques headed to the sideboard and sniffed inside the coffee pot, wrinkling his nose. "I was enjoying *apéro* at a friend's apartment and a few of us were going to go for American cheeseburgers for dinner – ironically, of course…hence this get-up. But now…well, here I am. If I'd known I wasn't going to be eating I'd have dug into the sausage, meats, and breads more deeply, because radish and cucumber *crudités* with an avocado dip might be good for my waistline, but they're not going to get me through to breakfast, are they?"

My tummy rumbled as I mentally ate my way across an entire table spread with imaginary *charcuterie* and *plats du fromage* – with a whole baguette to myself, of course – then I snapped back to reality, and stood to grab whatever I could to eat. Joanne might have judged the *madeleines* as being "dry", but – even if they were almost inedible – I'd dunk them in my tepid coffee, without caring about etiquette.

When I joined Jacques at the sideboard I said, "It's a shame your evening's been spoiled."

He looked me up and down as though I were one of the food items he was assessing then said, "Why are you two here again? You did leave, didn't you? I got the most dreadful telling off from that captain on the phone this morning for sneaking off last night, but we all agreed we were being of no use here whatsoever, and that if we all left…well, we'd dilute the trouble we'd get into."

I said, "The twins stayed."

Jacques rolled his shoulders. "They wouldn't say boo to a goose, those two. But Avril was correct – I've functioned much better today because I got a good night's sleep, and tomorrow's a Big Day. Or…well, do we have any news about what's happening at the exhibition? The last I heard was from Monica, late this morning."

I took my chance to ask, "Did she tell you about the discovery of Églantine's body?"

Jacques bit his lip. "Well, yes, that was the worst news of the day, of course." He looked a bit panicked, then added, "Please don't think I'm not devastated by her death – I am, and terribly worried, too. I mean – at least the place is surrounded by police officers, so I feel quite safe at the moment – but to think that you saw her…being strangled…through…there. Awful. And there we all were thinking she'd probably gone walkabout."

I added, "Or had been kidnapped."

Jacques relaxed, his hand on one hip. "Well, that was Avril's first thought…and I saw what she meant. And we'd all spent forever looking for Églantine, of course, so we knew she wasn't anywhere in the Maison, or the gardens, or even anywhere in the streets around here."

I knew I shouldn't reveal the fact that I'd had the chance to read what were, after all, supposed to be confidential police statements, so asked as innocently as I could, "You all…what, searched the whole place here, then some of you actually left the building to look for Églantine?"

Jacques nodded and started absently nibbling a piece of *palmier* he'd snapped off. "Oh yes – we were most diligent. I went with Joanne to check the garden, because she said that Églantine used to go there a lot. Look – I scratched my hand when I was beating one of the shrubs out there. We even beat the branches of the trees, in case she'd…I don't know…climbed up there somehow. It sounds rather silly now, but we were all so worried at the time."

I looked at the minute scratch that Jacques was showing me, then asked, "So other people searched here, while you searched outside?"

Jacques' expression told me he didn't fancy the *palmier* after all, and he dropped it. "We organized ourselves into teams, and tackled various areas. Joanne and I did the gardens, then the first floor. Though I did that alone, and quickly. It only took me about two minutes."

Joanne had obviously overheard our conversation, and called over, "More like ten…though, given the mess down there, Papa and I laughed about how relatively quickly you managed it. Papa said you're always telling him you know where to put your hands on anything there, exactly when you need it."

Knowing what Jacques had said in his statement, I asked, "It's just a storage area?"

Jacques did the hip thing again. "Well, it is…" He looked around, then leaned in and added quietly, "I didn't want Joanne in there with me, because I've got a bit of a secret project hatching, and I didn't want anyone to see it before the board meeting…not that that happened, of course, but you know what I mean."

I whispered back, "And what have you been up to, Jacques?"

Both Jacques and I jumped when a voice behind us said – too loudly, I felt, "Yes, tell us all what you've been up to – in secret – Jacques."

We turned to see Joanne hovering behind us; beyond her I could see Bud shaking his head helplessly.

She continued, "Have you been ordering up cheap velvet from new suppliers just so you can make some samples for a future ready-to-wear line, by any chance?"

Jacques gasped aloud. "How do you know about that? No one's supposed to know…Églantine made me promise. How on earth did you find out?"

Joanne adopted her now-familiar upside-down smiley face. "You know I work in textiles, Jacques. How many textile providers make velvet that's good enough that you'd consider using it, but cheap enough that you could afford to use it for off-the-rack stuff?"

Jacques rolled his eyes. "In this country – almost none…and Églantine wouldn't let me buy from anywhere else…or you. Oh, I see." It was clear that the penny had dropped. "It's a small world, and you all know each other, and someone told you – right?"

Joanne nodded. "I know I've been going back and forth about the ready-to-wear thing, but I thought you were dead set against it. What happened to change your mind?"

Jacques sighed. "It was Églantine herself. We had a long chat about how her career might have been different if she'd been young nowadays…and she helped me understand that the Maison could do both things well, and that I might enjoy it. And it has been a new challenge, I must admit. It's fun to deal with simpler shapes, to have to work out how to pare things down to the essentials, that'll have a broader appeal. And, as Églantine said, once things are simple, people can be encouraged to make them their own with all manner of add-ons…and that's where you can really indulge your creative side – and charge a lot, too. I openly admit that she was the one who suggested how I could incorporate simpler versions of our current line of couture accessories – scarves, wraps, kimonos, and so forth – with the standardized garments, and she even gave me several designs for new items in those ranges herself, challenging me to work out how they could be mass produced without compromising her vision. It's been – well, a breath of fresh air…though I've had to add it into my schedule of working with nit-picking clients, and that hasn't…gone down well with my partner."

I jumped in. "It sounds fascinating – I'd love to see what you've been working on. We couldn't nip down to the first floor now, could we, so I could have a quick look?"

Jacques put down the empty coffee cup he'd been holding, his eyes alight. "I don't see why not. Nothing's going to happen until that captain shows up – and your mother and father, Joanne. Oh…what are the twins wearing? And – more importantly – why?"

I turned to see that Monique and Monica had returned to the meeting room, and had changed their clothes. I assumed that everything they'd been wearing when they'd found Gustav's body had been taken away in evidence bags, but I could see why Jacques – and Joanne, by the look of it – would be puzzled by their appearance: it looked, for all the world, as though they were off to…the opera? Each was wearing a velvet tube – tight on both of them – and Monica was in teal, while Monique had opted for a deep burgundy. Each then had a matching crushed velvet shrug over their shoulders which fell in a waterfall tail down their back – Monica's was edged with silver, Monique's with gold – and yet their hair was still a bit messy. They were both barefoot.

Immediately they arrived, I saw their eyes dart toward Joanne, and both their faces lost all color; I realized I might help ease the situation – and keep the news of Gustav's death a secret for longer – by encouraging Joanne to join Jacques and me when we headed to the first floor.

I grabbed one of Jacques' arms, and one of Joanne's. "Come on – I bet you want to see what he's been up to, too, don't you,

Joanne? Let's all go together." I didn't exactly drag them to the door, but it wasn't far off. As we passed him, I said to Bud, "Maybe the twins would like some coffee? I'll be back…in a bit – let me know when Francine gets here." And we were gone.

Having crossed the landing on the first floor more times than I cared to recall, it was odd to finally stop there, outside the grandly carved, though somewhat squat, oak door. "Is it locked?"

Jacques produced a bunch of keys from his jeans' pocket with a flourish, and opened the door. "After you, ladies. The switch for the light's on the right."

I stepped into the doorway, reached to the right, and was immediately smacked in the face by a hand that shot out of the darkness. I reeled backwards, windmilling my arms at the shock of the attack. I must have stomped on Joanne's foot, because she screamed. I tried to turn away from what I sensed was another blow heading toward me, but managed to twist my ankle, then I felt my knee buckle beneath me…while Jacques was raising merry hell screaming "Police! Police!" as loudly as he could – which was extremely loudly.

Just as I was expecting my faceless adversary to lunge at me, or at least push me about as I lay, helpless, on the floor, I found myself surrounded by police officers with guns drawn, who leaped over me, and shouted their way into the darkness.

A moment later Bud was beside me. "Are you okay? What happened?"

I wasn't at all confused. Just sore. "Someone punched me in the face when I went inside there, then they hit out at me again, but I got a bit twisted around, and my knee went. I think I might have bumped into Joanne – is she okay?"

I looked across the landing, where Jacques was rubbing his elbow, and Joanne was twirling her foot. She said, "We're fine – but you went down heavily. Have you broken anything?"

Immediately I checked my wrist – the one I've already broken twice. That was fine. In fact, both my wrists and arms were okay, which I was pleased about, but there was something wrong with my left ankle.

The shouting inside the darkness stopped when someone flicked on the lights. Lying on the floor a few feet from me was a mannequin, with one detached arm beside it, and no head.

Oh, Cait – you complete idiot, you got smacked by a mannequin's arm, was what I thought; "If a few of you could help me up, please, that would be most helpful. I think I've sprained my ankle," was what I said.

Bud's face clouded with concern as he and two officers helped me up. They backed off as Bud encouraged me gently. "See if you can put any weight on it, Cait…but carefully. Take your time. There's no rush."

I tried. "That hurts. A lot."

Bud stroked my back. "I hope you haven't broken it."

Bravado kicked in as I said, "No, I'm sure it's just sprained – though if I could put it up, and get some ice on it, I think that might be a good idea."

Bud grabbed me under my armpits. "Can you make it to the elevator, if I support you here?"

"Hang on a minute," I countered, "I'm not going through all this to not see the inside of this place."

I heard Bud tut, and he said, "If Jacques would be so kind to lead the way then, and I'll help you hobble. Jacques? In you go."

Jacques and Joanne gave me a wide berth as they passed me. I thanked Bud for his support – both literally, and figuratively – and he tutted at me again, which I hoped was as scathing as he'd get.

Once inside I expressed admiration for the range of what appeared to be simple shift, jewel-toned dresses of different lengths, with straight or differing depths of V-shaped necklines, that hung on the rack in front of me. I concluded with: "I wish I could wear something like that, but I just won't let my bra straps show."

Jacques stared at me, then stared at the dresses. He whined a little when he said, "But if I add more than just the spaghetti straps the cutting and cloth costs go through the roof – and the finishing costs for a rounded neck are ruinous."

I replied, "Well, why not just add thicker, straight straps – that would solve my problem with them…and I bet it would broaden their appeal. There aren't a lot of women over a certain age who like to show their bra straps – and why limit yourself to those who either don't need a bra, or are too young to care that their straps are on display?"

Joanne grinned. "She's got a point, Jacques, and straight, wide straps would do it. I bet you could run up a few samples like that. By the way – who's been doing your cutting and sewing?"

Jacques said, "I did all the patternmaking and cutting myself – that's where I started, you know. But the sewing? Well, don't tell the twins, because they think she's grieving the loss of a loved one down in the south of France, but I convinced Leonora – from our *atelier* – to take a couple of weeks off and do it for me. I'm paying her, of course…but Églantine was passing the money to me to be able to do it."

I said, "They look…so lightweight, and yet that's not velour, is it – it's really velvet?"

Jacques beamed. "I worked with the manufacturer to create that. Joanne will know all about it, but you have to understand the way velvet is made. It's a complicated process, which is done on a double loom, because velvet starts out as two layers of cloth being woven at once, then the loop of the weave is sliced through, giving you the pile. By reformulating the underlying 'fabric' part, and cutting the pile close, we can create much more flexible and 'thinner' velvets, as you see here…incorporating the better properties available from velour. However, velour itself is an inferior material – it's created as one piece of fabric, in a pile-knit format, not at all like real velvet. Nowadays, there are new types of mixture threads we can use for weaving real velvet – double fabric velvet. Traditionally, all our velvets at the Maison have been silk-based…but now? The sky's the limit. And with all the new printing technology? Well, there are so many possibilities, either for pattern, or for *devoré*…though we've had to do a great deal of work reformulating the acids to burn through the newly devised top layers."

Jacques disappeared through the rack of dresses, then emerged with a piece of fabric in his hand that looked like a high-quality reproduction of the well-known Klimt portrait of Emilie Flöge…on velvet. He beamed. "This is just a sample – imagine what we could do with our own designs! Here's one dress where we've used the new fabric and the new acids. Églantine was incredibly excited about the opportunities."

Joanne spoke quietly, nodding. "I can see why she would have been. I'd be interested to see the specifications…especially of the acids you've used to create that *devoré*. Fascinating."

Jacques grabbed the dress away from Joanne's fingers. "Oh no – that's a secret. For now."

So many things are, was what I thought; "May I feel it?" was what I said.

Jacques held out the dress, and I stepped forward to touch it. Bud's grip loosened a little to allow me to reach, just as I lost my footing with my good leg…and I slithered – almost elegantly – to the floor. Again.

Bud all but snatched me up to my feet, "Good grief, Cait – are you okay? What happened?"

I explained, "I stepped onto something that…rolled under my foot. Like a pebble, or a rock – which makes no sense."

Bud looked at me in disbelief.

I could hear myself whining as I replied, "Honestly, I did." I bent down, as best I could, and started pushing away the dresses that skimmed the floor, trying to find whatever had caught me out this second time. "Look – there!"

Glowing in the dimness of the shadow being cast by the crosspiece at the bottom of the clothes rack was an oval-shaped stone, that was translucent – and amber.

I said, "I think that might have come from Églantine's famous amber collar."

Before I could say anything else, Jacques had bent down and picked up the stone.

I squealed, "Put it down – that's evidence."

Jacques stood there looking at the stone in his hand. "You just stepped on it, and we don't even know where it started out, only where it ended up. But how did it get here? When did it get here? If it's from Églantine's necklace – and it really looks like it is – does that mean she was killed…in here? But no – you said you saw her being strangled upstairs, Cait – then she was found at the exhibition. And yet this is…here. What does it mean?"

Jacques thrashed at the dresses on his rail and pointed. "Look – there's another stone, and another…they're all over the place. Oh – and what's that doing there? That's – oh my word, that's one of the pieces that should have gone to the exhibition."

I followed his gaze: a mound of crumpled, dark velvet, dotted with gleaming pearls, lay in a heap in a corner. When the twins had described the significant "One Night in Luxor" gown it had sounded entrancing – now it was no more than a messy ball in a dusty corner of a storage room.

Jacques leaped forward and grabbed the gown before Bud could get to him. "I must save it…oh no…will it ever be the same again?"

Bud shouted, "Drop it."

Both Jacques and Joanne jumped, and I was a bit taken aback: Bud rarely raises his voice, though I understood why he'd done it.

Jacques squealed, "But…but it's precious."

That's a bit Gollum-like, was what I thought; "It's also evidence," was what I said.

Bud took a deep breath, then used his calming voice when he said, "Cait's right…the amber stones from Églantine's necklace, and even that gown itself, could be vital to the investigation. Please just drop the dress, Jacques. We all need to get out of here and allow Francine and her forensics team to get to work. Who knows, they might even take up residence. Give me that original stone, Jacques, thank you, and I'm going to get Cait to the elevator while you both go up and tell Francine – Captain de Gaulle – that I need to speak to her when I get there."

I said, "I tell you what, Bud, you go on and do that, and I'll let Jacques and Joanne help me up the stairs. It's twice as far to walk to and from the elevator, and I'm sure if I take the stairs one at a time, I'll be fine. It's just a sprain."

Joanne jumped in. "Cait's right, we can help her, and we'll find some ice, and something to put it in, and we'll sort out a chair for her to put her foot on when we get up there."

Bud looked at me with love and concern in his eyes. "That's the same ankle you sprained when you broke your wrist in Kelowna, isn't it?" I nodded. "And that was the same wrist you'd broken in Nice, wasn't it?" I nodded again. "Not sure I should let you leave the house. Alright then, I agree." He kissed my forehead. "Take your time? I'll brief Francine." He turned to Jacques and Joanne. "Please take care of her." They nodded, both looking quite serious, then he left us.

I allowed myself to be supported by Joanne on one side, and Jacques on the other. I could feel my ankle getting hot, and thumping with pain, and every time I tried to put weight on my foot, I wanted to groan…but I didn't. The yards of marble that led to the foot of the stairs felt like half a mile, and yet I didn't dare stop until I had the balustrade to lean on, which I did as soon as I got there, releasing Joanne from her task.

She offered, "Let my carry your bag, Cait – it looks heavy."

I thanked her, extricated myself from it, then had a thought. "Hang on, let me pop my phone in there." When I pulled my phone out of my pocket, I thought I'd better check for messages, so I put in my code, and the photograph I'd taken of Églantine's newspaper clipping showing the young Lucienne appeared.

Joanne exclaimed, "Why do you have a photograph of my grandfather on your phone?"

We both stared at the picture. I said, "That isn't your grandfather."

She said, "I know my own grandfather, even if he is young in that picture. Is it from a newspaper? How did you get it?"

Joanne's grandfather? was what I thought; "You're sure?" was what I said.

"Yes. That's Avril's father. Dead now, and I never met him. But she had an album with pictures of her parents…and she's got loads of him all around her apartment. That was him – though he was a lot older than that, even when Avril was born."

I held onto the balustrade…for so many reasons. I knew that, in the moment, a response was needed, so I said, "It's from a newspaper clipping I came across." I tried to sound as vague as possible. "I wanted to ask Avril about it, but do you happen to know what your grandfather's name was?"

"He was Norman Tambour. Why?"

"Oh nothing…just curious, you know?"

Joanne frowned. "Me too – about that photo. But, come on…let's get you up these steps now."

Jacques asked, "Ready to start again?"

I was: I wanted to get to Bud as quickly as I could.

Vingt-trois

When the three of us arrived at the meeting room, everyone was there – including Avril, who I assumed had entered using the elevator while we'd all been on the stairs. On this occasion she'd decided to present herself in deepest black velvet, and had also managed to make herself look as though she were about to attend opening night at the theater, rather than a solemn occasion where she was about to be told that her ex-husband had died…though she didn't know that bit, of course.

While I explained to everyone what had happened to my ankle, making myself feel like an idiot all over again, Joanne helped me onto a chair and got another under my foot – Jacques had disappeared – and Bud placed a zipped plastic bag he'd filled with ice onto the lovely big lump which had now developed where I should have been able to see my ankle bone.

Wonderful.

"I'll keep an eye on you, Wife," he said, with feeling.

I kissed him on the cheek and whispered, "Could you sit opposite me, and watch anyone I might not be able to see?"

Bud shook his head. "Nope, not leaving you."

I sighed. "Look, I'm sitting down now, and I promise not to move…but – if things go the way I think they will – I'll want your input on how people react to…certain things. Please?"

Bud relented. "Okay, I get it, but I don't like it."

He skulked around the table and took a seat, which meant I only had to look up to see him…staring at me.

Joanne observed, "So you've graced us with your presence, Avril. How delightful. But I'd suggest that wearing much black's a bit over the top…even given the fact we're all here to acknowledge that we've lost both Églantine and Lucienne."

Avril bridled. "There's no such thing as too much black when you're in mourning, and we all are. Why you'd choose to come here wearing that get-up is the real mystery. Haven't you got something more suitable in your…meager array of clothing?"

Avril's acid tone made my toes curl: in the manner typical of narcissists – because that she most certainly was – Avril had managed to suggest that her daughter should feel guilty that she hadn't met an obligation to literally wear a physical display of her loss. I felt sorry for Joanne; I reckoned it must have been a huge challenge to have grown up in Avril's presence without becoming warped. Joanne didn't give off an aura of bitterness; she was clearly a woman driven by her professional focus and personal interests, which seemed to be many, and varied – relatively well balanced, then, given her mother's nature.

As if I'd needed more evidence that Joanne had – at least by this stage in her life – developed a way to manage her mother, she said, "I have no idea why you try to guilt me into doing things that you try to make me believe I should be doing – you know it doesn't work. You certainly can't threaten to take away my toys or stop me seeing my friends if I don't do as you say any longer…so you really have no leverage over me these days, Avril. And I was on my way out this evening, but rushed here immediately after I was called, hence my casual clothing. Jeans, a sweater, and a jacket are not the choice of the underclass these days, Avril. Not all of us took, literally, hours to decide what to wear…then, I dare say, you probably primped and preened in front of those massive mirrors you have all over that apartment of yours. At least we're all here now so we can start…whatever it is. Oh no…where's Papa? Is he here yet?"

As we all looked toward the double doors, Jacques ambled in looking bemused, followed by Pierre, then Francine, who stood at the end of the table and patted the air. Everyone who was standing, sat, and those who were fussing about, became still.

When she had everyone's attention, Captain de Gaulle said, "Thank you all for being here. You're all aware of the tragic circumstances which have prefaced us meeting tonight. I also know you've all lost people who meant a great deal to you. Let's have a moment of silence for Églantine George and Lucienne Durand, during which we can consider their lives, and our relationships with them." She closed her eyes, bowed her head, and clasped her hands together.

A few expressions of surprise flitted around the table, then there was absolute silence. Although an odd tactic, it proved effective: when everyone opened their eyes, and looked around, it was as though they'd taken the chance to truly focus on the matters at hand…and I suspected that was exactly what Francine had wanted.

She continued. "Thank you. It's never a bad thing to show our respect for the departed." Nods all around. "However, as you know, I am here to work out how these people met their deaths. I know you've all been able to help myself and my team to put together a full picture of everyone's movements over the past thirty-six hours – but I do have a few more questions. I've spoken to everyone who left here last night – in general terms, of course."

You've told them off for leaving, Francine – that's what you've done.

She continued, "Now I need to ask about what you did when you left here last night. Joanne?"

Joanne jumped. "I went home, to my apartment."

Francine asked, "Can anyone verify that?"

Joanne looked cautious. "You know I live alone, so, no. Sorry. I just…went home, and went to bed. I was tired…and upset about Lucienne, and…well, at that stage, I was still worried about Églantine being…missing."

Francine pressed. "And how did you get home?"

"I cycled. I'd come on my bike, so rode it home."

Francine sat. "Thank you. Jacques – same question for you. Where did you go when you left here last night."

Jacques' neck flushed. "Same answer – home. My other half's away for the weekend – but I used a ride-share app which'll tell you what time I got to my apartment."

Francine turned to the twins, who – unsurprisingly – chorused, "Home."

Monica added, "As you know, we share an apartment. We walked – it's just a few streets away, beyond the gardens. We needed…well, we both felt we needed the fresh air, didn't we?"

Monique nodded. "We did. But I don't think we saw anyone when we were walking, did we?"

Monica looked, and sounded, disappointed when she said, "No one I recall. But…our building has security cameras – you could check those." She appeared pleased with herself, and her sister patted her hand.

Bud said, "One of your officers kindly drove Cait and myself to our hotel, where we chatted with a receptionist named Dave, who works the late shift, I believe. We're at The Luxsey, as you know."

Joanne and Jacques both turned and stared at us, then at each other…and shared a half-smile that made their nostrils flare; I didn't know why.

Francine nodded her thanks at Bud, then turned to Anne-Marie and said, "And what of your evening, and night, Anne-Marie?"

The cleaner looked surprised. "Me? Well, I left yesterday morning – as you know. I was at home, with Guillermo, all afternoon and evening, then went to bed and slept all night, until I went to Mass this morning. And, no, no one can vouch for me, and I certainly don't live in the sort of building that has cameras."

Finally, Francine turned to Avril. "And you?"

Avril sat upright, ready to become the center of attention. "I dare say I shall sound like a broken record, but I went to my apartment, went to bed, and no one else was there."

Francine sighed. "As I thought."

I looked at the people sitting around the table, and did my best to spot…anything. There were the "obvious" patterns: Monica and Monique, Jacques and Joanne, Anne-Marie and Avril – initials of names, that was one; two sisters, a mother and daughter, but no family relationship between the cleaner and the designer, so nothing there; of course, there was the fact that everyone – with the exception of Jacques – had known Églantine and Lucienne for decades, but that led me nowhere.

I'm missing…something.

Francine stood, smoothed down her suit jacket over her waistcoat, and I suspected I knew what was coming next.

So this is how you're going to play it? Get ready, Cait – scan, encode, scan, encode…this will be important.

I looked over at Bud, and he returned my gaze. He'd worked it out, too; he was ready.

Having cleared her throat, Francine said, "I'm afraid I have some…solemn news for you all."

Monica and Monique grab a hand each on the table; they know what's coming. Both of them nibble the right corner of their bottom lip, simultaneously.

Anne-Marie leans forward, her shoulders droop – she also knows what's coming.

Jacques and Joanne exchange a glance – wide-eyed, puzzled, worried.

Avril rolls her shoulders, and leans forward, cupping her chin in one elegant hand, her black velvet gloved elbow resting lightly on the table.

Francine spoke gravely. "The body of Gustav Sutter was found in his office earlier today. We believe he was killed in the early hours of the morning."

I studied Joanne, Avril, and Jacques.

Joanne's brow furrows. "Papa? What?" She stares at Francine as though the captain has lost her mind.

Jacques' face breaks into a smile, as if to laugh off a joke…then freezes, and falls into an expression of horror.

Avril removes her hand from beneath her chin, and it slowly moves to cover her mouth which is shifting to make an O shape…then she's mouthing, "No," which she finally shouts aloud.

Beside me I hear a sigh — Anne-Marie is relieved that the news is out.

Francine's been watching everyone too, and our eyes meet for a second, then our gazes sweep past each other.

Joanne managed to croak, "You're telling me that my father is dead? Like this? Here — with all these people?"

Francine's tone softened. "I'm so terribly sorry, Joanne. But, at least your mother and you can support each other through this. Would you like some time alone? Ladies and gentlemen, let's give these ladies the room, shall we?" She looked at my foot – ice pack and all – and added, "Maybe it would be better if the two of you were to accompany me into the anteroom – I can give you all the information I have…privately."

Joanne leaped from her seat. "You did it this way so you could see how we all reacted. Do you think someone in this room killed my father? Is that it? Do you think I've done it? Or that my mother has? We're not rats in a laboratory, for you to experiment upon, you know! We're human beings…and I've lost…oh, I've lost everything that matters to me. Papa…oh Papa." The dead man's daughter buried her face in her hands as though she were ten years old, while Avril sat rigidly in her seat, fanning her face with her gloved hand, and gasping for air like a fish flopping about on the beach.

Francine barked, "Bertrand, immediately organize water for Mademoiselles Avril and Joanne in the anteroom, and make sure there are at least three chairs in there for us. Everyone else, let's take a little break, shall we? Under no circumstances is anyone to leave the building. I trust that on this occasion I've made myself absolutely clear on that point."

Having given all those sitting at the table her death stare, Francine moved to support Joanne and helped her toward the doors to the anteroom; Avril, realizing she'd have to make her own way there, did so tottering with grief and crying real tears. As I watched the mother and daughter leave the meeting room, I contemplated how sometimes backbiting and baiting can signify a strong bond.

Maybe Avril still had feelings for Gustav, despite their public tantrums?

Once the trio had left, Monica said, "Oh, I'm so glad that's out in the open. Not glad that it's happened, of course, but…well, I'm just not terribly good at keeping secrets."

Jacques squeaked, "You knew about this?"

Almost proudly, the twins chorused, "We found him."

Jacques clutched his chest then said, "How? I mean what…um…how did he die?"

As Monica began to describe what she and her sister had discovered, I pulled my phone out of my bag, did a quick bit of Googling, then motioned to Bud, who nipped around the table to my side. "What can I do for you, Wife?"

"Well, you can get me up, and help me to the washroom, first, and on the way there, you can tell me your impressions of the reactions to the news of Gustav's death, and fill me in on anything you managed to get out of Francine while you were alone with her."

He nodded and helped me to my feet, which was when I realized that – despite being almost numb thanks to the effects of the ice – my ankle was incredibly weak.

My husband knew me well. "That's not good, is it?"

I sighed. "It'll be fine. A bit of strapping, a good night's sleep, and I'll be right as rain. Now – come on – tell me what you saw, and what you've learned."

As I limped along, Bud spoke softly, and with urgency. "Okay – it seems that a huge amount of information is pouring in to Francine, which I'd expect at this point in the case. Here goes with the highlights, ready? I gave Francine the amber stone you found, and we agreed it would be a ridiculous coincidence if it, and the others we saw on the floor, weren't from Églantine's missing collar – which was definitely not found in the crate beneath her body, by the way. The laminated photograph we found in Lucienne's sofa? Her team has confirmed it was in fact Lucienne in the shot. Records showed he was in…oh, no – sometimes I wish I had your memory, Cait, or that I'd had time to take a note…I can't recall what part of the army she said he was in, and it doesn't matter, really, but Lucienne's service records tallied with the uniforms in the photo, so we definitely know it was him. Next, the knife used to kill Gustav, that I spotted on the floor in his office? Identified by the twins as an old leather-cutting knife he used as a letter opener, usually found on his desk. So, not brought to the scene by his killer. Oh – interestingly, Pierre texted me that he took Jacques up to his office to see what might have been stolen when it was ransacked – and Jacques confirmed that his office hasn't been touched, that it always looks like that."

I chuckled. "See, it's not just me who keeps a messy workspace, as I'm always telling you. I have a creative mind, in some ways, and Jacques is a true creative type. I'm glad you told me that, because the search of his office didn't fit with my overall view of the case – thanks."

Bud shrugged. "If he's played any part in all this, he could be lying…it might have been searched and he's covering for someone."

"Exactly – I knew you'd see that, Husband."

Bud took his win, and continued, "As for making any headway with identifying the person who was with Lucienne in the street, no luck there – on my part, nor on Francine's. The reflection you and I saw on that camera feed was too pixelated for me to make sense of it…it was barely a face at all, though Francine did say that she has a technical team using all their tools to try to clean it up, which might help if the face belongs to someone known within the investigation. What else? Oh yes – the post-mortem's been done on Églantine. Yes to strangulation, no to any defensive wounds – except for a few bruises on the tops of both her arms…so maybe an initial struggle, or power-move. Interestingly, the woman had not only had a complete hysterectomy, but she was also now suffering from Parkinson's disease. Her records show she'd consulted two different specialists who'd each confirmed the diagnosis, but there's no record of her receiving any treatment."

I said, "Ah, the hysterectomy explains a lot, and I'm not surprised about the Parkinson's…though it might have been a host of other types of disease. Thanks, Bud."

Bud shook his head and said, "No, of course none of that's a surprise – to you."

"Did Francine say anything about having looked into Églantine's will? It's not something she's mentioned to us, but I know we talked about 'who benefits'."

Bud smiled. "Yes, she mentioned that, but only in terms of how frustrating she was finding the process to discover Églantine's intentions – on a Sunday, when lawyers are not, apparently, keen to respond to any form of communication."

I nodded. "Okay, well…I'll give that one some thought, and maybe she'll be able to furnish us with some useful information before this whole thing gets…well, never mind. What next?"

Bud replied, "Finally, the reactions I saw to the news of Gustav's death? I'd say that Jacques looked suitably shocked, Avril was crying real tears, and Joanne seemed genuinely overwhelmed. The twins and Anne-Marie already knew –

though the twins both smiled when Francine announced it, which I took to be a sign of relief on their part."

"Excellent report, Husband." We'd reached the washroom. "Look…I need to do my thing for a bit – but I also need you to ask Francine if she could get all the pieces of physical evidence – all securely bagged, of course – to be available in the meeting room. Maybe you, as a retired officer, could suggest that to her? Everything I'll want to refer to will still be here at the Maison, I'm sure, because heaven knows the forensics people haven't had a chance to leave yet. They can stand guard over it all, if Francine wants – I just want items to be on hand, in case they need to be checked, or verified. Also…ask Francine to look into missing girls, aged around fourteen or fifteen, in this vicinity, about sixty-five years ago." I opened the map I'd pulled up on my phone, Googling, and pointed to the area I meant.

"Églantine's from that area, you reckon?"

"I do – and I just hope police records can prove it."

Bud smiled. "I'll do my best." He mugged a salute. "Are you going to do your wakeful dreaming thing?" I nodded. "Well, enjoy your trip to the place where that enormous brain of yours gets to roam free, and I'll do what I can at my end of things. But, listen – don't try to hobble back on your own – wait until I come to get you. I'll knock three times and ask for Madame Anderson, just so you know it's me, okay?"

We kissed, and he left. I locked the washroom door, took the only seat available, and started to hum: by allowing myself to enter a state of wakeful dreaming, my mind can make free associations between each stimulus I've experienced, without my logic or attitudes or judgement kicking in. It's sometimes the only way I can see the truth of a matter…I seem to be able to find the connections between that which feels nonsensical, in a way…and humming helps me do it.

Vingt-quatre

I'm not surprised that the first thing I realize is that I'm waiting for a fashion show to begin, which is being held in the circular garden outside *Maison Églantine*. The figures of the Three Fates on the fountain are alive, and are spinning green thread, passing it between them, then cutting it…and cackling as they do it…while I'm walking around them on a pathway where the cobbles are made of amber stones. Peacocks are flying through the air, each of them with a large peony in its beak, then they drop the flowers…and I'm being showered with acid, which burns my skin, so I run to hide beneath trees which morph from being a horse chestnut copse, to an evergreen forest.

I realize my feet are sore, but I can't see them…they've been replaced by baguettes which I try to kick away from myself because I know they are poisonous, but I fall…and fall…until Bud catches me. But he's not Bud, he's Gustav, and I'm a young version of Joanne and we dance around the amber path, humming "Clair de Lune" to each other…until I, as Joanne, realize it's Avril's face I can see on each of the figures of the Three Fates, and they're screaming as they each now wield a massive pair of shears, with which they cut the very air around us all, and I tumble through the slices in reality…and fall…and fall…until I hit the ground.

Now I'm myself again, and everything around me is black. I reach out my hands and know I'm trapped inside a velvet box. I push against the blackness, but nothing happens. I see a hole in the blackness…no, it's a ball made of glowing amber, and it's growing – it's heading toward me, then it smacks me in the face and I fall…and fall…until I'm in the anteroom, sitting in the chair where I saw a woman being strangled, but I'm the one being strangled. I'm not afraid. I don't fight my assailant…indeed, other than a pair of disembodied hands there isn't one…but there is a sound…of someone sweeping with a broom. Then a bell chimes – calling children to class – and I'm being not only strangled but also beaten about the head with a giant laminated photo by another pair of disembodied hands.

I leap out of the chair, and find myself standing on the table in the boardroom of the Maison. All the seats around me are occupied by mannequins, all wearing false beards, all wearing amber collars, and all swathed in *devoré* velvet. I have a bucket full of lurid green liquid in one hand and a ladle in the other. I splash a ladleful of the green dye onto one of the mannequins, and it screams from unmoving lips, "She loved me," then it begins to dissolve. I know instinctively that the liquid in the bucket is the acid that will reveal the truth…so I throw another ladle onto another mannequin, which screams, "I love her so much," then dissolves. I'm excited by this revelation, but don't know why. The next mannequin doesn't scream or dissolve – it leaps from its chair and joins me on the table and mocks me by mirroring my dismay and shock, then it matches me move for move as I try to fight it away from me, and off the table…but I'm the one who falls…and falls…until I discover I'm in a wooden boat, sailing over a sea made of duvets toward a woman who looks like Audrey Hepburn, but has the voice of Edith Piaf when she sings "Frère Jacques" at me…loudly and with great passion. I turn – knowing there's someone behind me – and see Lucienne, wearing his top hat…and he's holding a tiger by the tail and laughing, his rotten teeth exploding from his mouth to shoot toward me, piercing my flesh as I sail away.

I leap out of the boat to save myself…and fall…and fall…until I am in the reception area of the Maison surrounded by men with beards, in overalls, with army jackets over them, wearing top hats, and dancing the can-can while they hold trays of food above their heads, which falls, and burns like acid, so I run to a door that has opened in the side of the Maison, like the entire side of a dollhouse opening up, and I'm in the *Petit Palais*, hanging from the ceiling by one hand while the Martin twins twirl and pirouette below me, wearing magnificent gowns that I know are made entirely from amber beads…which then explode, the beads cascading around the two women, engulfing them until they disappear, then I see an arm stretch up from the surging waves of amber and I know it's Églantine herself, coming to save me…but I fall…and fall…until I land in a massive container of what I know is acid so, though I can't swim, I do swim, and I see a tiny version of Joanne bobbing about…and no matter how fast I swim toward her, she's always out of reach. She's holding up a long test tube that I know mustn't touch the acid, then she throws it to me to keep it safe, but I can't catch it. She disappears beneath the waves, and is replaced by her father, who cries so much that the level of the acid rises until I can step out of the container, which I can now see is so small that I can hold it in my hand.

I look into the container, and there I see Jacques, and Monica, and Monique, and Joanne, and Avril, and Églantine, and Lucienne, and Gustav, and Anne-Marie all splashing about and laughing…they're all so happy, so joyous…then Églantine grows and grows until she absorbs everybody, one-by-one…except for Lucienne, who she puts into one of the hundreds of pockets she has on the front of her velvet gown then she steps out, and kisses me on the neck with her cold, dead, pink lips…a kiss that rips painfully through my flesh…as she cackles, "The truth will burn, but it must be told".

I opened my eyes and found that I was holding my neck, and crying…then gathered myself and began to think through what I'd learned. There was a knock at the door.

Vingt-cinq

I called out, "Just a second," then took a moment to check how I looked in the mirror: passable, considering the day I'd had. I unlocked the washroom door, and Bud almost fell into my arms, which I wasn't expecting. I staggered backward – which put pressure on my ankle that I, frankly, didn't need.

As I let out an agonized yell, thankfully, Bud grabbed me tight, managed to stop me falling – again – and got me stable…on two feet-ish.

He peered at me with a look of utter disbelief on his face. "Good grief – are you okay? You don't look…right."

I pulled back, and stood as upright as my ankle would allow. "Thanks…in what way?"

"Well, I know you always look a bit dazed when you've been doing that wakeful dreaming thing – which is what I assume you did?" I nodded. "Right. But you look…a bit more out of it than usual, to be honest."

"Oh Husband…I'm tired, my ankle hurts, the last proper food I had was that lovely lunch opposite the opera – which was a heck of a long time ago – and, let's be honest, it's been a grueling couple of days, following on from an exhausting six weeks of preparation, then teaching. I'm just…worn out, I suppose…a bit ground down. But I really do think I understand what's happened, and why…and how – which is good. And all I have to do now is to push on for a little longer, right?"

Bud was already steering me along the corridor when he said, "I'm not so sure things are going to work out the way you'd like them to, Cait. When I managed to have a quiet word with

Francine, she did agree to take on board your requests, but she cut down any idea of you having a chance to ask questions in there. I know she's worked way outside her normal professional parameters by letting us be involved, but I don't think that you doing what you normally do is going to be…allowed."

I paused. "But I could really help her, Bud. I think I've worked it all out – and…well, it's not good, of course – but it fits all the facts, as I know them…and the psychological angles are all lined up."

Bud hugged me. "One of the things I love about you is that you always want to put right that which you can see is wrong, that you always want to fix what's broken. And murder is a situation where the most important thing that can go wrong has already happened – someone's life has been taken. I know that you and I both understand – only too well – that that's not something that can be 'fixed', but it is something that the right person, or people, should have to answer for. You know I support you one hundred percent when you need a bit of help to find out what happened, and then to bring that truth into the light. But, on this occasion, the local authorities – represented by Francine – have a job to do. And they're doing it."

I pounced. "But they're not doing a particularly good job of it, are they, Bud? And that's because their procedures – even if Francine has bent them a bit so we can be included – aren't going to be able to pull together all the facts in the way I have."

The expression on Bud's face told me, before I turned, that Francine was behind me. I wasn't surprised when she said, "Oh, I'm not up to the job, am I, Cait? I'll have you know that I'm about to take the killer into custody. My team back at headquarters has identified the person who so generously gave a poisoned baguette to Lucienne Durand in the street. We used teamwork and technology, and – mostly – the proper procedures to achieve this."

I can't let this go…does she really get it? was what I thought; "So you understand why Joanne thought she was looking at a photograph of her grandfather when she saw one of the young Lucienne?" was what I said.

Francine looked shocked. "When did she say that? Did she say it to you? Why didn't you tell me that? And – no…I…I don't know what it means – tell me."

I replied as calmly as I could. "She spotted it on my phone when she was helping me upstairs. It was there because I found this in Églantine's dressing room." I handed her the envelope containing the newspaper cutting. "You called our gathering to order immediately after you arrived, so I didn't have a chance to tell you any of this, then you went off with Joanne and Avril. So I'm telling you now – as soon as I can – because it's what gave me the key to unlocking this whole thing…which, by the way, is quite the story."

Pierre appeared through the doors and joined us in the corridor. "Captain, I have a…message for you."

Francine glared testily at Pierre, "Can it wait, Bertrand?"

Pierre shifted his weight from foot to foot. "No, not really."

Francine sighed. "Out with it."

Pierre swallowed. "It's from Commissioner Bovet. He will arrive here…shortly. He…he told me to tell you that he expects you to update him personally. He…he mentioned that he received a call from…the highest level…about this case."

Francine's nostrils flared, and she swore quietly. "If he's coming here on a Sunday night it's for blood, not an update. He spends his weekends entertaining everyone who's anyone in the world of French jurisprudence and Parisian politics at his country house – he won't be pleased to not be dining with them. Get everyone into the meeting room, Bertrand, post officers on every entrance and exit to this building and to the meeting room, and ensure that each crime scene is obviously secured."

Pierre replied, "All already done."

"But too late to save me," muttered Francine. She tossed her still-immaculate hair and looked me in the eye. "You think I've missed something, don't you?"

I nodded. "It took me a while to put it all together, and it was Joanne's reaction to that photo of Lucienne that helped."

The captain added, "But…we've got a good shot of the person who gave Lucienne that sandwich…at last, and that's what helped me."

I said, "Let me guess – it turns out to be a man with a full beard and moustache?"

Francine nodded. "Same description as the 'extra' removal person – the one wearing the disguise. And there's only one person that can be…though I was struggling for a motive until I was told about that ready-to-wear range. I hear you went down to the first floor to see it, and that's where you found that stone from Églantine's necklace, and the dress that should have been in the crate that contained Églantine's body. All of that? That's how I know I've got the right person."

No, no, no, was what I thought; "But I still think you haven't grasped the whole story…nor do you understand the motivation," was what I said.

Pierre was hovering, looking most uncomfortable. He started to blink almost uncontrollably when Francine swung to face him and said, "What do you think, Pierre? I've told you my theory, which fits all the facts. Do you think I've messed up?"

Forget "deer in headlights", you look more like a small furry creature being held, wriggling, above a mincer in motion, Pierre.

He shuffled about a bit, gripped his precious tablet tighter, then closed his eyes and squeaked out, "Cait's known for coming up with motive-based solutions to knotty problems, where the true nature of the victim…or victims…has proved illuminating. You researched her and Bud – so you know that too. On the other hand, Captain, you have a well-earned reputation for solving complicated cases, and all the members in all the departments you oversee applaud the way you use the machinery of our criminal investigative organization. I don't know what Cait's theory is, but you did put up an excellent argument for your planned arrest, Fran…Captain."

I thought Pierre had done an excellent job of not insulting his superior's abilities, and I also hadn't missed how he'd almost used Francine's name instead of her rank when he'd done so.

I said, "You believe Jacques Novello is guilty of all three murders, don't you, Francine?"

Francine nodded. "I do. You worked it out, too?"

I said, "But Joanne told us she was searching for Églantine with Jacques at roughly the same time that the person on the timed recording was sharing a baguette with Lucienne."

Francine took a deep breath. "He's coerced her into saying that…she feels a loyalty toward him that I believe is based upon a strange, but mutual attraction, or possibly camaraderie."

I said, "Love certainly plays a role in all this, but not in the way you believe, Francine."

She nibbled her lip, and sneaked a glance at Pierre – who seemed to be studying the ceiling. Her demeanor shifted. "I have a plan that might work…but I would need to paint you as someone I am allowing to ramble on, pontificating, to infuriate the killer into exposing himself. If that played out in front of my superior's superior – Bovet – that would allow me to leap in at the end and prove my point, while you would have a chance to…test out your theory. But – would you play that part in my little theatrical presentation, I wonder, Cait?"

You think I'm full of it, and want to be the one who comes out smelling of roses by proving me wrong in front of someone who can make or break your career, was what I thought; "I'd be delighted to have the chance to explain my side of things," was what I said.

I heard Bud breathe out, heavily, then he asked, "So when does this all begin?"

Francine was already in motion. "As soon as Commissioner Bovet arrives. Bertrand, let's get the place sorted out before then, and let's make sure all our proofs are lined up."

Alone again, Bud whispered to me, "Francine's fighting for her career – you're not going to…do anything rash, are you?"

I hugged him. "I only want to speak on behalf of the victims who can no longer speak for themselves, and see justice done. I have absolutely no intention of trying to make Francine look like a fool in order to achieve that – because she's certainly no fool, and I can see why she believes Jacques did it all, alone, and why, because we've both seen how passionate he is about that ready-to-wear collection. But she's missed how pivotal Joanne's role in all this was…though, when I explain that, I'll make sure I point out how Francine's leadership was what got me to where I shall, I hope, be able to lead everyone else. I won't undermine her, Bud. She doesn't deserve it. Her efforts, and sacrifices, also deserve their own sort of justice."

"Good. Now – let's get you installed in a chair, with that foot of yours up, and iced, then you can think yourself into the zone and…you know…do you."

"I love you, Husband."

"Love you more, Wife."

"Love you most. I win." I did my sweet-smile thing.

Bud chuckled. "You usually do."

Vingt-six

Commissioner Bovet arrived at *Maison Églantine* looking as though he'd left a shooting weekend at a stately home, which, for all I knew, he had. I suspected that whatever creatures had been his quarry out in the French countryside – and quite a posh bit of it, if the cut of his clothing was anything to go by – he now had Captain Francine de Gaulle in his sights. He looked thoroughly irritated when he stomped into the meeting room; he summarily declined all offers of refreshment, and surveyed each face within our group, surrounding the table, as though he might be assessing a gathering of mass murderers.

I was only too well aware of the facts of the matter from his point of view: the murder of a well-respected French fashion icon – with a direct impact upon the plans of the President of the country, no less; a brazen killing in a Paris street; a murder taking place at a location that should have been secured by a police presence. None of it bode well for Francine. I supposed that at least he didn't know that one of his captains had allowed two foreign "amateurs" to stick their noses into the case as well…though I suspected that Francine was about to guide the poised guillotine toward her own neck by telling him just that.

I wonder how she'll handle this?

Francine greeted Bovet deferentially as he walked around the table, and she'd got someone – possibly Pierre – to rustle up some name cards for everyone, so it really looked as though we were all at some sort of conference as we sat there with water bottles and glasses, name cards, and…well, most people had a rather bemused look on their face.

Bovet accepted a seat at the table, Francine cleverly positioning him at its head, while she took the chair to his right.

She began, "Thank you for coming here tonight, Commissioner Bovet, I know we're all honored by your presence – and it's particularly timely that you should arrive now, because we were all just about to give our attention to Professor Cait Morgan here. A professor of criminal psychology at the University of Vancouver, she was specially requested to teach courses at our illustrious *Sorbonne Université* recently, and presented herself yesterday as a witness to a crime, which, it transpired, was the killing of Églantine George. Having thoroughly checked her credentials, and having established that she has consulted on various high-profile murder investigations in her Canadian home, I took advantage of her expertise and have allowed her some limited access to our procedures in this instance – a valuable insight she has told me, with gratitude, that she has found most illuminating." Both Francine and Bovet nodded in my direction.

Thanks for talking me up, to cover your own backside…and that's an interesting decision to not mention Bud at all, was what I thought; "I am, indeed, grateful for a unique opportunity to see the professionalism of your teams in action," was what I said.

Francine continued, "Cait was just about to tell us all how she's seen this case from her own, academic, perspective. I'm sure we'll all be pleased to take this – brief – opportunity to hear her remarks."

Bovet's body language warned me he was just about to tell Francine that he had no intention of doing any such thing, so I jumped in. "As you can see, Commissioner, I'm slightly incapacitated at the moment, but I can assure you that my mental abilities remain unaffected. I'm sure that when I return to my university the week after next, my Chancellor will be most impressed to hear that my time as a visiting professor at the *Sorbonne* was augmented by being allowed to help interpret a case which has proved so interesting that I believe it might end up being cited in a future academic paper. Such papers are, of course, read and discussed around the world. I would be happy to credit you, personally, with having accommodated me in this instance. However, if you'd prefer that I didn't, then it would be ethically necessary for me to specifically mention that the paper had been written without your cooperation – that you'd turned down my offer to listen to what I believe are valuable insights into these heinous murders."

Hoping I'd wrong-footed the man, I watched his micro-expressions with interest as he mentally weighed his options. He looked at his watch, then said, "My evening belongs to you two women now, it seems. But let's get this over with as efficiently as possible. And do try to remember there are people in this room who might not be as well versed in academic jargon as we…professionals."

Lovely – pompous with a hint of misogyny thrown in for good measure, was what I thought; "I won't waste any of your valuable time, Commissioner Bovet, nor that of anyone else who's here, and I'll use…non-academic language," was what I said.

Francine's shoulders settled; Pierre's tablet was raised ready to record events; I wriggled in my seat a little so that I could see most of the people around me.

I began. "I'm sure your schedule's been too full for you to do anything but give the reports about this case the most cursory glance, Commissioner, so I'll summarize the situation to begin with – with an introduction to the people in this room, and an explanation of their role within this tragic set of circumstances. Firstly, allow me to introduce my husband – he's joined me from Canada." Bovet nodded. I continued, "The reasons for all three murders that have touched *Maison Églantine* go back a long way – the people in this room know different parts of the story I'm about to tell you, some will know none. I shall tell it all."

Bovet interjected, "Briefly."

I nodded. "As briefly as possible, of course. So…about sixty-five years ago, a teenaged girl was found badly injured – probably thrown from a moving vehicle and left for dead, in fact – and nursed back to health at a convent near Buguet-sur-Marne, outside Paris. The girl eventually regained consciousness, learned to walk and speak again, and 'acquired' the name Églantine…which she'd seen on a Toulouse-Lautrec poster in an art book she'd been given. The girl loved art, it seems."

I noted that the twins, Jacques, Avril, and Joanne all looked shocked by this revelation.

Monica said, "Églantine had been attacked back then…as…a teen? Is that where she got her scars? Not when she was experimenting with acids?"

Joanne asked, "Églantine had scars? Is that why she always wore that collar thing? I thought that was because…well, because it was beautiful, and because – you know – she never wore any other jewelry and that was a valuable piece. Amber's an incredible result of chemical polymerization, the result of millennia of pressure upon tree sap, so amber of that quality, and put together in such an elaborate and well-matched way, is worth a great deal of money – and rightly so. I always admired it."

Jacques sighed. "It was magnificent, wasn't it? It was so sad to find it in pieces. Though what you said about it earlier today really touched me, Joanne. It wasn't something she simply wore – it was a part of her. It was her neck. It was her chest. I've tried, but I can't imagine her without it. It would be like seeing someone who was…more than naked."

Monica jumped in. "It's broken? But you've found it? Where? When?"

Avril asked, "Who says Églantine was attacked in her youth? That's nonsense. She'd have mentioned something like that."

Bovet held up his hand. "Stop talking, everyone. Let the woman get on with it."

I nodded toward the pink-faced man, and said, "Thank you, Commissioner. We know all of this because Anne-Marie Lefebvre was a novice at that convent at the time, and later became a Sister there. She was allowed to care for Églantine, who eventually left, and was not heard from again. Some years later, Églantine George convinced a young Avril Tambour to model a gown she'd designed, and it was a huge success. The Martin twins became the people who were able to create Églantine's designs, and Avril's boyfriend at the time, Gustav Sutter, stepped up to handle the business side of things. Avril and Gustav married, and they had a daughter – Joanne – who also became involved in the world of fashion, though on the technical side of textile production, rather than here at the Maison itself. Over the years, the business became what we know today – *Maison Églantine* is renowned the world over for its luxurious creations in velvet, and has managed to maintain its reputation within a fashion business that's in a state of flux."

"Thank you for the introductions," said Bovet relatively graciously…though I noted that he was staring at Jacques with some curiosity.

I continued, "As you know, Commissioner, an exhibition is due to open tomorrow evening – at an event that will be attended by the French President himself – celebrating the history of French fashion, and *Maison Églantine* will take its place there. However, despite the fact that the business has run successfully – and relatively unchanged – for decades, Églantine realized she wasn't getting any younger, and that she needed to bring in someone to take over as head of design. Jacques Novello's arrival heralded a chance for the continuation of all that's good about the Maison, but there have been moves afoot to shift the focus of the business – to expand its efforts into the ready-to-wear market – which were supported by Églantine herself. Specimen garments for such an endeavor have been developed by Jacques…and a full proposal would have been put to the board by Églantine yesterday, had that meeting gone ahead. It's fair to say that not everyone on the board was in favor of this new, potential, direction. The other thing that's worth mentioning is that there have been some suggestions that Églantine's mental capacity had been…wavering a little, of late."

I paused, and Bovet said, "Thank you for the summary and introductions. And your conclusions?"

I saw Francine shift impatiently in her seat, but ignored her and said, "As the reactions in the room suggest, most people here weren't aware that the person we all know as Églantine George had been nursed by nuns through the injuries that, thereafter, caused her to wear her signature amber collar throughout her life, to hide a shocking scar that had been inflicted upon her when she was attacked with acid, which also all but robbed her of a 'normal' voice. What Anne-Marie was also able to tell us was that – when Églantine was brought to her convent – she was unconscious, and remained in a coma for about a year. The police couldn't discover who she was, nor even where she was from, at the time, due to the fact that she was unable to answer any questions, but it became obvious – as the months passed – that she was pregnant. Eventually, Églantine was delivered of a child by cesarean section."

There were gasps around the table.

Monica said, "She had a child? She never mentioned one. Oh Monique, I thought she trusted us. Why didn't she tell us?"

Monique looked dumbfounded. "Well, I never. We often talked with her about us not wanting children – and she always agreed that it was possible for a single person to be complete without a family…though she was, sometimes, jealous that we had each other, don't you think?"

I jumped in. "Églantine wasn't aware she'd had a baby for some time…possibly not until years later. However, by the time

Anne-Marie came back into Églantine's life and told her what had happened – that the child had been born, then taken away for adoption – Églantine had already worked out what the cesarean scar on her belly meant, and she'd even managed to track down her child…and had given them an opportunity to be close to her. However, I don't believe she ever told them about their origins. That would be a great burden for any child to bear, I'd have thought – to know they'd been born of rape."

"How awful," said Monique. "Who was her child? Is it one of us? Well, not me and Monica, of course, because we're too old, and she only had one baby, correct?"

Anne-Marie looked doubtful. "I wasn't allowed to watch the delivery – well, the operation really – but I think one of the Sisters would have mentioned it if there'd been twins…and I don't know how old you are, but the child would be sixty-four now – though who knows if they'd have been assigned their correct exact birthdate after they'd been taken away."

Joanne looked at her mother and said, "You're a bit older than that, Avril…but I suppose you could have been her daughter. She sort of treated you like one."

Avril snapped, "Don't be ridiculous, Joanne…though I'm not that much older than sixty-four."

Joanne snorted. "There are police here, Avril – you don't need to lie about your age, they don't care."

Avril pouted. Loudly…if that's possible.

Her daughter added, "Papa was a little younger than you, wasn't he? He could have been…oh, Cait, are you saying that my father was Églantine's son? Was that why you had a photo of my grandfather on your phone? Oh, no – that was Avril's father, not Papa's father. Was Papa adopted, Avril? Oh no, I'm confused, now."

I could tell that, because of all the interruptions, Bovet, too, was getting confused, and I didn't want that.

Take control, Cait.

I said, "Hang on a moment, Joanne – I'll get there, I promise. Because it is important, and it's why everything happened. But, first, let's consider what did happen. The fact of the matter is that I witnessed the strangulation of Églantine George, around the noon hour, on Saturday. Bud and I came here and met Lucienne Durand shortly thereafter, and he told us something that was later discovered to be untrue – he told us that the room where I saw the attack take place was being used by caterers at that time. I've considered that lie of his a great deal, and I believe he was covering for someone who'd done 'something' that – maybe – not even he really understood at that time. Some sort of 'incident' we don't know about. Yet."

I cast my eyes around the table, but couldn't see any signs of guilt at all.

I pressed on. "Gustav told us that Lucienne claimed to be feeling unwell later that day, that he left the Maison shortly after we did – and we all know that he was found dead by strychnine poisoning that evening. Through the diligent work carried out by Captain de Gaulle's teams, it's been discovered that the baguette which poisoned Lucienne was given to him by a bearded man an hour or so after Lucienne left the Maison. This man matched the description of an unknown 'fourth man' who removed a packing crate for the twins at the Maison on Saturday, that was later discovered to contain Églantine's remains. We also know that Gustav Sutter met his death while sitting at his desk, here at the Maison, some time after he left this very room in the early hours of Sunday morning."

"An evil perpetrator, to have killed three people so rapidly, and coldly," said Bovet with some gravitas. "And the person who did this was?"

I wouldn't be pressured. "If Églantine was killed around noon, but the caterers were in the anteroom by just gone twelve twenty – which Captain de Gaulle has hard evidence to support – then Églantine's killer had to get her body out of the anteroom quickly. I believe the fact that beads from Églantine's amber necklace were found in the storage room on the first floor means that's where the killer took her body – initially. Knowing that crates full of garments headed for the exhibition were being moved around the Maison, a disguise allowed for the collection of a crate from the twins on the fourth floor, which was taken to the first floor, where the gown it contained was swapped out for Églantine's body. The crate was then taken to the side door of the Maison where it was collected either by a company that believed it was just making a simple pick-up and drop-off, or – more likely – by a vehicle responding to a ride-share-style request to make a delivery. I know Francine's people can check that out, and are probably doing so right now."

I noticed that Francine's back stiffened when I said this, though she hid her surprise extremely well.

I continued, "Unfortunately for Lucienne, whether he did or didn't suspect Églantine's killer of having attacked her, and whether he did or didn't see the crate in question being taken from the Maison didn't really matter – because no chances would be taken…Lucienne had to go. By the way, the relaxed nature of the luncheon – where people were wandering in and out of this room – meant there was ample opportunity for the crate to be dispatched. When Églantine failed to appear for the board meeting, there was a general consensus to search the Maison and the surrounding area for her…which I understand took some time. It was during this period that the person that Captain de Gaulle's team eventually picked up on camera obtained the poison and sandwich that killed Lucienne, and met up with him in the street, inviting him to accept the poisoned food. Once everyone had been questioned that evening, someone slashed Gustav's throat, in his own office – with his own letter opener, no less – then that same person searched Églantine's apartment for something they believed might be hidden among her books. I suggest this was a search for a photograph that's now been found."

Jacques said, "But no one was alone when we were searching for Églantine – we all searched in pairs, for most of the time. Me and Joanne were hardly apart."

Monica added, "And Monique and I never left each other's sides, did we?"

Her sister rolled her shoulders haughtily. "No, we didn't."

Avril bleated, "I was with Gustav the whole time…poor Gustav."

Joanne tutted loudly, and glared at her mother. A frown crossed the commissioner's face as he grappled with the dynamic between the mother and her child.

I said, "Well…Joanne could have been covering for Jacques, or vice versa. Monica and Monique? I bet there've been times in your lives when each one of you has pretended to be the other – allowing people to believe that two of you are generally present when one is really absent. And Avril – we only have your word that you and Gustav were in each other's company all the time. You see…any one of you could have left the Maison to go out and poison Lucienne…as long as just one other person was prepared to lie for you."

A general hubbub broke out, which was what I'd hoped for, and I took my chance to watch each face and study the micro-expressions of everyone I'd named: both the twins were nibbling their upper lips; Joanne and Jacques were both a bit pink in the face; Avril's eyes couldn't settle on…anything. I knew right then that I stood a good chance of cracking a killer's alibi.

Francine patted the air – a motion she used to great effect. Everyone calmed down, though with expressions of varying degrees of having been offended by my comments.

I continued, "Rather than accuse someone of lying about that particular aspect, let me tell you about a question I had to ask myself – what was it that drew my eyes to the scene I saw in the window of the anteroom just through those doors yesterday at noon?"

Pause for effect, Cait.

Monique said, "And…what was it?"

I replied, "There was a flash of light – that's what initially caught my attention. It was close to noon, and a pleasant, sunny day. I dare say a few people were pulling open their windows, and even contemplating a bit of spring cleaning, it being a Saturday lunchtime. Captain de Gaulle – your officers interviewed everyone living in the two blocks abutting each side of this building, correct?" I knew they had.

Francine nodded. "We did. In some cases, twice. Initially we were seeking information regarding any sightings of Églantine George – when we believed her to be missing, possibly kidnapped. However, everyone was questioned again – or for the first time, if they'd been impossible to get hold of – when her body was found, and it became clear we were dealing with a murder…that had taken place in the anteroom. On the second occasion, particular attention was given to those living in the building across the road which would have allowed a view into the window where the attack took place. No one saw anything they could characterize as unusual around the time in question. Essentially, we drew a blank."

The commissioner let out a low, non-committal rumble.

I said, "But what if someone *had* been looking out of their window at the time that Églantine was being attacked, then strangled? What if they'd been so shocked by what they were seeing that they'd pulled open their window to 'get a better look'? The sun might have flashed on that pane, drawing my attention to the vicinity, where I was able to see what was happening in this building…as they could. And what if they knew not only the victim but also – having a different line of vision than I did – the attacker too? What might they do?"

Jacques blurted out, "If I knew the attacker I might not call the police – sorry – but I'd get over here as fast as I could to try to…find out what had happened, or something. I mean – I might not believe my eyes. Wouldn't anyone try to…act?"

Monica and Monique did the metronome nodding thing, while Joanne and Avril looked…stunned. Francine's eyes began to dart around the table, and Bovet looked pretty disgruntled.

I said, "I saw hands around Églantine's neck…around the glowing gold of her amber collar…but she wasn't struggling. I've given that fact a great deal of thought, and – now that I've gained some insights into the woman – I believe she didn't struggle because she knew she stood no chance of stopping the person who was killing her. They were too strong, and they had too much to lose to allow her to live."

Bovet exploded. "So who killed her?"

I replied, "Gustav Sutter strangled Églantine George to death."

There was a sharp intake of breath from Joanne who pushed back her chair, leaped to her feet and shouted, "Don't you dare say that about Papa. He's not here to defend himself. Why are you saying he killed her? Why would he? No…no, he wouldn't. Nothing could make my father kill…anyone. He was…too gentle for that. Too loving. He was a truly kind man."

I'm so terribly sorry, Joanne – especially because I know that what you're about to hear will break your heart…even more.

Bovet barked, "Sit!"

Joanne looked as though she'd been slapped in the face, and sat down hard, tears welling in her eyes – signifying both anger and sadness, I suspected. Jacques passed her a handkerchief, which she accepted with a forced, upside-down smile.

I spoke softly, "I believe you're right, Joanne – your father was, usually, a gentle, loving man…but I also believe that's exactly why he did what he did. Thanks to Anne-Marie, we know that he argued with Églantine a few days ago, telling her that something she was planning to do would destroy his family, and probably ruin the company. Now, we know that Gustav was a supporter of the idea of a ready-to-wear collection, and I bet he knew what was going on as far as the secret work to prepare a selection of samples by Jacques was concerned…so that couldn't have been what Églantine was going to bring up that could have led to ruin. However, despite him begging her not to do it, I reckon Églantine had decided to follow the path she believed was the right one. I never met the woman, though I've been honored to have had the opportunity to see where, and how, she lived, and I've been entranced by the astonishing garments she created, which this house – in the shape of the Martin twins – has created. I wish I could have met her, because I can tell you – from what I've learned about her – that she was an extraordinary woman. Imagine what she overcame – the trauma, the loss of her youth – and yet she made…all this, by using her talent, and applying her desire to draw people to her whose lives she also built up, even as she built her empire. I believe it would have been highly unlikely that she'd have changed her mind about anything at all, ever…let alone something she believed to be so important, even if she knew that might not be…healthy for her. You see, she knew Gustav well. Well enough to believe he would fight for his daughter…which is, I believe, why she wasn't struggling with him, when he was squeezing the life from her – she knew she wouldn't win, because he wouldn't let her. Equally, Gustav knew her well – knew that what drove her was the desire to have things done the right way…her way. He knew she'd not be persuaded to remain quiet…not if she'd decided to speak out. So he felt he had to choose her – or you, Joanne. He killed her to save you, his beloved daughter."

Joanne's eyes were wide. "Save me from what? What could Églantine possibly do to me?"

Come on Cait…this is it.

I said, "Well, back about forty years ago, Églantine spotted a photo in a newspaper, and recognized the face of a young soldier, because it was so similar to the face of the man who'd attacked her, left her for dead, and impregnated her. She believed him to be her son. She tracked him down, gave him a job, and he's been close to her since then – though unaware of their relationship. Another example of Églantine doing what she believed to be the right thing, the right way. It's notable that she made Lucienne grow a beard, and keep it, as a condition of retaining his post – I believe this was because she didn't want to be constantly reminded of her attacker's face. Now, trust me when I tell you this, folks – it's a horribly sad, but true, statistic that most rape victims know their attacker…that they are raped by someone within their close, or extended, circle. It's not a great leap, therefore, when I say I believe she'd actually known the person who'd attacked her. In fact, I believe that Églantine not only recovered her ability to walk and talk when she was at that convent, but that she also – eventually, though maybe not for some time – recovered her memory of the night she'd been attacked. And she decided – in her own way, again – to act upon what she knew."

Bovet looked at his watch and said, "This is all very interesting, but you have named the culprit, and he is dead. He killed twice, then took his own life. He has paid the price."

I could see that Francine was about to say something, so snapped, "But you have to understand why Gustav did what he did. You see, he was the boyfriend of a girl who was befriended by Églantine, who was set on the road to stardom by Églantine, and guided on that path until she was the world-famous face of Églantine's entire business. As you said, Avril, people bought gowns they'd seen you wear when they had no idea who Églantine was – but I believe that Églantine knew who you were…in a way that not even you did. In recent months her mind was wandering – she'd been heard to refer to people in confusing ways, and I understand she'd been told she had Parkinson's disease. That explains things like her less acute sense of smell, her weight loss, the fact she was shuffling about more these days…changes spotted by those of you close to her. I believe that her mind might have been losing its ability to keep all the secrets she'd held close for decades. She'd never told Lucienne that he was her son, but she was about to do so…and that's why Gustav killed her."

Joanne stared at her mother, then me, then shouted, "Rubbish."

I sighed. "Églantine had told your father that she was going to bring this truth out into the light…and more. Your father believed that knowledge would hurt you, and…well, I think it's pretty clear to all of us that there's not much of a loving bond between you and your mother, nor did there appear to be one between your mother and father, but I believe that Gustav foresaw the anguish that such a revelation would cause you *and* Avril. He wasn't a spiteful man – he was a loving one – and I don't believe he wanted either of you to be so wounded. Now, I admit that I don't know why Églantine thought this was the right time to reveal her secrets – but I have come to learn that she'd acknowledged her age, and probably her disease, in several ways. She'd brought in Jacques to take on her design responsibilities. She was supporting a new direction for the company that would allow it to grow. She was involved with making plans to allow Monica and Monique to have a good retirement…and I believe she'd have been making changes to her will. I've heard that the shares in *Maison Églantine* that were owned by her are due to be distributed on a basis that reflects current holdings – but what of this building itself, I wonder? It must be worth many, many millions, and I understand that it was the personal possession of Églantine. What will happen to that? Were you able to make any headway with Églantine's will, Captain de Gaulle?"

Francine gained everyone's immediate and avid attention. She shook her head. "Unfortunately not. Every attempt has been made to connect with the lawyer holding her will, but to no avail. It's almost as though he's dropped off the planet – or maybe he's just somewhere where there's no signal. My team will follow up in the morning."

Bovet snapped, "You'll follow up yourself."

Francine smiled, stonily.

I continued, "Let's just say, for now, that maybe Églantine was aware of the slips she was making – referring openly to Lucienne as her son, on one occasion, for example – and was 'putting things in order', as she saw it. I believe that when she and Gustav argued again on Saturday morning – someone had been smoking a cigar in her apartment more recently than days earlier – this was when she and he thrashed through the topic again."

The room had become unnaturally quiet. Even the twins were perfectly still, which was unusual for them.

A wave of utter sadness washed over me, but I had to keep going. "Nothing happens in isolation. Every action has a cause. When a person decides to take the life of another, they always 'have their reasons'. In this instance, I believe that reason was love. Gustav loved you, Joanne, more than he loved anyone, and Églantine was threatening to make your life as miserable as…as I'm about to make it. I'm so sorry. I can't know this, because your father's no longer here for me to ask him, but I suspect that he and Églantine met in her apartment yesterday morning, after the twins had left it, and that he and she then came down to the second floor in the elevator, possibly with Églantine saying she would, unusually, join the group for lunch, because she saw that as a way to keep herself…safe, until she was able to speak to you all. However, they moved into the anteroom instead of this room, and that's where she made it clear that she'd be telling all at the board meeting – that she'd create fireworks, as she'd put it to Anne-Marie. The gloves I saw on the strangler's hands? Well, I was never one hundred percent certain that they were gloved hands, so maybe they weren't, and there really was no premeditation at all – but what I do believe is that there was a struggle that I didn't witness prior to that final, deadly act…and I believe that was seen by someone who lived in the building across the road, on the second floor – who'd have had an excellent view into that window."

Avril actually whimpered, and everyone stared at her. She looked up from picking at her exquisitely manicured nails, those eyes of hers reminding me of Princess Diana again – seemingly naïve, but hinting at hidden knowledge.

She said quietly, "I couldn't believe what I was seeing – I opened my window across the road, as though that would make a difference. Then I rushed over here – came in through the front door, saw Lucienne, and ran up to the anteroom. Églantine was dead…and Gustav was…was crying like a baby. None of it made any sense to me, and he wouldn't tell me what had happened. All I knew was that people would be arriving at any moment, so we had to do…something. He kept babbling that it was all for you, Joanne, but I didn't know what he meant. Anyway, we agreed we'd better hide…the body…so we took it down to the first floor in the elevator – well, I did, your father wouldn't fit – and I checked that Lucienne was getting some air, out on the front steps where he could see nothing going on inside. We got the body into the storage area, placed it under a couple of rolls of cloth, and locked the door behind us. We didn't have a plan past that, and Gustav couldn't stop crying so, I admit it, I slapped him, and shouted at him…which Lucienne somehow heard. He ran inside, then up to the first floor, but we told him we'd just had a silly fight – which he believed."

Monica said quietly, "He was a kind man."

Avril mused, "Maybe that was the 'incident' Cait referred to – which led him to lie about there being caterers at the Maison earlier than there really were…I don't know. But it was good of him not to mention what I believe we convinced him was just a spat that…got out of hand."

Monique nodded. "Yes, Lucienne would have done that – covered for you and Gustav, to…strangers."

A pointed glare from Bovet led both twins to tut loudly.

Avril cleared her throat, and everyone returned their attention to her. "Anyway, we both came up here, and decided that we had to do…something. We knew about the men taking the crates to the exhibition, and Gustav suggested we could somehow get Églantine's body out of the Maison and off to the *Petit Palais*, then he'd come up with some way to be able to get it out of there on Sunday, before any of the crates were opened. So that's what we did."

Monique said, "But it wasn't Gustav who collected the crate – we'd have recognized Gustav, wouldn't we, Monica?"

Her sister replied huffily, "Of course we'd have recognized Gustav. The man we saw had a beard, and a moustache, and a hat, and glasses, and he limped, and…oh dear, he was wearing a disguise, wasn't he? And we didn't see through it."

The sisters grabbed each other's hands on top of the table, and exchanged a look of horror.

I nodded. "And he was whistling 'Clair de Lune', which had been playing in Églantine's apartment that morning."

The twins nodded. Monica said, "Yes…that was what he was whistling."

Anne-Marie whispered, "Oh no…oh dear…how shall I ever be able to listen to that piece again?"

I said to Avril, "So your experience from your early modelling days paid off. I'm betting you rushed across to your apartment, where you not only collected make-up, a wig, and supplies of false facial hair, but also changed your clothes. Did you feel dirty?"

Avril looked shocked. "I…I did. But how did you know?"

I replied, "Lucienne told me and Bud that you'd been wearing a gold scarf when he'd first seen you, but you were wearing a blue dress with silver piping when we met you – and I can't imagine that someone like you would wear a gold scarf when your embellishments were all silver."

Avril lifted her chin. "Quite right."

I continued, "You sent Gustav up to collect the crate, wearing a heavy disguise, then the two of you got Églantine's corpse into it on the first floor, he returned his appearance to normal, and you hailed – what, a ride-share removal van?"

Avril nodded. "I know I'm going to get into trouble, Commissioner – but I admit that I helped my ex-husband. By this time, Gustav was thinking much more clearly – he seemed to have got over the fact that he'd taken someone's life, and had become completely focused on not being found out. I'm sorry that I helped him, Commissioner, but you have to understand that we were married for a long time, and were happy, once…and we had you, Joanne. I still didn't know what he meant about it all being about you, but I could tell it was important to him so…I'm sorry. I know I broke the law…a bit."

I didn't want Bovet – or Francine – to say anything, yet, so jumped in. "And which one of you decided that Lucienne had to die, Avril?"

Avril didn't smile, but she did grit her teeth. "Gustav wouldn't tell me anything about anything, but he was terrified that, because Lucienne had seen us 'fighting', his suspicions would be aroused when it was discovered that Églantine was missing. But, honestly, all Gustav said was that he would 'sort it out', as long as I covered for him. He told me that he'd sent Lucienne home for the day, and then I made a fuss – as he told me to – about us all going around the place searching for Églantine when she didn't arrive for the meeting. This was so that Gustav could get away from the Maison for a while to…well, honestly, I thought he was just going to talk to Lucienne, or maybe offer him money, you know? So I agreed that I'd say I'd been searching with Gustav while he went to…see Lucienne. I was horrified when I found out what had happened. What Gustav had done. After we all found out about Lucienne being dead, I confronted him, and Gustav told me that he'd done it – which terrified me. You do understand, don't you, Commissioner? The man who was the father of my child had killed two people. What if I didn't back up his lies? Would he kill me too? He told me that he'd got strychnine to kill Lucienne from his own apartment. It seems that Joanne has been storing all sorts of nasty things there for years…things she's picked up from one stinky laboratory after another, and that's what gave him the idea. When everyone left that night, Gustav told me he had a few things to do. Given what Cait's said, it sounds as though he went up to search Églantine's apartment for that photograph…but he still hadn't told me…anything. I went back to my apartment and decided that I'd make him tell me all about it properly – help me understand why he'd done what he'd done – after he'd gone to the *Petit Palais* and made Églantine's body…umm…disappear the next morning. This morning. But…he never did…because he…oh dear, he shouldn't have killed himself. And certainly not in that horrid way." She dissolved into tears. They were quite genuine, and her make-up wasn't waterproof, it seemed.

Joanne was also crying, but silently – not in performance mode like her mother. Jacques looked awkward as he reached an arm around Joanne's shoulders, then even more so when she wriggled away from him.

Joanne asked plaintively, "Why do you say that Papa killed himself, Avril? How could anyone…do that…like that?" She stared helplessly at Francine, her eyes bloodshot, her voice trembling. "Is that even possible? To…to cut your own…to slice open your own…" She broke down, her ability to form words evaporating.

Francine and Bovet shared a professionally guarded glance. Francine said, "I believe it is possible to cut one's own throat, if a person's determined enough…though it's hardly a frequently used method of taking one's own life."

I bet you're glad you didn't move to accuse Jacques, now, Francine.

I said quietly, "Not a frequently used method, Joanne, no. In fact, it's psychologically and medically a completely atypical method to use…needing not only physical but also emotional strength. And, although there wasn't a single hesitation mark on your father's neck, there was an injury on his hand, which is…significant."

Anne-Marie crossed herself, kissed the rosary she'd pulled from her handbag, and her lips began to move silently.

I asked, "Anne-Marie, did Églantine confess her plans to you to reveal the truth about her pregnancy and Lucienne's identity? With your background, and your shared history, she might have believed you'd keep her secret, until she was ready to share it with everyone."

Anne-Marie spoke quietly. "She did, but only in part. God forgive me for not having told you when you asked, but I believed I should keep her confidence, you see. She told me yesterday morning that she was going to tell you all at the board meeting about the fact that she had a child, and would reveal their identity. She sought my counsel about her plan, but I told her that I couldn't advise her, because she refused, even then, to tell me more, so I couldn't assess what her revelation might mean. She…she seemed quite determined. She said that people deserved to know the whole truth – because they were all like her family. She didn't seem angry, or upset, just calmly set upon her path, and…resigned to it, in a way. If she was sick, as you say, Cait, that might explain…oh dear, such a lot."

Avril had regained her composure sufficiently to be able to say, "I understand that you'll have to charge me with something, Commissioner, but please believe me when I tell you that I was acting out of loyalty to my ex-husband."

Joanne managed, "So you covered everything up for Papa? But…but you hated him. The vitriol you've hurled at him over the years can't mean…nothing." Joanne peered at me through smudged spectacles. "But I still don't understand – why would Églantine telling everyone that Lucienne was her son hurt me? I mean – it's sad, but…but sort of wonderful, in a way…but it's got nothing to do with me."

Here we go. Do your best.

I said, "Well, it does, actually because of who Lucienne's father was. Joanne, when you saw the photograph on my phone that you believed was of your maternal grandfather, it was, in fact, a photograph of Lucienne as a young man, when he was in the army. It was the photograph that Églantine spotted in a newspaper, which led her to him decades ago. But you saw an immediate and significant similarity between that photo and the ones you'd seen of your grandfather. Your certainty that I was lying when I told you it wasn't your grandfather was quite genuine."

Joanne blubbed, "But…but…well, so what?"

I turned to Francine. "Were you able to find out anything about what Bud asked you to check? A girl of the right age who disappeared in the area I noted, at about the right time? A possible real identity for the woman we all knew as Églantine George."

Everyone, including the commissioner, stared at Francine, who nodded. "Due to the fact that a recent upgrade has been made to our computerized records, we did locate such a person. One Mireille Audubon disappeared at the right time, and she was the right age. Fourteen, at the time she vanished. The records state that she was reported missing by a teacher at the school where she'd been a problem student, in Montlyon – the only school in the village. Statements taken at the time show that both her parents believed that she'd run away, which was why they didn't report her as missing. The inquiries into her disappearance were…well, it was a small village in a deeply rural area where there wasn't any real police presence, so next to nothing was done. Indeed, the records suggest that the parents never followed up after some cursory inquiries…nor did the police."

Avril muttered, "There was no Audubon family in Montlyon. I grew up there and it was a small village. I would know."

Francine looked across at Avril and said, "I have the date when the girl went missing, and I have your date of birth on file. She was last seen several months after you were born. Her family left the area a few years later."

Avril snorted. "You see? I was right."

Joanne said, "You say the missing girl – who became Églantine, I assume – went to school in Montlyon? That's where your father was the janitor, Avril. So she'd have known him…" Joanne's face lost any color it had, and she stopped speaking.

I took a deep breath and said, "The photograph of Lucienne as a young man looked like your grandfather, Joanne, because your grandfather – Avril's father, Norman Tambour – raped Églantine when she was a young girl, then did his best to kill her, by pouring acid onto her…janitorial supplies can contain some horribly caustic products. He dumped her on the side of the road like so much…garbage. The N3 is a road that runs not far outside the village of Montlyon and almost through the village of Buguet-sur-Marne where Anne-Marie's convent was located…far enough away to avoid any easy connection, but close enough to allow him to make the return journey on one wet night – when the ditches were full, which was what, ironically, saved Églantine's life…because the water washed off the acid. It is this knowledge that Gustav was trying to protect you from, Joanne. Églantine actively sought you out, Avril, and supported your start in the world of fashion…to save you from the man who raped her. With both Lucienne and Églantine's remains available, I believe that DNA analysis will prove he was her son. I dare say that if either Avril or Joanne would agree to a test, it would then be possible to show that Avril's father was also Lucienne's biological father."

Joanne had stopped sobbing, and was staring at her mother intently when she said, "So Lucienne was Avril's half-brother? My…half-uncle? And my grandfather was…a rapist, and an attempted killer. And my own father murdered two people, then took his own life? This is all…this is…too much…" She was hardly breathing.

Avril didn't even look up. "This is the first I'm hearing of it all. My father was never like that…had no interest in young girls…he was a kind and loving man. Everyone knew it. I was his princess. He loved me a great deal." She held her head high, tears streaming down her face.

Come on, Cait…

I said, "Avril, it's clear that I've done what Églantine had planned to – I've exposed your late father as a man capable of the most heinous crimes – and all the damage that knowledge can, and will do, has already begun. I'm so sorry about that…but not as sorry as you are, I'm sure."

Joanne looked from me to Avril, and – for the first time since we'd met – I saw evidence of a softening of her heart toward her mother. "Don't worry about me, Maman, I'm stronger than I look. I've never been one of those people who believe that we're responsible for the actions of our forebears…we can't be. So let me take all this on board as I can, over time. But you? I know you worshipped your father – you always had so many photographs of the two of you together around the place. Never with your mother, which I always thought unusual…until I realized that you and she were like chalk and cheese. She never forgave you for running off to Paris like you did, did she? And by the time you were famous enough to go back there after I had been born, to show them what you'd made of your life, your father was dead. I don't remember her well, of course, and I never met him…but I'm sorry that you've found out this…terrible thing…about him. None of this is your fault, Maman. Maybe I can stay with you for a while? We've never spent much time together since I went away to school. Maybe we can deal with this together? We've both got a lot to consider when it comes to the actions that our fathers have taken…though – thanks to Cait's explanations – maybe I can understand why Papa did what he did, whereas I can see already that the news about what your father did has shocked you to your core."

I watched as Avril appeared to crumble under the weight of her daughter's love. Saw the mask slip as she navigated her own emotional turmoil, and knew it was time for me to deliver the final, devastating blow.

I said, "I found the photograph that Églantine told Gustav about, though I don't believe she showed it to him, because everything on top of it was covered with dust when Bud first found the place where it was hidden. We also discovered that Lucienne had his own copy…which was ironic, because – in his eyes – it was just a photograph of him and some old army buddies, not a passport to his birthright. But the fact that Églantine had a son, isn't the only secret here today, is it?"

Eyes darted. No one spoke.

I focused on Joanne. "I know that you and Jacques spent most of the time searching for Églantine together, but you both agreed that he would check out the first floor on his own…which meant that you were alone for a short time, too. But you weren't alone, were you, Joanne? You mentioned something to me about a conversation you had with your father, while Jacques wasn't with you."

Joanne's furrowed brow told me she was thinking back to the period when everyone had been hunting for the missing Églantine. Eventually she said, "Yes, Papa and I had some time together here in this meeting room, then Jacques joined us, and we all…oh yes – I was alone with Papa for a while, but Avril was…where were you then?"

Avril said nothing.

I jumped in. "Avril, I believe what you told us about seeing your ex-husband attack Églantine, and even the part about you disguising him so he could move that crate. But it wasn't Gustav who rushed to his apartment and got hold of some strychnine from Joanne's old science supplies, nor was it he who encountered Lucienne in the street with a baguette – it was you, disguised to look like a man. You killed Lucienne, Avril. I personally witnessed the shock on Gustav's face when Francine announced that Lucienne was dead, and I believe that shock was genuine. He had no idea you'd gone off to murder the man. You talked Gustav into covering for you during that entire period when people were searching for Églantine – or you managed to 'steamroller' him with what he told Joanne were your 'womanly wiles'. That was a clever idea, by the way, to get everyone to search…designed to allow you the chance to sneak away."

Oh, careful, Avril…I nearly got you with that one…you almost looked proud there for a moment.

I straightened my back a little in my chair, then said, "Gustav had told you what Églantine was about to tell the world…and you were just as horrified to hear what your father had done as he was. Probably more so. But your first thought wasn't to save your daughter from the damage that news might cause…you wanted to save your own reputation. Because you only really care about yourself, Avril, the way any narcissist does. Églantine had remembered – possibly years after she'd left the convent – who'd attacked her, and went back to his place of work…her old school. She'd probably known that a baby girl had been born to her school janitor's wife not long before he attacked her – something that might have been a psychologically triggering factor for Norman Tambour – but, whether she did or not, there you were, Avril, a seemingly carefree teen…who she decided to 'rescue'. She believed that the right thing to do was to take you out of harm's way. When you learned all this from your ex-husband – who'd already allowed himself to become so enraged by the idea that his beloved daughter's life would be wrecked that he'd robbed Églantine of hers – you didn't hesitate…you acted. I suggest that you were the one who was thinking clearly enough to come up with the plan to move Églantine's body out of the Maison, and that you were the one who decided to kill Lucienne. Once Gustav told you that Lucienne was Églantine's son, and your half-brother, you could see your own father's face in him, couldn't you? Imagine having to see Lucienne every single day, a constant reminder that your father – who loved you so much – had once raped Églantine…who'd been no more than a child at the time. Not only might Lucienne have possibly seen or heard something that could tie Gustav to Églantine's killing – and you've admitted to us that he at least knew that you and Gustav were at the Maison when Églantine would have 'gone missing' – but his mere presence here might, somehow, allow the truth to become known. So he, too, had to be killed."

Avril finally spoke. "I've never heard such nonsense. I hope you're taking notes, Commissioner – this is slander."

Bovet's eyes slid toward me, then back to Avril, and I could almost feel the chill in the air.

Good.

I said, "Then? Well then there was only Gustav left alive who knew the truth…and he'd never talk, would he, Avril? But you'd seen him dissolve after he'd killed – you've told us how he was emotionally affected by the fact that he'd taken a life, and I'm pretty sure the man I met yesterday afternoon had already been drinking a fair bit, and he continued to do so. You must have wondered if he'd be able to hold up through an interrogation. No, you couldn't take any chances, so…you killed him too. Why would he question it if you joined him in his office for one last nightcap? Or if you picked up his letter opener? There wasn't a mark on his neck other than the fatal one – and I believe that's because you didn't hesitate, even when he put up his hand in a last-moment attempt to stop you. Then you went up to Églantine's apartment and searched through all her precious books trying to find the 'evidence' she had. You'd witnessed her distress at having misplaced a book that was deeply meaningful to her on one occasion…so I think you believed that was where she'd secreted the damning photograph. You did what you did to protect your own reputation – not to help Gustav out of a tight spot, nor to save your daughter. Be honest – you might as well be now…all the rest of it is out in the light."

Avril rose slowly. Everyone's eyes were on her – no longer seeing her as a model or a muse or a mother, but as a murderer.

She crowed, "It's all out in the light? Are you kidding? You have no idea. Yes – you're right about it all…but what you don't know is that my father was…was…already abusing me by the time Églantine came along and offered me a way out. He had been for years. He damaged me psychologically in ways that have led me to…do all this. I can't be blamed for what I did…I reacted to Gustav murdering that…that woman…the way I did because of how my father had treated me, for years. He was an evil, evil man."

Joanne's face was rigid with disbelief as she stared at her mother. "You…you surrounded yourself with photos of an evil man? I don't believe you. But that you killed my papa? Oh Avril…I hate myself for saying it, but I can believe that…only too easily."

Avril roared, "My father was evil, I tell you. And your father was…weak. Always weak. I was the one who was trying to save you, my darling child, not him."

Francine glanced across the table toward me, and we exchanged a half-raised eyebrow that told me she understood exactly the way that Avril was about to play things, going forward. Commissioner Bovet nodded silently as Francine spoke firmly to Avril Tambour – explaining her situation and her rights – then two officers escorted her to the door. Avril held her chin high as she walked confidently out of the room, and didn't look at anyone…not even her stunned daughter.

I could see Joanne's hands clenching and unclenching on the table as she gazed across the room with unseeing eyes. Her voice cracked when she said, "I never knew why Avril was so…detached from me, as a mother. Papa was always my rock, always the one giving me support and direction. I have no idea if what Avril says her father did to her is true…maybe that will all come out, now. And, if he did, was that maybe the reason why she's been the way she has been with me my whole life? But

– whatever her early life might have been like – does that provide any justification for her killing my father? And Lucienne, of course. Oh…Maman."

Jacques reached out, took one of Joanne's hands, and she let him hold it, though she straightened her back, and finally looked Francine in the eye. "I'll speak for Maman if needed. She's only ever been cold toward me, not bad. Not until…Lucienne, and…Papa. Oh Papa…why did he think he had to save me? He spent so much of his life teaching me how to be able to save myself…I'd have coped."

"And you have friends," said Jacques gently. "So, especially until all this…comes out, you have people in this room who know the truth, but won't speak of it. You can turn to us if you need to talk about things – or not. You know – maybe we can just be quiet together."

Joanne did her downward smile thing. "Friends who enjoy a companionable silence? And what would your partner think of that, Jacques? Doesn't he nag you already about how much time you spend here, or out with friends?"

"He loves me. He'll understand. Love's a wonderful thing…until…it isn't."

Joanne finally let her tears flow, and she nuzzled into Jacques' shirt; it was clear that neither of them cared that it would probably be ruined.

Monica, Monique, and Anne-Marie exchanged tearful glances.

Anne-Marie said, "I wish I'd known about…well, what could I have done?"

Monica said, "If she'd told us, we'd have understood…but how would that have helped with…any of this? Poor Gustav. Though, he shouldn't have killed Églantine, of course."

Monique asked, "What was her real name, again?"

I replied, "Mireille Audubon."

Anne-Marie smiled sadly. "How…odd."

Monica asked, "Why's that odd?"

Anne-Marie shrugged. "She was always so entranced by Toulouse-Lautrec. I know that's why she took the name Églantine, and I dare say she loved the fact that Avril was named as she was, because of the number of times Lautrec depicted the famous can-can dancer, Jane Avril, who belonged to Mademoiselle Églantine's troupe. But it's quite a coincidence that he was also thought to have had a favorite among his prostitute friends who was named Mireille."

Monica said, "I had no idea you were such an art afficionado."

Anne-Marie winked. "We old nuns, you know…still waters run deep, my dear."

Monique said, "Does anyone know if this means that the exhibition can go ahead?"

Commissioner Bovet was huddled in a corner with Francine, and this question made him turn. "What? The exhibition? Of course it'll go ahead – that's why I'm here. To make sure it does. Schedules of important people can't be changed for…well, an investigation that's now over, thanks to this Cait Morgan."

I jumped in. "But it wasn't all me, Commissioner. Without the work carried out by Captain de Gaulle and her team, I wouldn't have had the facts to be able to…apply my academic process. I'm incredibly grateful to the captain for allowing me to do…what I do. It was her professionalism and foresight, and that of her stalwart aide, Pierre Bertrand, that allowed this resolution to be reached. I'm so grateful that she gave me the opportunity to…act as her cat's paw…to try to draw out a confession from Avril. She had faith in me, and I agreed to put her plan into action."

Bovet swung around to face Francine. "Your plan? You knew what was going to come out all along?"

I spotted a millisecond of hesitation on Francine's part, then she replied, "I did, but I have Officer Bertrand to thank for that. I don't know if you're aware of his role within our department, but he's been doing some fascinating work with regard to victim profiling, a field that's growing in reputation – thanks to the academic work of people like Professor Morgan, as I originally explained. You might want to have him present his theories and practices to yourself and your senior colleagues, sir. We need every tool that can be of use to us – especially in cases like this where a psychological lens is just what we need."

Bovet nodded, glanced toward me, then returned his attention to Francine and Pierre. When he reached out to shake their hands, I wondered if Pierre might faint. "Good job. Good teamwork. Yes…congratulate the entire team. And get going with all that evidence – it'll be needed. Sounds like she might be aiming to put up a fight, that one. She's slippery, I'd say. Damned fine-looking woman in her day…my wife will be devastated to hear about all this. Loves the stuff that comes out of this house, she does. Ah well – we'll see where the whole thing goes from here. Goodnight." Then he left us all standing there – seemingly delighted that "he'd" achieved so much in such a short time.

There was a great deal of activity in the meeting room for the next half an hour or so. Eventually, Joanne approached me and said, "Thank you. I know you might not think I mean it, but I do. The truth is unfeeling, but it's pure…and it's needed if there's to be any healing."

I dared, "It won't be easy, Joanne. I can see you have friends here who'll support you all they can, but don't be afraid to seek professional advice, too. There'll be people who can help you navigate all the challenges you'll have to face. I'm sorry to say that this is exactly the sort of story that the media will lap up, so you might need to plan to stay out of the way for a while."

Joanne touched my arm gently. "I Googled you, Cait – and I know you understand how caustic the attention of the media can be…you had to endure a great deal when they found your ex-boyfriend dead in your apartment in Cambridge, didn't you?" I nodded. "So thanks for warning me about that. But I'm not you – they won't find me interesting after a while. I'm just…me. Not a criminal psychologist whose abusive ex-lover had been found dead, when there was no one else in the place. Yes…that must have been difficult."

I said, "I was completely cleared – the post-mortem proved I didn't kill him…you read that too, right?"

Joanne nodded and did the upside-down smiling thing. "Yes, I read that too. But, you make a good point. Francine has told me that Papa's wife, Sylvia, has been informed of his death. She's all alone now, too – so I'll go there tonight. We can talk about Papa…it might help us both. And she's out in the countryside, away from all…this."

I agreed that might help both her and Sylvia…then she left us, and returned to the huddle of those grappling with shock and grief – as well as the practical responsibilities of getting an exhibit ready to open, and to keep a company running…somehow.

Bud hugged me close. "Let's go. I'll help you to the elevator. If that ankle's no better in the morning, we'll work out how to get an X-ray done. You might have broken it."

I stood and winced. "I'm sure it'll be fine, Bud, really I am. Besides, there are so many more places I want to see before we leave Paris – thank goodness we did the boat trip and the opera house before any of this happened. And…well, I wouldn't mind seeing the rest of the places that bus would have taken us – in fact, that would be a great way to get around without me having to do too much walking. What do you say – shall we have another go at it tomorrow?"

Bud shook his head. "Oh, Cait – let's see how you're doing then, shall we? Meanwhile, let's say our goodnights, and ask about what Francine might need of us, before we make any plans at all."

As though she'd heard us chatting – which she might well have done – Francine grabbed Pierre's arm, and dragged him toward us.

She was looking haggard, but relieved. "You two should go. Since you've refused my advice to accept medical attention – twice – you should at least get that ankle up, and iced, Cait. Pierre and I want to thank you – both informally and formally – though you'll need to come into our offices to give a full statement at some point tomorrow, please."

Pierre beamed. "I'll see you then. I'll continue to work on this case, thanks to Commissioner Bovet. He's going to invite me to present to the top brass…it'll be…um…a wonderful opportunity."

I reached up to pat him on the arm. "You'll be great. And we'll come whenever you say, of course. But you're right – I need to look after this." I pointed to my foot.

"And I need to look after her," said Bud.

The journey back to our hotel was painful, but blessedly brief – there was almost no traffic, and it had obviously rained while we'd all been stuck inside the Maison, which meant that Paris glittered as we drove through it, the lights reflecting off the wet streets, making the place look like so many paintings that romanticize the city…though it really doesn't need to be romanticized at all.

With Dave at the reception desk to greet us when we arrived, I had to explain my limp…though it was something of a relief to be able to do so in English. Once again, we accepted bags of popcorn from him, as well as a few bags into which we could dump ice, and he sent us on our way with: "As guests you're automatically invited to the opening tomorrow evening, by the way."

Bud and I paused at the door leading to the elevators, and exchanged a puzzled glance.

My thoughts flew to the exhibit at the *Petit Palace*. "Yes, it's definitely going ahead, but…well, what do you mean, we're invited?" I was confused.

It was Dave's turn to look puzzled. "Yeah, of course it's going ahead. The DJ's gonna be setting up in the courtyard if it's dry – which it's due to be – so there'll be no dinner service there tomorrow evening, and the artist himself will arrive at nine. The after-party's in the cocktail bar upstairs from eleven onwards."

Bud and I both shook our heads dumbly. Dave handed us a flyer, which featured a portrait created by an artist who clearly favored the naïve approach to painting.

I read the text. "There's a gallery here? In the basement? And an exhibition opening? And a DJ?"

Dave nodded. "It's what we're known for – we're huge supporters of local artists. Our group of hotels isn't big, but the first one was in the East End of London – in England, not Ontario – and it built a great reputation among the hotbed of the arty set there. That's why there's always such a great buzz about this place – we attract the right crowd. The after-party'll probably go on for hours – and you two are clearly nightbirds, so I thought it might be your kinda thing."

Bud and I thanked him, and the astonished looks we'd received when we'd mentioned where we were staying became a little less opaque.

"Let's get that foot of yours up, and iced…then it's some sleep for us, Wife," said Bud, as the elevator doors opened.

"Yes please, Husband."

Vingt-sept

It had taken a week after we got home for me to finally empty my suitcase; life hobbling about in one of those boot things slows to a snail's pace, apparently, and I'd refused all of Bud's offers to help me unpack and get my washing done, though I'd at least let him sort out his own luggage and laundry.

I didn't get up from my desk when I got the email, but shouted, "Bud – I've got something you'll want to see on my laptop."

Marty made it to my side in my office before Bud got there – of course. I petted his beautiful, velvety head, and wonky ear, as we both waited patiently. Well, I waited patiently, but Marty panted like a steam train and looked so deliriously happy that I could feel him quiver. When Bud ambled in, he was greeted with licks – which suggested the pair had been apart for two months, rather than the two minutes it had been.

Bud grinned when he saw my screen. "What's this then? The Martin twins have been given some sort of an award?"

"They have. Jacques sent me this – it was taken on the opening night of the exhibit, in Paris…but he's only just received permission from the twins to send it on – they didn't want to seem boastful. Look, they've received medals for services to the French fashion industry. What a wonderful, and suitable, end to their long careers. He accepted the one that was awarded to Églantine, posthumously. He says the twins have already picked out a farm in their beloved countryside to buy for their cat sanctuary, and they're getting the whole thing fast-tracked – though what that means in France, I don't know. He also says that the offer made to them for their shares, by that conglomerate that's taking over *Maison Églantine*, was – as the saying goes – 'too good to refuse'…so they didn't, and now they can afford half the world's supply of cat food, he reckons. Oh, and he says that Anne-Marie is volunteering at a place where they house cats and dogs that are up for adoption – and getting a better apartment, with that money Églantine left her."

Bud said, "Good for all of them," as he smooshed Marty's ears and petted his head. Marty responded with more excited licks. "It's great to know they're going to be able to realize their dreams in their retirement. And I know Jacques told us that he's going to stay on at the Maison, while the new owners expand the entire brand, but is there any news about the building itself yet? With Lucienne having been named as the person due to inherit it in Églantine's new will, and her having specifically disinherited her parents – which, frankly, I felt was overkill, but I do understand that such things matter, due to the way French law works – what's happening about that? The building, I mean. It's got to be worth a fortune. The lawyers won't get it all, somehow, will they?"

"I don't know. Jacques doesn't say, though I think the French are pretty set on property inheritance having to work through a bloodline. Maybe, somehow, it'll find its way to Joanne? I mean, she was actually related to Lucienne by…well, a horribly unfortunate 'association' through her grandfather. But, honestly, I don't know. I suspect they'll have to wait until there's a verdict on Avril – who'd otherwise inherit ahead of her daughter – but wouldn't be allowed to benefit from her crime of killing Lucienne…if she's found guilty of that. Luckily for us, that's not our problem. Jacques does say that Joanne's still holed up with Sylvia out in the countryside, and that she's coping well with coming to terms with what her parents did…so I'm pleased for her in that respect."

"Any more news from Pierre about how the case against Avril is progressing?"

I checked. "Nothing – but it's early days yet…it's not been a month since they took her into custody. I mean, we know that the case against her is, in fact, progressing, but that's all. I expect that, as here, the legal wheels grind slow. As far as Pierre's transfer to that centralized training unit goes? No more news on that front, either…though he sounded excited that it might happen 'soon', in his last email."

"You knew he'd be moving out of that specific post of his pretty quickly, didn't you?"

I chuckled. "Oh come on, Bud – the attraction between him and Francine was obvious, and also obviously mutual…and he's done the logical thing by asking to transfer out to a place where his skill set can be put to good use across the entire police service. I can't imagine that a relationship between superior-inferior officers is something that's either allowed, or encouraged. Francine's good – she'll go far – and I believe Pierre will too. It would be lovely if they could take the personal part of that journey together, somehow, don't you think?"

"No argument from me, Wife."

"Of course not."

"How's that ankle today? I said you should have got it X-rayed in Paris, but no, you had to hobble around on it for a week until we got home, didn't you? Just as well the doctor in the ER here said that you hadn't done any more damage to it by being stubborn…that a chipped bone is stable."

"Oh come on, Bud – we had a good time, didn't we? The hotel people couldn't have been nicer to us…lending me that walking cane was just what I needed, and that bus pass thing was brilliant…we went around the *Arc de Triomphe* using it six times! I don't think we missed anything we'd wanted to see. I know I never jumped onto it, or even off it, but I managed to get about…slowly. And we did walk under the Eiffel Tower holding hands, and across the *Trocadéro*…and we even managed to get a good, slow stroll through the *Jardin des Tuileries*. But, you know what? Renting that wheelchair so you could push me around the *Musée d'Orsay* on my birthday was truly inspired…I'll never forget my fifty-second birthday, Bud…thank you. And I'm really glad we were staying where we were – and that's thanks to your research. Those two elegant courtyards, that bustled and crackled with people who were truly interested in life and each other…so excited about art and the creative process that they actually talked to each other in groups – rather than just scrolling on their phones like so many folks do these days? And that wonderful restaurant they had there – so we didn't have to go hunting for places for breakfast and dinner? And the staff…who just couldn't have been more attentive? That was just what I needed. A real break."

Bud rubbed my back, gently, while still petting Marty's head. "Well, don't go 'breaking' anything else for a while, okay?"

"I promise to do my best, Husband."

"You always do, Wife. You always do."

Acknowledgements

One of the questions I'm frequently asked is: "Where do you get your ideas?" I often find that a difficult one to answer, because I rarely manage to stop thinking about potential victims, suspects, locations, and methods of murder; in my defense, that is my job, after all. But, on this occasion, I *can* answer that question: I was sitting on the top-deck of a bus touring Paris, and wondered, *What if I looked into one of these wonderful windows we're driving past and saw a murder being committed?* And I was off…

I first visited Paris in the spring of 1979. I arrived at about five in the morning, and it had been raining, and – even now – I find it difficult to describe the feeling I had of having "come home". It's extraordinary to visit a place for the first time and feel so utterly comfortable there, but I did. When I was living in London through the 1980s to 2000, I was able to visit Paris often and was never, ever disappointed by the city, or the people. Once I moved to Canada, it was more difficult to get back there, but I've spent what I can only call "quality time" there during the past couple of years, and knew that I had to send Cait and Bud there as soon as I could work that into the arc of their lives. So here it is – at last – Cait and Bud get to do (some of) the things I adore doing in Paris. I hope you enjoy/ed your time with them there.

Of course I've referenced historical figures and real places in the book, but *Maison Églantine* is a complete fabrication. However, Cait and Bud's chosen hotel is based on The Hoxton, Paris – which is both real, and wonderful. Thanks to everyone we've met there over the years: our time with you (so far, and there will be more visits, because we'll never, now, stay anywhere else!) has been completely magical.

I'd also like to note that Merrill Young, a true champion of Canadian crime fiction – and fellow fan of *art nouveau* gowns and *objets d'art* – allowed me to use her Grandma's name in the book: Emma Kraft migrated to Canada from Norway and inspired Merrill's love of all things sewing-related.

Once again, my editor Anna Harrisson has helped make this book better – thank you, Anna. Also, Sue Vincent is my stalwart proof-checker – thanks, Sue. As a team we really do our best to not allow a single mistake to sneak through – so, if you spot one, please let me know? (My email address is at my website.)

Living with an author isn't easy, but my husband supports me, allows me the time I need to do this, and is my cheerleader in every way. Honestly, if he didn't do what he does, I wouldn't be able, or happy, to write. Thank you. Love you most. (I officially win, forever, because it's printed in a book.)

Somehow you found this book – so my thanks to all the reviewers, bloggers, people who've given the book a social media shout-out, librarians, booksellers…or anyone you've met, or know, who's told you about it: getting the word out about a book's existence is a challenge, so, without all that amplification, I know my little voice wouldn't be heard – THANK YOU ALL! (Yes, I am shouting.)

Finally, my thanks to you – for choosing to spend time with Cait and Bud. I hope you enjoy/ed it (and, if you did…please consider telling a friend!).

Cathy Ace, September 2025

About The Author

CATHY ACE was born and raised in Swansea, Wales, and migrated to British Columbia, Canada aged forty. She is the author of *The Cait Morgan Mysteries*, *The WISE Enquiries Agency Mysteries*, the standalone novel of psychological suspense, *The Wrong Boy*, and short stories and novellas. As well as being passionate about writing crime fiction, she's also a keen gardener.

You can find out more about Cathy and all her works at her website: www.cathyace.com

www.ingramcontent.com/pod-product-compliance
Lightning Source LLC
Chambersburg PA
CBHW061227310726
48971CB00007B/1970